I0637732

BAD LOVE BEYOND

KEVIN L. SCHEWE, MD, FACRO

Jan-Carol
Publishing, Inc

"every story needs a book"

Bad Love Beyond
Kevin L. Schewe, MD, FACRO

Published November 2020
Broken Crow Ridge
Imprint of Jan-Carol Publishing, Inc.
All rights reserved
Copyright © 2020 Kevin L. Schewe, MD, FACRO

This is a work of fiction. Any resemblance to actual persons,
either living or dead is entirely coincidental. All names, characters
and events are the product of the author's imagination.

This book may not be reproduced in whole or part, in any manner
whatsoever without written permission, with the exception of brief
quotations within book reviews or articles.

ISBN: 978-1-950895-74-8
Library of Congress Control Number: 2020950529

You may contact the publisher:
Jan-Carol Publishing, Inc.
PO Box 701
Johnson City, TN 37605
publisher@jancarolpublishing.com
jancarolpublishing.com

DEDICATION

I have been a board-certified cancer specialist practicing radiation oncology for 34 years as of July 1st 2021. I am the youngest of three children and have two older sisters, Kathy Williams and Denise Bourg. My first novel, *Bad Love Strikes* was dedicated to Kathy, who remains in remission from her breast cancer. The second novel, *Bad Love Strikes* was dedicated to Denise Bourg, the middle child in our family of three siblings. I am the proud parent of two children: Ashley Daugherty is my oldest daughter and Christie Schewe is my youngest daughter. This third book, *Bad Love Strikes* is dedicated to Ashley.

Growing up, Ashley was a fun, athletic and active child who embraced her risk-taking genetics and loved adventure of all types. There was not a roller coaster or theme park ride too fast or too daring for her to try—and then try again and again! She learned to ride hunter-jumper horses at a young age and competed in the Midwest circuit earning innumerable ribbons and trophies along the way. I remember watching her at horse shows. They would show her the route to take one time and then she would ride and jump her horse through that route trying to set the fastest time without knocking down fence rails. I was so impressed. I couldn't imagine memorizing the expected route that fast, much less jump fences against a time clock!

Ashley was an outstanding student and cheerleader. Throughout her school years and into adulthood, she has shown an amazing ability to create and draw pictures of all types. She has that artistic gene that is now spilling over to her children and could someday lead to illustrating children's books. She met her soulmate and now husband, Chad Daugherty, in California. Ashley and Chad have built an outstanding marriage together and they are the proud parents of my two grandchildren, Gracie and Olivia Daugherty. They live in southern California where Ashley is an incredible Mom to Gracie and "Livy" and actively volunteers at the girls' school. Their future shines brightly in front of them.

Ashley always dreamed and fantasized of being a secret spy agent growing up—one of our all-time favorite movies together is *True Lies*. She loves the *Bad Love Book Series* and would fit right in with the Bad Love Gang. I love you, Ashley, and could not be more proud of you and all that you have accomplished and will certainly undertake and realize in your future.

PRAISE FOR
BAD LOVE BEYOND
Book 3 in The Bad Love Series

"In *Bad Love Beyond* the gang propels us to another galaxy—and Planet Azur—and the interaction with the inhabitants produces an immensely creative and entertaining venture as well as a novel transport of anti-cancer meds to the USA. Skillful writing (both historical and fantastical), a zesty sense of humor, an appreciation for pop culture, and the ability to create memorably entertaining characters combine to make this an immensely impressive novel—and experience! Very highly recommended."
>   —Dr. Grady Harp, Amazon Top 50 Hall of Fame Reviewer, 5 Stars

"Young adults will love the dinosaurs, time travel, and stunning creations in *Bad Love Beyond*."
>   —Mike Ball, Erma Bombeck Award-Winning Author, 5 Stars

"Vividly detailed and historically accurate, Dr. Schewe sends his readers on an unforgettable roller coaster of a time travel story, guaranteed, I believe, to rival the classic *The Time Machine* by H. G. Wells. Highly recommended!"
>   —Susan Keefe, *Midwest Book Review*, 5 Stars

"The madcap/fun-loving crusaders in the Bad Love Gang are back in *Bad Love Beyond* complete with dancing, danger, and dinos. Everyone from pre-teens to seniors will LOVE IT!"   —Marlene Grippa, Retired Children's Librarian, 5 Stars

"Bringing his signature sense of humor, love of music, expansive grasp of history and attention to detail to bear, Schewe tells a romping and action-packed tale of space travel, alien culture, and relationships. The descriptions and historic elements of locations and included playlist of songs which run throughout the narrative really draw the reader in and set each scene. If you enjoy history and sci-fi, or have ever wished that Frank and Joe Hardy and their friends were more interesting, you'll love the Bad Love Gang and their adventures!"   —Jessica Tofino, Educator and Writer, 5 Stars

ALSO BY KEVIN L. SCHEWE, MD, FACRO:

BAD LOVE STRIKES
BAD LOVE TIGERS

BAD LOVE
BEYOND

ACKNOWLEDGMENTS

For 33.5 years I have worked on the front lines of cancer care as a radiation oncologist in private practice. Receiving a diagnosis of cancer, and then facing the realities of staging, treatment, side effects of treatment, and recovery are challenges that are larger than life. Living with a cancer diagnosis after treatment requires a new view on life and life's priorities. I want to acknowledge the thousands of cancer patients that I have cared for these past 33.5 years—all of whom have taught me valuable lessons of life and have shown me courage beyond measure, sacrifice, love, humility, victory, real-life miracles, and acceptance. I am eternally thankful to all of these patients, their families, and loved ones—all who have shown me and continue to show me the meaning of life here on earth.

The writing of *Bad Love Beyond* has taken place during the continued COVID-19 experience here in my beloved home of Denver, Colorado. While I have been treating cancer patients during this unprecedented global pandemic, my dauntless colleagues in medicine have fought an epic and courageous war against a vicious virus attacking our society and way of life. I want to acknowledge all the frontline responders to this pandemic who have sacrificed so much in a heroic effort to save lives—your sacrifices and bravery shall never be forgotten.

The *Bad Love Book Series* is rich in actual history uniquely blended with the adventures of time-traveling, 1970s teenagers and laced with the unforgettable music of the 1960s and 1970s. During this difficult time of a global pandemic and its various consequences, these books offer hope and inspiration to a world filled with new challenges.

AUTHOR'S FOREWORD

RECOMMENDED ACTION FOR ALL YOU TIME AND SPACE TRAVELERS!

In order to get the full sensory effect of traveling through time and space with the Bad Love Gang, I highly recommend that you download the 31-song soundtrack listed on the next page by using your Spotify, iTunes, Pandora, or Amazon Prime account. Alternatively, you can use YouTube to play each song as you are reading. As each song is boldly introduced throughout the novel, take the time (no pun intended!) to listen to the music and enjoy the full sensory effect of being an honorary member of the Bad Love Gang. Do not be afraid to lip sync, sing, and/or break out and dance, play your air guitar or tap your feet as the music moves you!

Back from their mission as the Bad Love Tigers to secure the secrets of Area 51 and the White Hole Project, *Bad Love Beyond* starts as the Bad Love Gang are summoned to the Oval Office by President Gerald Ford. They receive his blessing to use the White Hole Project to attempt intergalactic space travel in their search of the cure for Hannah Lieb's breast cancer. Fighting off the KGB and their arch-enemy, Borya Krovopuskov, the group returns to Area 51 in 1942 using the White Hole Project. They reconnect with their alien friend, Blue Nova One, on Earth's sister planet, Azur, 11.5 billion light years away. The music from the 1960s and 1970s paves the way as the Bad Love Gang deal with dinosaurs, the forces of nature, the mystery of The Bermuda Triangle, and alien politics in their race to get the cure for Hannah. Buckle-up for the time and intergalactic space ride of your life!

SOUNDTRACK TO *BAD LOVE BEYOND*

1. "Easy Livin'," Uriah Heep (1972)
2. "Two Lane Highway," Pure Prairie League (1975)
3. "Paint It Black," The Rolling Stones (1966)
4. "Bad Moon Rising," Creedence Clearwater Revival (1969)
5. "You Really Got Me," The Kinks (1964)
6. "Devil with a Blue Dress On/Good Golly Miss Molly," Mitch Ryder and the Detroit Wheels (1966)
7. "Johnny B. Goode," Chuck Berry (1958)
8. "Higher Ground," Stevie Wonder (1973)
9. "The Good, the Bad and the Ugly," Ennio Morricone (1967)
10. "For What It's Worth," Buffalo Springfield (1966)
11. "Rocket Man," Elton John (1972)
12. "Aquarius/Let the Sunshine In," The Fifth Dimension (1969)
13. "Summer in the City," The Lovin' Spoonful (1966)
14. "Back in the U.S.S.R.," The Beatles (1968)
15. "Dream On," Aerosmith (1973)
16. "Get Down Tonight," KC and the Sunshine Band (1975)
17. "Brandy (You're a Fine Girl)," Looking Glass (1972)
18. "Blue Suede Shoes," Elvis Presley (1956)
19. "I Am Woman," Helen Reddy (1972)
20. "Indian Reservation (The Lament of the Cherokee Reservation Indian)," Paul Revere and the Raiders (1971)
21. "Going Mobile," The Who (1971)

MAIN CHARACTERS

THE BAD LOVE GANG FROM OAK RIDGE, TENNESSEE

1. **Kevin "Bubble Butt" or "BB" Schafer:** Age 17. Borderline genius, has one foot in reality and one foot in destiny. Great sense of humor. Loves strategy, adventure, and popular music: has a "music brain." A pilot, he discovered the White Hole Project time machine with Bowmar. Plans adventures for the Bad Love Gang. The narrator of the *Bad Love Book Series*.

2. **Nathan "Bowmar" Williams:** Age 17. Bubble Butt's best friend. African-American certified genius, with an IQ somewhere north of 140. Discovered the White Hole Project time machine with BB. Understands time travel and plans adventures with Bubble Butt.

3. **Brianna "Cleopatra" Williams:** Age 18. Bowmar's sister, a total social butterfly with a high social IQ. Becomes the queen of any social circle she enters. Tries to keep her brother Bowmar grounded. Very independent. Crisco's best friend.

4. **Jimmy "Goondoggy" Blanchert:** Age 17. Bubble Butt's next-door neighbor from early childhood who has absolutely no concept of fear. Loves the outdoors and adventure. Always ready for the next adventure into the unknown, and will try anything at least once. Highly energetic and very smart.

5. **Billy "Willy" Blanchert:** Age 19. Goondoggy's older brother. A pilot, he learned how to fly with Bubble Butt. The polar opposite of Goondoggy. Analyzes Bad Love Gang plans to calculate odds of success. Struggles to overcome caution and fear. Has a gentle spirit, and usually caves in to the group's plans. Very smart.

6. **Donny "The Runt" Legrande:** Age 18. French-American, shorter in stature than the rest of the Bad Love Gang. Son of a talented aircraft mechanic. A resourceful mechanical genius who can fix or improve any and all internal combustion engines. Not afraid to take on a fight. Loyal friend.

7. **David "Crazy Ike" Eichenmuller:** Age 19. German-Irish American who can speak perfect German and English. Covered head to toes with freckles. A bit of a troublemaker who generally ignores rules/laws. Can steal anything and lie his way out of trouble. Smart, always entertaining, and just a little bit crazy. Starting college in journalism school.

8. **Karen "Crisco" O'Sullivan:** Age 15+. Irish-Catholic American and the oldest of eleven children. Overly mature for her age, a good athlete and street smart. Interested in nursing and photography. Super cute with blonde hair, blue eyes, mature voice for her age, and a perfect body—other than a slightly disproportionate booty. Cleopatra's best friend.

9. **Frankie "Spaghetti Head" Russo:** Age 17. Italian-Catholic American, a relatively new addition to the Bad Love Gang. Strong Italian family background. Speaks with an Italian accent and adds a Mafia-style touch to the gang. Has incredibly thick, curly, dark hair. Good at calculating damage and destruction.

10. **Gary "The Pud" Jacobson:** Age 16. Great at doing tedious and/or time-consuming jobs. Understands wireless communication devices backwards and forwards. Got his nickname for being average in every sport as a kid. Resourceful, dependable and reliable—gets the job done. Cynical sense of humor.

11. **Aaron "Meatball" Eisen:** Age 17. From an American-Jewish family. A jack of all trades who can fix anything mechanical or electrical. Always ready to lend a helping hand. Has a true heart of gold. A problem solver and totally street-smart. A great cook. Fell in love with Hannah Lieb and fathered a child (Elijah) with her during time travel in Bad Love Strikes.

12. **Paul "Waldo" Thompson:** Age 44. A Korean War Medal of Honor recipient. Works in procurement at Oak Ridge National Laboratory. A gun collector and firearms expert. Loves to camp, play cards, and talk about everything under the sun. Married and devoted to Mary, with no children. Together, they virtually adopted the entire Bad Love Gang and serve as surrogate parents. Their home is always open to the gang.

13. **Mary Thompson:** Age 43. Married to Waldo and surrogate mom to the Bad Love Gang. Incredibly nice, sweet, nonjudgmental and a peacemaker. Worries about the gang's adventures and encourages Waldo to protect their "children." Uniquely, never assigned a nickname by the Bad Love Gang. Devoted to Waldo. Knows how to handle firearms.

14. **Danny "Tater" Ford:** Age 17. A southern boy to his core, from a military family. Born in Columbus, Georgia and moved to Oak Ridge, Tennessee at age eight. The Bad Love Gang's continual

source of southern-fried humor. Terrific sense of humor and uncanny wit. Always entertaining, always ready for adventure.

BAD LOVE GANG ADDED FROM THE 1944 RESCUE MISSION

1. **Jack "Bucky" Smith:** Age 27. West Point graduate, 1940. USAAF Captain and Special Forces WWII pilot. Personally chosen by President Franklin Roosevelt as the first White Hole Project test pilot. Has top-secret clearance to Area 51. Was lost in time on his inaugural time-travel mission until rescued by the Bad Love Gang. Returned with the Bad Love Gang in November 1974 and has become BB's "big brother." Smart, courageous, handsome, great at strategy and hard to kill.

2. **Darby "Pumpkin" Nelson:** Age 23. British by heritage from London, England. Adopted, his parents were both killed in a Nazi bombing raid on London. Navigator extraordinaire and trained as a pilot. Joined the Bad Love Gang along with Bucky during the Phantom Fortress mission, and returned with the gang to November 1974. Adopted Jewish orphan boy Benzion "Ben" Kaplan. Great British wit and a total team player. Face turns orange when embarrassed.

3. **Benzion "Ben" Kaplan:** Age 9. Jewish orphan boy on the run from Nazi authorities during the Holocaust. Rescued by the Bad Love Gang in November 1944 and brought back to the future, along with Bucky and Pumpkin. Adopted by Pumpkin. Smart and growing up fast. Inquisitive and good at math. Wants to become a pilot.

MAIN CHARACTERS FROM PLANET AZUR

1. **Queen Azur:** The supreme ruler of the Blue Azurians on Planet Azur.

2. **Blue Nova One:** The prime princess to Queen Azur. The chief diplomat for the Blue Azurians, second in command to the queen. Made first contact with the Bad Love Gang in the forests of southern China. Blue Azurian confidant and friend to the Bad Love Gang. Extremely intelligent, intellectually on par with Bowmar. A capable Azurian spaceship captain who explores other galaxies in search of blue exotic matter.

3. **Blue Max Ten:** Captain of the crashed Azurian spaceship at Area 51. Husband to Queen Azur, father to their two children, Blue Bellatrix "Bella" Ten and Blue Badar Ten (who both befriend Ben). Brother to Blue Zaniah Ten.

4. **Blue Zaniah Ten:** Systems engineer of the crashed Azurian spaceship at Area 51. Sister to Blue Max Ten and sister-in-law to Queen Azur. Shared assistant to the queen and Blue Nova One.

5. **Danvinio "Dan" One:** Elected and trusted prime minister of the Republic of Azur and its diverse people, the Gazurians. In year seven of a single ten-year term as Prime Minister. A devoted public servant of the Republic faced with an impending cataclysmic, volcanic, extinction event. Loves music and the arts. Six feet tall, he is a handsome, athletic black man with salt and pepper hair in his 50s.

6. **Stareveret "Star" Three:** Elected vice prime minister of the Republic of Azur and the right-hand diplomat to Danvinio One. A military veteran loyal to Dan and the Republic. A trusted and experienced pilot of Gazurian Helium airships. Captain of the Republic's Titan One Airship. In her mid-30s, she is a fair-skinned, freckled, redhead with green eyes.

7. **Jadedominic "Jade" Eleven:** The Republic's best search and rescue pilot. Captain of the Helium rescue airship Libero Three. From a small tribe in the Republic, her ancestors were forced to immigrate when their planet faced extinction. A striking green woman with incredibly bright green eyes and black hair. Smart and courageous.

TABLE OF CONTENTS

CHAPTER ONE:

PRESIDENTIAL INVITATION

"If Lincoln were alive today,
he'd be turning over in his grave."
—Gerald R. Ford

Friday, June 27, 1975 at 8:35 AM local time,
the White House, Oval Office, Washington, DC

W e first met Navy Lieutenant Gerald R. Ford at age 31, while
he was in the midst of transferring from the Navy Pre-Flight
School at Saint Mary's College in Moraga, California to the Naval
Reserve Training Command, Naval Air Station (NAS) in Glenview,
Illinois. On Sunday, April 15, 1945, Bucky, Waldo, and I had met
with Lieutenant Ford in Commander Staples' office at NAS Glenview and reviewed key details of his future life. We said that we would
contact him through the White House switchboard in 1975, and he
would know that it was us because the message would say, "The
Denver Project needs you." Thirty years later, on Tuesday, April 29,
1975, we placed our first call to President Ford. It was the very day of
the Fall of Saigon and the end of the Vietnam War. President Ford
returned our call on Wednesday April 30, 1975. We told him about
the extremely smart and dangerous Russian spy, Borya Krovopus-

kov (aka Russ Krovo), heading the oldest Soviet Union KGB sleeper cell spy unit in modern Soviet/American history. We requested that Borya and his local network in the Oak Ridge and Knoxville areas be apprehended, an action we felt was necessary in order for the Denver Project (which now included security for both the White Hole Project and Area 51) to remain safe and undetected. President Ford indicated that he would promptly deal with the Russian spy cell, and discreetly invite us to the White House in the near future. The president was anxious to meet with us, but had some unsettling news.

On Friday, June 27, 1975 at 8:35 AM, President Gerald R. Ford met with White House Chief of Staff Donald Rumsfeld in the Oval Office. Ford gave him instructions to contact Korean War Medal of Honor recipient Captain Paul Thompson (Waldo), who now worked in procurement at Oak Ridge National Laboratory (ORNL) since retiring from the Army. Rumsfeld was to instruct Thompson to bring the Denver Project leadership directly to the White House for an off-the-record meeting with the president at 7:00 AM on Tuesday, July 1st in the Oval Office. Rumsfeld was told to assist Thompson in any way needed to make their White House visit unnoticed but comfortable—including reservations at the Hay-Adams Hotel, across the street from the White House. The president made it clear to Rumsfeld that the only guests that would be present in the Oval Office for this discreet meeting would be the president, Captain Thompson and his guests, and FBI Special Agent Charlie "Chuck" Brooks.

Charlie Brooks was a 26-year-old African-American/Latino whose father (Joseph) was an African-American FBI agent who worked for the Special Intelligence Service in World War II. The Special Intelligence Service was a covert counterintelligence branch of the FBI, located in South America during World War II. It was established under the direction of President Franklin D. Roosevelt in June of 1940 to monitor Axis activities in Central and South America. The FBI Special Intelligence Service placed more than 340 undercover agents in various regions of Latin America. They operated for seven years, and by 1946 nearly 900 Axis spies had been discovered. Joseph Brooks was assigned to La Paz, Bolivia from 1942 until 1945. While there he met and fell in love with a beautiful Bolivian woman named Pilar Flores. Her family had been engaged in silver mining in the 1800s but switched to tin mining in the early 1900s, and profited greatly from that strategy. Joseph and Pilar married and moved to Virginia in late 1945, when his tour in Bolivia was finished and World War II was ending. Charlie/Chuck was the first of three children, born to Joseph and Pilar in 1948.

Chuck Brooks grew up idolizing his Father's career with the FBI and was determined from a very young age to follow in his father's footsteps. His mother, Pilar, loved dancing, music, the arts and travel and was able to support her love of these things through her family's endowment. Chuck had the blended genetics from his career-focused father and his vivacious and passionate mother. He went to Howard University in Washington, DC, starting as an undergraduate in pre-law in 1965 and graduated from Law School in 1972. He immediately joined the FBI and enrolled in the FBI Academy at Quantico, Virginia with his eyes on Russian counterespionage as his first career step. Quantico opened in 1972 and Chuck was in the first graduating class. He was fluent in Russian and Spanish, and despite his somewhat unorthodox methods, he had quickly distinguished himself by getting results in undercover anti-KGB investigations in and around Washington, DC. When President Ford had called FBI Director, Clarence M. Kelley, and requested his recommendation for a young, rising, smart and aggressive special agent to assign to a covert anti-KGB mission in Tennessee, Kelley recommended Brooks without hesitation.

Chuck was a baby-boomer, the product of going to high school and college in the 1960s: a crazy, tumultuous decade defined by the civil rights movement, the Vietnam War, antiwar protests, sex, drugs, the rise of rock and roll, political assassinations, and the emerging so-called "generation gap." Regardless of Chuck's career path, desire, and dedication to follow in his father's footsteps, he also inherited and learned his mother's dancing footwork and passion for music growing up. He loved rhythm and blues, jazz, soul, funk, early hip hop, and of course, rock and roll. The combination of his African American and Bolivian Latino heritage—along with his love of music, 1960s social life experiences, and well-honed skills learned during FBI training—made him the perfect fit for his upcoming assignment with the Bad Love Gang. His classmates at Quantico had given him the nickname "Dick Tracy" for his crime-solving skills. The Bad Love Gang was bound to expand upon Chuck's nickname status if he joined their ranks in any capacity.

At 10:00 AM on Friday, June 27, 1975, Donald Rumsfeld was back in his private office and called retired Army Captain Paul Thompson (Waldo) at Oak Ridge National Laboratory. Rumsfeld explained that President Ford was requesting to meet with him and the leadership of the Denver Project in the Oval Office at 7:00 AM sharp on Tuesday, July 1st. He told Waldo to check in at the Hay-Adams Hotel across the street from the White House on Monday June 30th for a two-night stay, and asked Waldo how many rooms would be required. Waldo, remembering the encounter with Ford at NAS Glenview, decided to throw Rumsfeld a bit of a curve ball to test the president's memory.

"We'll need four rooms at the Hay-Adams. Tell the president that I am bringing Bucky, Bubble Butt, and one other guy named Bowmar. Got it?"

Rumsfeld answered, "Yes, I got it. Is there anything else that you will need?"

Waldo smartly replied, "I'm bringing my best damn car. Tell those guys at the Hay-Adams they better keep a close eye on it!"

Rumsfeld chuckled for a moment and said, "I think that we can take care of that. See you Tuesday morning."

Unfortunately, and unbeknownst to both Rumsfeld and Waldo, the phone that Waldo used at Oak Ridge National Laboratory to take Rumsfeld's call was bugged.

Rumsfeld met again with President Ford at 5:30 that evening and mentioned that he had reached Captain Paul Thompson. Thompson had confirmed that he was coming, and would be bringing "Bucky, Bubble Butt, and Bowmar—along with his best damn car."

Ford half-laughed, shaking his head, and said, "I don't know Bowmar yet, but I can't wait to see those guys again. They definitely know how to leave a lasting impression; that I can say!"

Monday, June 30, 1975 at 7:00 AM local time,
Oak Ridge, Tennessee

Waldo, Bucky, Bowmar, and I pulled out of Waldo's driveway in Oak Ridge, Tennessee on Monday June 30, 1975 at 7:00 AM in Waldo's 1968 Dodge Charger R/T Hemi bound for Washington, DC. It would be a 500-mile drive, mostly north up Interstate 81. Waldo and Mary had seen the Steve McQueen movie *Bullitt* in late October of 1968. The movie had one of the greatest car chase scenes to ever grace the silver screen. While driving his dark green Ford Mustang Fastback, Steve McQueen, playing Detective Frank Bullitt, followed a black Dodge Charger driven by two hitmen. An extended chase developed through the hilly, curvy streets of San Francisco. The camera action was so realistic onscreen as the two cars flew up and down the bumpy hills of San Francisco that the viewers could feel it in the pit of their stomachs. It was almost as if the cars were jumping ski slopes, and you were watching the action from the tips of the skis. The sound effects of the engines roaring and gears shifting were intoxicating! The chase ended in Brisbane, California on the southern edge of San Francisco when the Dodge Charger crashed off the road, killing the two hitmen in a fiery explosion. The following weekend, Waldo went and custom ordered his 1968 Dodge Charger R/T 426 Hemi.

Waldo ordered the car in Dodge Racing Green with a black interior, black vinyl roof, and transverse bumblebee tape stripe in white. He had to have the four-speed Hurst Competition-Plus stick. The 426 Hemi engine in 1968 added $605 to the Charger R/T's $3506 base sticker price. In other words, that engine option added nearly 20% to the price of the car—but that 426 Hemi engine was priceless! The 426 cubic inch V8 Hemi head Mopar engine had two Carter aluminum four-barrel (AFB) carburetors, producing 425 horsepower and 490 pound-feet of torque @ 4000 rpm. That second generation Dodge Charger was the pinnacle, the epitome of 1960's American muscle cars. The Runt had helped Waldo install after-market competition headers and Willy had installed the latest Sony AM/FM cassette stereo system with graphic equalizer in early 1975. We were all pumped for the day's road trip to Washington, DC, and I had pleaded with Waldo to let me drive first. Driving that car made me feel like I had thrown a saddle over a giant block V-8 engine and was riding like a cowboy up the highway! We made a quick stop in Knoxville to fill the tank and grab some ice-cold Coca-Colas, then took Interstate 40 to connect to Interstate 81 for the long drive north.

Waldo was riding shotgun, claiming that riding in the back would make him car sick, with Bucky and Bowmar in the back seat. Waldo preferred country-western music to the Bad Love Gang's modern rock and roll, but knew that he was generally outvoted unless Tater was around, so he tolerated our music choices for limited periods of time. I had already picked out two songs to play to get this road trip underway. One was hard rock, so I could slam the Hemi pedal to the metal and feel that raw, Mopar muscle power. The other song was a brand-new American country rock tune, chosen to try and appease Waldo ever so slightly.

Waldo kept the Charger garaged in the winter and with our recent time-travel mission, hadn't had it out much. As such, this was Bucky's first ride in a true American muscle car; I was anxious to see his face once I got into it. We pulled onto the entrance ramp to Interstate 40 North and I plugged in the first song as I put those 425 ponies and 490 pound-feet of torque to work. The Hemi engine roared and we bolted forward like a bat out of hell, the acceleration forcefully laying everyone back in their seats. The stereo blared out **"Easy Livin'"** by Uriah Heep, and the Charger Hemi blasted off like an Apollo rocket! **"Easy Livin'"** was the band's first hit in the United States, reaching number 39 on the US Billboard Hot 100; the song peaked at number 25 in Canada in 1972. It reached number five in the Netherlands, and made the top 20 charts in Germany, Finland, Norway, and Denmark. The pounding rhythm of the song always made me want to crunch the accelerator pedal through the floorboard of whatever car I was driving. After the speedometer needle went past 110 miles per hour, Waldo looked at me sternly and shook his left index finger back and forth. I smiled and winked at him, knowing it was my cue to come back down to earth.

In July of 1975, the speed limit on US interstate highways was 55 mph. In response to oil price spikes and imported oil supply disruptions during the 1973 Arab oil embargo and oil crisis, Congress enacted the National Maximum Speed Law. States had to agree to the 55 mph speed limit if they wanted to receive federal funding for highway repair. The legislation required 55 mph speed limits on all four-lane divided highways. Subsequent studies of fuel consumption suggested at most a 1% savings, and the non-compliance rate with the 55 mph speed limit typically exceeded 80%. Clearly part of the noncompliant 80%, I calmly said to Waldo, "I was only going double the speed limit; what's your problem there, Baldo?"

Waldo looked at me and responded, "Listen here, Bubble Brains, you don't just get a ticket for going that fast. They throw your ass in jail, and I don't want you to be wearing striped pajamas when we go to see the president tomorrow morning."

Bucky broke in, "That was great! I loved it! If this thing had wings it could fly, no problemo! I wanna drive when you're done, BB!"

Bowmar jokingly interjected, "I think your 1945 driver's license might have expired by now, Bucky Boy."

"Bubble Butt and I are working on that. I just haven't had time to take a Tennessee driver's license test with my new, altered ID. Hey, Waldo, how about I take the test in this car?"

"You better keep a lower profile when you take that test," Waldo replied. "You'd have a hard time staying under the speed limit driving this hot rod. But when you're ready to go out and impress the 1975 women, let me know; maybe I'll make you a lucky man."

I declared, "Bucky doesn't need any help in that department! He's got Peggy Sue Harding waiting for him back in 1945; the Chinese agent, Li-Ming Sun, is enthralled by him; the Indian spy Nisha Singh is hoping for his favor; and our very own Crisco has a crush on him. I'm sure someone on Blue Nova One's planet is waiting for him as well."

Bucky smiled and shrugged his shoulders as Bowmar added, "I'd say that sounds like a little bit of envy or jealousy, BB."

We all laughed as I halfway agreed. "Well, I guess I am taking some notes as we travel through time together."

Bowmar then looked at Bucky and enquired, "I'm curious about this thing called love. I know that you're from a different era, but what is it that makes you attractive to women? I might want to try it out someday."

Bucky thought quietly for a moment and then answered, "It's confidence, but never in a conceited or overly-inflated way; it's having healthy confidence in yourself and what you do—and it goes both ways for men and women."

"Peggy Sue Harding calls him 'Captain Denver.' Maybe we should switch that to 'Captain Confidence,' the caped, time-traveling crusader who never flinches, is easy to love, and is hard to kill!" I commented sarcastically.

"Very funny, Bubble Balls. I actually like it, but I think I'll skip the cape for now!" Bucky retorted.

We continued for a while longer in silence and I found myself daydreaming about the two-lane highways that we traveled on our epic road trip in April 1945, crisscrossing America for our recent time-travel mission. Coming out of my trance, I announced our next song. "I'm playing a brand-new song that was just released this month. It's from the third album by Pure Prairie League, and the song is called **"Two Lane Highway."** I think you'll like this one, Waldo; it's considered country rock." The song was mellow, and so easy to sing and daydream about while driving. The cover art for the album was great; it showed a cowboy sitting on a rock in front of a cactus, trying to hitch a ride on the side of a two-lane highway running through the desert. There was no telling what happened to his horse, but he had all his cowboy gear on and a scraggly mustache that covered his whole mouth. I would have liked to hear his stories! By the end of the song, the four of us were all singing the refrain together.

Waldo remarked, "It's not exactly Johnny Cash, Merle Haggard or Waylon Jennings, but I think I can live with it—especially with you driving, Bubble Butt."

We stopped in Roanoke, Virginia to refuel and get lunch. Waldo guided us to a historic Virginia restaurant called The Roanoke Weiner Stand, which had been a legend in southwestern Virginia since it opened its doors in 1916. We all ate hot dogs topped with chili, mustard, and onions along with fresh French fries and Coca-Cola, and it all was just fabulous! There is nothing quite like a classic American hot dog on a summer day in the Blue Ridge Mountains! Life felt normal again for the moment, but we would soon get a reminder of how our lives had changed since discovering the White Hole Project time travel machine.

After lunch, Waldo took over the driving duties; Bucky rode shotgun, and Bowmar and I sat in the back. We got back on Interstate 81 North, listened to some of Waldo's country western music, talked about our upcoming visit with President Ford, and generally relaxed while Waldo drove. Just after we passed through Lexington, Virginia on I-81, Waldo got our attention. "Gentlemen, we are being followed by a red 1966 Pontiac GTO. I have been watching these guys off and on since twenty miles north of Roanoke. I didn't think much of it at first, but when I slow down, they slow down; when I speed up, they speed up. My intuition tells me that we have company, and they are *not* our friends. Everybody buckle up tight, because we are going to show this Goat what real speed is when I suck him up our tail pipes and spit him out across the median." The original Pontiac GTO, launched in 1964, was nicknamed "the Goat" for its defiant, stripped-to-the-basics muscle car persona and the letters in its name. The animal was known for eating anything and the Pontiac GTO could eat anything on the street. Adding to the fun, the acronym for GOAT was turned into "Gas Oil And Tire" burner.

Driving the red 1966 Pontiac GTO behind us were two Russian KGB agents: Nikolai Kozlov, known locally as Nick Kolo, and Maxim Meknikov, known locally as Max Miller. Both men were stationed in Charlotte, North Carolina and had been called upon by Borya Krovo-puskov's successor to intercept us on June 30th. Their plan was to send a message to the rest of the Bad Love Gang and the powers that be in Washington, DC. Both men were well-embedded in Charlotte: Nick worked in the banking industry, and Max worked in the energy sector. Nick had cultivated a love for American muscle cars and his Russian last name, Kozlov, literally meant *goat*. He thought it would be clever to own a classic Pontiac GTO Goat and make good on his muscle car ambitions. In 1973, he purchased a barely-used red hardtop 1966 Pontiac GTO XS coupe. Pontiac introduced the XS option in mid-1966, a modification that added even more strength to the famous Pontiac tri-power 389-cubic-inch engine. The XS featured a new 744 high lift cam and RAM air intake. With stiffer valve springs, hotter cam, and a cold air induction system, the XS package boosted the GTO's already impressive engine performance from 360 horsepower up to 380 horsepower. Lastly, Nick's Goat had the four-speed manual transmission, as opposed to the two-speed Pontiac automatic. Just as Waldo was getting suspicious, Nick had downshifted and slammed his accelerator foot to the floor. The 389 XS roared into action with the deep-throated dual exhaust bellowing. Max readied his West German Heckler & Koch P9S semi-automatic 9mm. Their plan was to send a non-lethal message.

Looking in the rearview mirror, Waldo suddenly exclaimed, "God-dammit, I knew these bastards were up to no good!" We were driving at 55 mph as Waldo forcefully threw the Hurst competition four-speed into second gear, and the Mopar 426 Hemi engine screamed to life. The positraction rear end differential squealed, laying down a small amount of burnt rubber at 55 mph. The tires then gripped the highway hard as we bolted forward like a ground-to-air missile. The g-force pressed us back into our seats as the sounds of competition headers and dual exhaust turned the immediate surroundings into a 1960s dragstrip.

Nick and the GTO had a head start and were coming up on our tail as we began to forcefully accelerate. Waldo was already red in the face, all the way to the top of his male pattern balding head. In other words, he was pissed to the max. He yelled, "BB, reach under my seat! And Bucky, reach under your seat!" Bucky and I did as we were told; pulling out the matching Smith and Wesson .44-caliber Magnum pistols that Waldo had hidden underneath the seats.

In the 1971 movie *Dirty Harry*, actor Clint Eastwood introduced the world to the double-action Smith & Wesson Model 29, .44 caliber Magnum revolver, dubbed "the most powerful handgun in the world." Waldo had bought a matching pair with the 8 and 3/8-inch barrels and as always, never left home unarmed; this trip was no exception. I smiled to myself, thinking how glad I was that Waldo was on our side. Just as we grabbed the pistols, Max fired his first shot, which directly hit the driver's side rearview mirror—a foot away from Waldo's left shoulder. Waldo murmured, "Those sons-of-bitches are gonna pay for that," and then more loudly told us to hold our fire. The 1968 Dodge racing green, 426 Hemi Charger R/T began to pull away from the red 1966 Pontiac GTO XS. Max fired another shot that hit one of our tail-lights, but it was too late; we were accelerating out of their range of fire.

I quickly examined my newfound Dirty Harry .44 Magnum pistol as we out-accelerated the red GTO. The sound in the Charger cabin was intoxicating, merely from the roar of the 426 Hemi being pushed to its limits. I leaned forward and looked over Waldo's right shoulder, staring at the speedometer. The needle was hovering between 140-145 mph, on a dial that topped out at 150 mph. It was surreal, going so fast, and it felt a bit like we were floating down the road. But really, we were practically flying!

Waldo, keeping his hands on the wheel and eyes on the road, yelled back to Bowmar, "That Goat tops out at a hundred twenty miles per hour, and we're doing one forty-five. How long before I have a five-minute lead?"

Bowmar quipped, "BB and Bucky get the Dirty Harry matching pistols and I get a word problem to calculate like I'm in math class? What kinda deal is that, Waldo?"

"Just do your brainiac shit and give me an answer, smartass!"

I interrupted, "Waldo, you're not planning to go back after these guys, are you? We are outrunning them, hands down."

"Listen Bubble Butt, there is a time to run and there is a time to fight; this is not the time to run. You and Bucky are gonna go ahead and 'make my day' with those two pistols just as soon as I swing your asses into position. No one puts bullet holes in my Charger and walks away," Waldo growled.

Using my best John Wayne impersonation, I replied, "Well, OK there, Pilgrim; I've got six big bullets and an itchy trigger finger. What's the plan?"

Bucky chimed in, "Those aren't bullets, those are cannon shells! I've never seen a handgun so big! This thing is a hand-held Howitzer!"

"Bowmar, give me that calculation!" Waldo barked.

Bowmar answered, "He's traveling two miles per minute, so you will be ten miles ahead of him—or have a five-minute lead in another thirteen minutes, assuming he hasn't slowed down a bit. You sure as hell haven't."

"OK, time it and let me know when ten minutes has gone by. Here's the plan: when we have about a five-minute lead, I'm crossing the median to the other side, then crossing back behind them. We will turn the tables and catch them from behind. I think these guys are trying to send a message rather than actually kill us, because that shot to my rearview mirror was so dead-on not to be planned. BB, trade places with Bowmar and I'll get you and Bucky in firing position on their driver's side. Shoot their tires, dashboard, windshield, and engine compartment, but don't kill them. We'll send a louder message in their direction."

I traded places with Bowmar and was soon sitting directly behind Bucky, thinking, *There went our peaceful little trip to the White House.* Bowmar cued Waldo at ten minutes, and Waldo watched for a smooth patch of median to cross onto I-81 south. Once he identified a smooth enough crossing, Waldo put the Charger into a violent four-wheel drift of skidding deceleration, then accelerated at the perfect moment across the median, heading back south on I-81. We all kept our eyes peeled for the red GTO. Bucky was the first to spot it, coming north on I-85 at high speed. They were going too fast to notice us over in the southbound lane, and Waldo deftly crossed back over as they went by. The chase was on; Waldo drove the Charger like we were on the NASCAR circuit, or maybe the Cannonball Run!

We approached the Russians at high speed from behind. When the red GTO started to come back into clear view, Bucky and I got prepared, rolling our windows down and getting the .44 Magnums ready to shoot. We agreed that I would gun for the rear tires and rear windows, while he aimed for the front tires, windshield, dashboard, and engine compartment. These guys were going down, albeit alive. Waldo barked, "The very instant I pull alongside this Goat, fire away!

Don't hesitate for a second, as I said earlier; make my day, and make these bastards pay!"

As Waldo started to make his move, my music brain kicked into high gear as I thought about shooting ugly black bullet holes into that beautiful red 1966 Pontiac GTO XS. My brain started playing **"Paint It Black,"** by the Rolling Stones. The song was released in May 1966 and it reached number one in both the Billboard Hot 100 and the UK Singles Chart. It also went to number one in Canada and the Netherlands. It described the extreme grief suffered by someone stunned by the sudden and unexpected loss of a spouse, lover, or partner. In this case, it was going to be the extreme grief of losing one hell of a hot car! It was playing loud and heavy in my brain as I visualized making war on the red GTO with the Dirty Harry .44 Magnum in my hands.

Going roughly 100-110 mph north on I-81, Nick and Max had been focused on the road straight ahead and avoiding the sparse afternoon traffic. As Waldo made his move to pull up along their driver's side, Nick saw it coming at the last moment. He tried to swerve to stop Waldo's advance, glancing the GTO off the Charger. Shocked as I was that Waldo allowed his Charger to be damaged, he forced the Charger forward, scraping the GTO as he put Bucky and me in immediate position to fire. Max was trying to get a shot off, but I could see him struggling to position himself either in front of or behind Nick, and that caused a defeating delay.

Bucky and I opened fire on the GTO with the .44 Magnums, and every shot sounded like artillery fire booming at close range. The air was filled with the howls of muscle car engines and booming .44 Magnum cannon explosions. Bucky blew a hole through their radiator and took out the dashboard, windshield, and left front tire. I blew away the rear window, got the left rear tire, and put a couple of holes in the driver's side door. In my music brain the red GTO went to black as Nick lost control, running off the highway and spinning out wildly. The GTO crashed sideways into a small grove of trees. A message had been sent, but it was not the message that Nick's and Max's superiors had planned on.

CHAPTER TWO:

MAKING HAY

"Friends are the sunshine of life."
—John Hay

"Friends are born, not made."
—Henry Adams

Monday, June 30, 1975 at 7:00 PM local time,
the Hay-Adams Hotel, Washington, DC

We arrived at the Hay-Adams Hotel across the street from the White House at 6:00 PM on Monday. Waldo's Charger had suffered collision damage to the right front bumper, right front fender, passenger door and rear quarter panel, not to mention the destruction wrought by bullets impacting the driver's mirror and left taillight. The manager of valet parking, Chester "Chet" Brown, met us when we arrived and Waldo gave his name for check in. Chet was a tall, thin, good-humored man dressed in a crisp uniform, with a weathered face from smoking too many cigarettes. He briefly stared at the body damage to the passenger side of the Charger, and then directly addressed Waldo as he approached: "Good evening, Captain Thompson. I'm Chet Brown, and a friend of mine at the White House gave me explicit instructions to personally take care of your car during your visit to the Hay-Adams. I love the '68 Charger, but I wasn't expecting to see that you'd used it for a demolition derby. It looks like a little abstract Christmas decoration there, with the red and green paint mixed together on the passenger side!"

Knowing he was being teased by a peer his own age, Waldo responded, "Well Merry Christmas a little early there, Chet. How about a nice punch in the face for your present this year?"

They shook hands and chuckled together as Chet told Waldo that he too was a Korean War veteran. Waldo didn't go into details, but explained, "We had a little misunderstanding on the road to DC, and the other guy's car won't be making any more road trips anytime soon." Chet assured Waldo that the Charger was in good hands, and to enjoy his "stay at the Hay."

The Hay-Adams hotel, located at 16th and H Streets NW, occupies the site where the 1885 homes of John Hay and Henry Adams once stood. John Hay and Henry Adams were well-known active statesmen in Washington, DC in the latter half of the nineteenth century. Hay was the private secretary to Abraham Lincoln and subsequently served as the US ambassador to the UK, as well as being the secretary of state for Presidents William McKinley and Theodore Roosevelt. Henry Adams was the grandson of John Quincy Adams (the sixth US president), a distinguished writer, and an aficionado of the arts. The two men were notable scholars and an active part of the Washington DC cultural circuit. The two men, their wives, and a geologist named Clarence King were a close group of friends who dubbed themselves "The Five of Hearts," and had fine china and stationary letterhead printed with that moniker. They hosted splendid gatherings and magnificent parties at their homes that attracted important society figures—particularly authors, including Dolly Madison, Mark Twain, Henry James, and Edith Wharton.

In 1927, Washington developer Harry Wardman bought and razed both their historic homes, building the 138-room hotel across the street from the White House in the Italian Renaissance style. The hotel opened in 1928 as the Hay-Adams House and immediately attracted society's most prominent travelers, such as Charles Lindbergh, Sinclair Lewis, and Amelia Earhart. The hotel went through several changes of ownership, and the name was changed to the Hay-Adams Hotel in 1973.

We noted that the hotel had great views of the White House, Lafayette Square, and St. John's church. The impressive lobby was full of beautiful details that included vaulted archways, ornate filigreed ceilings, handsome walnut paneling, grand oil paintings, sparkling chandeliers, and elaborate oversized flower bouquets. The reservations were in Waldo's name, Captain Paul Thompson. At check-in, the hotel manager met us, gave us the keys to our rooms, and told us that White House Chief of Staff Donald Rumsfeld had arranged for the four of us to dine in the hotel restaurant. We would have dinner in the Lafayette Room at 7:30 PM, with views overlooking Lafayette Square and the White House. He also handed us an envelope marked *Confidential*. I looked at the group with a smile of relief and commented, "Hmm, I guess our luck is coming back around again."

We went straight to the restaurant while our small amount of luggage was delivered to our rooms. After we sat down for dinner together, Bowmar—in his classic encyclopedic fashion—proceeded to tell us the story of the haunting of the Hay-Adams Hotel. "Local legend holds that Henry Adams' wife, Clover, committed suicide here on December 6, 1885 and now haunts the hotel. Marion 'Clover' Hooper Adams lived in one of the original houses that sat on this hotel site. She fell into a deep depression after the death of her physician father in April 1885. She adored her father, and after his death she was no longer interested in her hobby of taking and developing photographs. There were also rumors that her husband had several affairs and/or a mistress, which may have further contributed to her melancholy. Retiring early one afternoon complaining of a toothache, she was later discovered by her husband sprawled on the rug in front of her fireplace. There was an open bottle of potassium cyanide nearby, a poisonous chemical she used to develop her photographs. There were conflicting reports about her death; some people wondered if she could have been murdered. No one knows for sure exactly how she died. In a fit of grief, Henry destroyed all of Clover's photographs and belongings. Henry and Clover are buried together under a monument the public called *Grief*. The staff of the hotel complain that the ghost of Clover is most active during early December, around the anniversary of her death. She makes her presence known by opening previously-locked doors in unoccupied suites, causing radios to spontaneously flicker to life, and leaving the faint aroma of almonds behind—the scent of potassium cyanide. Housekeepers have reported that she whispers their names in empty rooms, asking 'What do you want?' She even wraps her invisible arms around them in gentle embraces."

"Wow. That is quite a story, Bowmar!" I blurted. "I know it's not December, but I hope that you wake up tonight with her arms wrapped around you and not me. I don't think that Waldo, Bucky, or I can help you fight off ghosts. But if you start to smell almonds, I recommend that you keep your mouth shut. Don't yawn, and definitely don't swallow."

"Oh, thanks, I really appreciate your divine spiritual help there, Bubble Buddha. I think I might watch TV all night."

Bucky joined the conversation. "I suggest you get some sleep tonight, Bowmar. We need your computer brain to be fully operational tomorrow in the Oval Office. Let me know if you want me to come and read you a bedtime story, or sing you a little song: *Rock-a-bye baby, in the treetop...*" Bowmar frowned and kicked Bucky under the table.

"You may be hard to kill, Captain Denver, but I'll be using my persuasive powers to send that ghost your way tonight. We'll see how far your manly confidence goes with a woman from the beyond!" Bowmar retorted. He then changed the subject, asking, "So BB, how do you see this conversation with President Ford going tomorrow morning?"

"I have been giving that some thought, and I am looking forward to seeing him again. He had such a likable personality when we met him in April 1945," I replied. "He decided on the timing of this meeting, so he must have something to tell us. I suspect it may have to do with those two Ruskies in the red Goat chasing us today, or maybe how it went when they apprehended Borya Krovopuskov and his spy cell. Then again, maybe there's something going on at Area 51 that we don't know about. Well...come to think of it, President Ford might not even know that we were put in charge of security for Area 51, unless that information was passed down from the Roosevelt and Truman administrations somehow. I'd say from our perspective that we use this as an opportunity to bring him up to speed about our recent mission, to establish security and maintain the integrity of the White Hole Project and Area 51. Assuming that we are roughly on the same page and there are no major surprises, then maybe we can brainstorm together about our next mission."

Waldo, Bucky and Bowmar all looked at me cross-eyed and simultaneously cried out, "*What* next mission?!"

I felt six eyes piercing me from three corners of our table as my music brain started playing **"Bad Moon Rising,"** by Creedence Clearwater Revival. Released in April 1969, it was a global chart topper and definitely not about "a bathroom on the right." It was *the* song that made Creedence Clearwater Revival's name take off like a rocket ship worldwide. The lyrics came straight out of the tumultuous end of the 1960s, with references for catastrophic climate conditions or possibly an apocalypse that would be visited upon the Earth. "I can't get Blue Nova One off my mind, and the whole purpose of two alien ships coming to opposite ends of Earth simultaneously. What was their mission? Were they in trouble on their planet, or are we in trouble here?" I asked.

Bowmar quickly weighed in. "Why do you think there has to be trouble brewing here or there? Maybe it was just a peaceful expedition of exploration. Based on your description, she wasn't very different from us."

"When problems arise, we typically wait until we are in crisis mode, then we react because we have no choice," I answered. "Blue Nova One seemed very calm and deliberate, but their mission was aborted because they ran into unexpected problems. Not only that, but she knew me, Bucky, Pumpkin, and Goondoggy. And said she missed you, Bowmar."

Three voices spoke together. "What do you have in mind, Bubble Butt?"

"I have an idea percolating in my brain about us going to visit Blue Nova One and her planet, using the White Hole Project to link time and space travel. We haven't been back from our last mission long enough for this idea to fully germinate, but I'd like to get together with Bowmar and Bucky after we get back home to talk this through. I have done some research into space travel, given what we know about the White Hole Project and our visit to the alien ship at Area 51, that I would like to share with you. Tomorrow, I might test the waters with the president just a little, depending on how the discussion goes."

Bucky replied, "I've already been lost in time; I'm not sure that I want to get lost in space too. You'll have some convincing to do, that's for sure." Then he enquired, "Waldo, what does that envelope marked *Confidential* have to say?"

Waldo opened the letter and read it to us. "It says, 'Welcome to Washington, DC, Captain Thompson. Give me a call on this private phone line after dinner. Sincerely, Donald Rumsfeld.' Maybe he heard about our little encounter with the Ruskies earlier today. I think that I'm gonna give him the bill for my car repairs!"

After we finished dinner, we all retired to Waldo's suite and listened in on his phone call to Rumsfeld. Waldo dialed the number and said, "Good evening, Don; it's Waldo, and I'm here at the Hay-Adams with Bubble Butt, Bucky, and Bowmar, all with the Denver Project as you requested. Thank you for the fine accommodations and the terrific dinner in the Lafayette Room."

Rumsfeld replied, "Of course, it's our pleasure, Waldo. I don't have much for you. I wanted to make certain you arrived and let you know that a Secret Service agent named Dan Cotton will meet you and your group at six thirty AM, sharp, in the hotel lobby. He will take the four of you through all the security check points and directly to the Oval Office. I will not be attending your meeting with the president, but special FBI agent Chuck Brooks will be there. Is there anything else that you need?"

Waldo answered, "Yes, as a matter of fact, there is. I need my beloved '68 Charger repaired! We were ambushed by Russian operatives driving a red 1966 GTO on Interstate 81 North this afternoon. We did prevail, but my car looks like shit right now! The head of valet parking, Chet Brown—whom I assume you must know—asked me if I used the car in a demolition derby."

Rumsfeld responded, "I am sorry to hear that and quite frankly, a bit shocked. I received no such notifications in my late afternoon briefings today. I suspect the Russians cleaned up their mess before the local police or authorities heard anything. However, I am sure that you will get some answers when you meet with the President tomorrow morning. I know that he is very anxious to meet with you. Our Secret Service has specialty garages to deal with automotive damages big and small—and they can work very fast when the appropriate authority is exercised. With your permission, I will get your Charger picked up within the hour and repaired while you are here."

"Hell *yes*, you have my permission! Just tell those repair guys to treat it like it's one of their own precious children, and I'll be happy."

Rumsfeld chuckled and completed the call, "The President said you and your group always leave a lasting impression. I'm starting to understand why. Get some rest, and we'll see you tomorrow."

CHAPTER THREE:

PRESIDENTIAL BRIEFING

"When a man is asked to make a speech,
the first thing he has to decide is what to say."
—Gerald R. Ford

Tuesday, July 1, 1975 at 7:00 AM local time,
the White House Oval Office, Washington, DC

S ecret Service Agent, Dan Cotton, met us in the lobby of the Hay-
Adams Hotel at 6:30 AM as planned and escorted us directly to the
White House Oval Office. As we made the walk, my mind pictured
the grandeur, history, and power of the Oval Office and the fact that
we would soon be there to discreetly meet with President Gerald R.
Ford. In my lifetime, I could recall a few Oval Office images, such as
President Kennedy addressing the nation with the news of the Cuban
Missile Crisis in 1962. We had trained in grade school to get under our
desks—or if time permitted, to get to a tunnel under the road by our
school playground—in the event of a nuclear war (like that would keep
us safe). In my mind's eye, I could see President Nixon speaking with
the Apollo 11 astronauts after they landed and walked on the moon in
1969, and when Nixon announced his resignation from office in 1974,
paving the way for our current meeting with President Ford.

The modern history of the Oval Office dated back to 1909, when
President William Howard Taft expanded and extensively remodeled

the White House West Wing. Taft changed the shape of the old rect-angular office to a full oval, creating the Oval Office in the center of the West Wing as the official working office space for the President of the United States. He furnished it with silk velvet curtains and a check-erboard floor made of mahagua wood from the Philippines, decorated in an olive-green color scheme. The West Wing caught fire in 1929 and the original Oval Office was gutted, along with most of the rest of the building. It was rebuilt to the same design, but our deeply respected friend, mentor and President, Franklin D. Roosevelt, renovated and further expanded the West Wing to accommodate additional staff in 1933. He moved the Oval Office to the southeast corner, where there was better natural light from windows to the east and south, as well as easier access to the presidential residence. FDR's mandated changes made the Oval Office two feet wider and two feet longer, with the great presidential seal set in the ceiling. Since Roosevelt's renovation, the modern Oval Office had changed very little except in its furnish-ings. Most Presidents have at least chosen a new rug and drapes, and decided what historic presidential desk they want to use. Interestingly, President Eisenhower left everything the same when he took office, and President Kennedy's new decor was just being installed the day he was assassinated.

As we came through the door to President Ford's Oval Office at precisely 7:00 AM, the president was seated behind the Wilson desk. One of only six desks used by Presidents in the Oval office, the large mahogany Wilson desk was used by Presidents Nixon and Ford. It was a beautiful double-pedestal desk with drawers in both pedestals, and the knee-hole extended all the way through the desk. A sheet of glass covered the entire top of the desk. Red drapery flanked the windows behind the president, and a yellow floral rug covered the middle floor, flanked by two striped sofas facing each other. There were two yellow wing chairs and two Queen Anne-style armchairs on either side of the sofas; a hinged mahogany butler's tray table stood between the two sofas. Uniquely, Ford had first placed the incredibly handsome Seymour tall-case clock in the Oval Office. (I was a big fan of antique grandfather clocks, and quite taken by the elegance of the Seymour clock). FBI Special Agent Charlie "Chuck" Brooks was seated in a chair to the President's right with his back to us when we entered.

Once Waldo, Bucky, Bowmar, and I were through the door and standing inside the Oval Office, agent Dan Cotton introduced us. "Mr. President, these gentlemen from the Denver Project are here to meet with you as requested. I will return at seven forty AM, before your next meeting with the CIA and National Security Affairs."

President Ford rose from his seat, as did FBI agent Chuck Brooks. "Thanks, Dan, I'll take it from here, and see you see you in forty minutes." And with that, Dan shut the door behind him. We were once again face to face with President Gerald R. Ford, only this time he was sixty-one years old; when we met him in April 1945, he was thirty-one years old. Thirty years had passed by for him, but only ten weeks had gone by for us since we first met him.

Ford paused in silence for a moment behind the Wilson desk, staring at the four of us as we stared back. Then he smiled, and was the first to speak. "Gentlemen, I have waited with both patience and anticipation for thirty years for this very moment. You told me at our meeting in Commander Staples' office that you would look exactly the same when you saw me again—and by God, you were right!" He tightly pinched his right cheek between his right thumb and index finger. "Yep, I can feel that! I have to tell you from my perspective; this is both eerie and exhilarating. Whatever Fountain of Youth you all have been drinking from, I'd like to get some of that for me and Betty!" We all laughed and relaxed a bit. "Bubble Butt, Waldo, and Bucky, it's great to see you; and welcome, Bowmar." He then made the only remaining introduction. "This is FBI Special Agent Chuck Brooks. Chuck, introduce yourself and let's have the group take a seat on the chairs and sofas while I grab something from my desk."

The four of us shook hands and made our introductions with Chuck, then the five of us took seats. Waldo and Bucky sat on one sofa, while Bowmar and I sat facing them on the other. Chuck sat in one of the yellow wing chairs. The President grabbed a piece of paper and a small leather-bound book from his desk drawer and joined us, sitting in one of the Queen Anne-style armchairs at the head of our circle of engagement. The President put the book in his lap and unfolded what appeared to be a very old piece of paper. "I have something that I need to show you, and something that I need to read to you," he informed us. In that moment, I had the sensation of déjà vu. I felt like we were back in Warm Springs, Georgia, talking with President Roosevelt in his bedroom at the Little White House. The remarkable conversation with President Ford that followed would be permanently seared in my consciousness.

The President continued, "That Sunday when we met at NAS Glenview, on April 15, 1945, when Peggy Sue Harding took me back to the officer's barracks, I quickly sat down and wrote this note to myself. You will recall that I was already a lawyer when I joined the Navy; I know how to take good notes. This is dated April 15th, 1945." He then read from the sheet of paper. "You will run for Congress in 1948, get married during the campaign, and honeymoon attending campaign rallies. An American President will be assassinated, and you will be part of a committee investigating that assassination. You will represent your Michigan district in Congress for twenty-five years. You will never be elected Vice President or President, but you will serve as Vice President and President. You will face a difficult decision to use your pardon power as President. I was visited by a two-star general named Paul 'Waldo' Thompson, a young-looking Colonel named Kevin 'Bubble Butt' Schafer, and Captain Jack 'Bucky' Smith, who suggested they were time travelers and in charge of a top-secret military program called the Denver Project. They also called themselves the... Bad Love Gang? Waldo initiated the conversation but Bubble Butt did most of the talking. On the ride back to the barracks, Peggy Sue said she knew Bucky from high school in Denver, and had not seen him in ten years. They will contact me in 1975 through the White House switchboard using the phrase 'the Denver Project needs you.' I liked these guys, and kind of wished I could have tagged along with them."

He handed the old piece of paper to me to pass around to the group. Sure enough, it looked like it was thirty years old and bore the wear and tear of having been looked at many times during those three decades. As I started to pass the note to Bowmar, Chuck Brooks broke the silence in the room with a wide toothy smile on his face, "Mr. President, my mom is originally from Bolivia and has that Spanish romantic passion thing going on. I don't think she would have stayed with my dad if he took her to political rallies on their honeymoon!"

We all chuckled, including the President as he responded, "I think I told these guys that I was more romantic than to spend my honeymoon on the campaign trail. I must have reread that note a hundred times after marrying Betty during my first campaign. It was then that I began to secretly believe that this was all true, and I would become President one day. Everything in that note has come true without fail; it really is spooky, when you think about it."

"You also said that you were way too nice of a guy to ever be President of the United States. We didn't write it down, but we were all impressed that you were so likeable at age thirty-one. I hope that all these years of politics haven't tainted your fun-factor too much," I said with a smile. "We do call ourselves the Bad Love Gang, and our motto is 'Live dangerously, have fun, don't die.' I think the strangest part about our meeting here this morning is that for you, it has been thirty years since we first met...but for us, we met you only ten weeks ago, when you were thirty-one years old."

"I like that motto!" Chuck exclaimed. "The FBI could use something like that. Our motto is Fidelity, Bravery and Integrity, F-B-I. We deal with a lot of serious shit all the time, but people need to lighten up a bit and not act like the world is ending every five flippin' minutes! I think I might want to join the Bad Love Gang as part of this assignment."

Bowmar spoke up, "Listen, bro, you might not realize what you're getting into with that request. The first thing that is going to happen is they/we are going to give you a new nickname and it's not going to be flattering. And then you'll have to live with it for the rest of your life!"

"Speak for yourself there, Brainiac boy. After all these years of watching over you little shits, the name 'Waldo' is starting to grow on me just a bit!"

Bucky quickly weighed in. "I was Special Ops in the Air Force in 1945, got rescued by these guys in November 1944 on my first time-travel mission, and now I'm living in 1975 as a bona fide member of the Bad Love Gang and the Denver Project. How crazy is *that*?!"

We just got started, and I'm already having fun. Now I get to share something that might surprise these guys for once, President Ford mused. As his weathered personal note circulated back to him, he unbuttoned and opened the leather-bound book in his lap and interrupted our banter. "This book I am holding is called the *Book of Presidents*. It contains presidential writings of the deepest secrets of every US administration all the way back to George Washington." I felt a cold shiver run the length of my spine. "It is passed directly from president to president at the transition of each new administration, and every president is sworn to keep it to their eyes only. I am at liberty to read to you from it, but only my eyes can see it. Richard Nixon privately revealed this book to me before he left office, and made sure that I knew to carefully date every new entry I made. That is how each new president can easily use this book to validate and/or research our nation's profoundest secrets. I am going to share a couple of specific dated examples that have helped me know how to deal with the Denver Project and the Bad Love Gang."

Ford had placed a couple of tabs in the book to mark where he would read from. He continued, "President Roosevelt made the following entries:

"June 18, 1942: Last night, an alien spaceship crashed at Indian Springs Airfield at Groom Dry Lake in Nevada. I have designated this airbase as our nation's highest-level top secret. We will build a hanger around the spaceship and try to learn its mysteries.

"July 1, 1942: Received a letter from General Claire Chennault of the AVG Flying Tigers indicating that an alien spaceship had crashed east of Kunming, China on Thursday afternoon June 18, 1942. The Bad Love Tigers (sent by me?) led by Captain Jack 'Bucky' Smith arrived on Sunday June 21, 1942 and discovered the crash site the following day. They rescued Flying Tigers downed pilot Allen Wright. They fought off Japanese ground forces and completely destroyed an incoming Japanese bombing mission, taking out ten enemy planes. The alien spaceship left on Wednesday evening June 24, 1942."

Chuck leaned over and gave Bucky a high-five and said, "That's some awesome shit, and you're sitting here with us right now? Wow!"

"Bubble Butt was the real hero that day," Bucky protested, "and we'll tell you about that in a few minutes."

President Ford continued reading selected FDR entries.

"October 1, 1942: I met with Vannevar Bush and Albert Einstein tonight and commissioned them to build the White Hole Project in Oak Ridge Tennessee, a time machine made possible by using something we are calling blue exotic matter, extracted from the alien spaceship in Nevada. If Hitler gets the atomic bomb first, we will use the White Hole to go back in time and stop him. I have made the White Hole Project our nation's utmost secret—even more secret than the atomic bomb project. We can never let time travel fall into the wrong hands.

"October 28, 1942: Vannevar Bush and I had dinner with Captain Jack 'Bucky' Smith, who personally witnessed the alien spaceship crash on June 17, 1942, then boarded the alien ship and saw the aliens depart. He gave a credible eyewitness report of the events from that night. I like and trust this young special ops pilot. I have assigned him as the first test pilot for the White Hole Project.

"March 17, 1945: St. Patrick's Day, and my fortieth wedding anniversary. I was notified that the first White Hole Project launch failed; Captain Jack 'Bucky' Smith is presumed dead. I spoke to his parents, Jim and Liz. We are launching a detailed failure analysis. I feel terrible, and am depressed about losing Bucky; I personally chose him. The White Hole Project is on hold until we determine what went wrong.

"That was Roosevelt's last entry about the White Hole Project. The next entry is from Harry Truman.

"April 16, 1945: After searching hard, we found Captain Jack 'Bucky' Smith alive in St. Louis, Missouri. He is decidedly not dead. Tonight I spoke to Bucky, who is in charge of the Denver Project, which is more secret than the Manhattan Project. I read Franklin's last letter in this life, which was addressed to me and urged me to give Bucky and his team whatever resources they need to carry out their mission. Bucky's team is called the 'Bad Love Gang.' God help us, with a name like that!

"April 19, 1945: Earlier today, Bucky and his team the Bad Love Gang took out nearly the entire Colorado Russian spy network just west of Kit Carson, Colorado. I was told they left quite a scene of destruction. They are on their way to stay at the Broadmoor Hotel and train to fly P-40 Warhawks at Peterson Army Air Base in Colorado Springs. They have my full support. I contacted Peterson Air Base with orders to fully cooperate with Bucky, and give him and his group everything that they need. I also called Charles Tutt Jr. at the Broadmoor, and told him to treat that group like gold. Vannevar Bush is going to brief me in detail about the Denver Project after General Leslie Groves briefs me about the Manhattan project on April 24th."

Being intrigued with World War II history, I was day dreaming just a little bit as I came to and added, "I want to meet Winston Churchill and have a discussion with him. How great would that be?!"

President Ford broadly smiled and said, "How do you know with certainty that you haven't met with Winston Churchill? Maybe you will get your wish, Bubble Butt. I have only read a few select excerpts from this book to you. I will tell you this much: The White Hole Project, the Denver Project, Area 51, and the Bad Love Gang are mentioned more inside this book than what I have just shared. That is why I trust you, your intentions, and your role in protecting the secrets of the White Hole Project and Area 51, and have no intention of doing anything but supporting you and continuing to carry out FDR's directive to give you everything you need to succeed. That said, Bubble Butt, I want you to give me the abbreviated, high-level version of your overall mission when you tracked me down at NAS Glenview so I can get a better feel for your 'recent' mission. I want you to tell me what your plans are for the White Hole Project. Then I am going to explain exactly why agent Brooks is sitting here with us, and how we need to move forward from here."

Holy shit, I am about to give the president of the United States a briefing about the Bad Love Gang using the White Hole Project and its future, I thought. *I haven't completely thought this through. I'll just have to wing it. I'm so glad Bowmar, Bucky, and Waldo are sitting here with me!* As I gathered my thoughts to speak, my music brain briefly played **"You Really Got Me,"** by the Kinks. Normally, I am *overconfident* if anything; teachers whom I respect the most have called me brash. But for a brief moment, President Ford really got me caught a bit off balance and I was thinking *What am I doing here?* Somehow the music in my brain helped me recover and remember that we are always more afraid of what we don't know than of what we do know. I was about to share an idea with the president about what we didn't know, and that was what temporarily made my heart and brain race.

CHAPTER FOUR:

THE DESTINY OF THE WHITE HOLE PROJECT

"Things are only impossible until they're not."
—Captain Jean-Luc Picard,
Star Trek: The Next Generation

Tuesday, July 1, 1975 at 7:15 AM local time,
the White House Oval Office, Washington, DC

After a brief lapse of mental composure that no one in the room really noticed, I proceeded to summarize our recent time-travel missions for President Ford, trying to keep the chronology tied to the "present" times.

"As Bucky mentioned, we took our first time-travel mission in November 1974. We time-traveled to November 1944 and rescued thirteen Holocaust victims from Nazi-occupied Poland, using a famous B-17 Flying Fortress known as the Phantom Fortress. Bucky had been sent to the Phantom Fortress by President Roosevelt but was stuck in time when we arrived. He returned to 1974 with us. So did his navigator, Darby 'Pumpkin' Nelson, and a Jewish orphan boy named Benzion Kaplan. We had been back just over five weeks and really had not planned any other missions.

"Six months ago today, the entire Bad Love Gang had assembled at the White Hole Project to celebrate New Year's Eve. We were having a great time until, at the stroke of midnight, we were ambushed by Russian KGB agent Borya Krovopuskov. We all might have been killed, but Waldo's baseball-sized prostate saved our lives." Waldo frowned at me and everyone else laughed out loud. "He was out of sight answering the call of nature at the stroke of midnight; after the ambush became apparent, he was able to sneak up and get the draw on Borya, wounding him twice. Waldo took a bullet to his own left shoulder."

Waldo added, "I wasn't shooting to kill, otherwise that bastard would be shoveling coal to stoke the furnaces of hell. I wanted to interrogate his ass."

Ford laughingly remarked, "Spoken like a true Medal of Honor recipient. Continue on, BB."

"Borya got away and we were faced with a decision: go directly to the authorities, or take matters into our own hands. Bucky, convinced that the breach in security started when the White Hole Project was built, recommended that we speak to President Roosevelt and then decide how to proceed. Our most recent mission—when we met you, Mr. President—started on April 12, 1975 and did not fully end until a week ago. We met with FDR on the morning of April 12, 1945—the day he died—at the Little White House in Warm Springs, Georgia. He confirmed breaches of security in the Manhattan Project, and put us in charge of securing the White Hole Project in addition to Area 51. He handed us an envelope with a hand-written letter to General Claire Chennault of the famed Flying Tigers, and instructed us to meet with Chennault in June of 1942 and deliver the note. We left Warm Springs and took an epic 1945 road trip, starting at the White Hole Project in Oak Ridge, Tennessee. We sealed the entrance to the White Hole Project, then drove to Chicago to meet you at NAS Glenview. We knew we would need your help now in 1975 to apprehend Borya and his spy cell, and decided the best way to enlist your help was to meet with you long before you would become president."

"No one would believe this story, but the way you did it made it undeniably memorable and believable," President Ford agreed. "Go ahead."

"After we met you, we continued on to Peterson Army Air Base in Colorado Springs, Colorado to train to fly P-40 Warhawks. We were tailed by Russian, Chinese, and Indian spies the entire trip, and we had a major shootout in Colorado with the Russian spy cell who called themselves the Vodka Cowboys. We were forewarned by a Chinese spy named Ming Sun, and Waldo devised a battle plan knowing we would be ambushed. The Bad Love Gang established its reputation with the Ruskies that day as we prevailed against two-to-one odds. Peggy Sue Harding, whom you met, was nearly killed that day—but Colonel Carter Clarke of the Vennona Project helped us to get her medical help just in time.

"Four of us trained to fly and fight in P-40 Warhawks and we finished that leg of the mission at Area 51, familiarizing ourselves with the crashed alien spaceship hidden there. A week and a half ago, seven of us from the Bad Love Gang used the White Hole to time-travel to China in June of 1942 and volunteer for the AVG Flying Tigers. We met with General Claire Chennault, as instructed by FDR. An alien spaceship had crashed in south China at the exact same time as the crash in Area 51. We realized that Roosevelt sent us there to protect the secrets of Area 51. Calling ourselves the Panda Bear Squadron of the Bad Love Tigers, we found the UFO crash site, rescued AVG downed pilot Allen Wright, joined friendly Chinese ground forces to repel a Japanese ground assault, and then destroyed an incoming Japanese Army Air Force squadron sent to bomb the alien spaceship."

Bucky interposed, "That is when BB was the real hero. There were four of us flying P-40 Warhawks, and ten Japanese enemy aircraft. We managed to shoot nine of the ten Japanese planes down, but we all ran out of ammunition. The remaining Japanese fighter plane decided to make it a kamikaze mission and crash his plane into the alien spaceship. Bubble Butt put his P-40 into a terminal dive and rammed the Japanese Oscar before he could complete his kamikaze intentions."

"I am lovin' this story, and it's giving me some goosebumps...but if BB rammed his plane into the Jap plane, how is it that he is sitting here with us right now?" Chuck enquired.

"I knew Bowmar was recalling us at 5:00 PM, so I tried to time my dive into that Jap plane at exactly 5:00 PM," I replied.

Chuck asked, "What if Bowmar was late? What if your timing was off?"

Bowmar answered, "We all wear synchronized military watches, and I'm never early or late."

I added, "If he was late or my timing was off, then you would be talking to a ghost right now."

"Excuse me, Mr. President, but I have to say that is some of the most insane, craziest shit I have ever heard!" Chuck exclaimed.

Bucky, Waldo, Bowmar and I all simultaneously turned and faced Chuck Brooks who acted surprised that we all turned in synchrony. I winked at Bowmar and he responded for us as a group. "It may be insane, crazy shit. But it is all *very true* insane, crazy shit. President Roosevelt and I were holding hands the morning of April 12, 1945 when I got zapped back to 1975 by the White Hole. These three guys were sitting there with Roosevelt as he was suddenly left empty-handed and his hands dropped to his lap. How crazy is that? Listen to me, bro; whether you allow yourself to believe it or not, you are sitting here in the Oval Office with four time travelers—and that is the truth."

President Ford rejoined the conversation. "I know you are telling the absolute truth, because I personally met three of you in 1945 and you are written into the *Book of Presidents*. I think Chuck's doubts are normal, only natural; that is why I wanted him here with us this morning. So BB, finish your story and tell me what you want to do with the White Hole Project."

"Well, Mr. President, I saved the best for last," I replied "The night before we left the forest in south China, we spied on the damaged alien spaceship that had crash landed there. It was me, Bucky, the navigator we mentioned named Pumpkin, and a guy we call Willy. After darkness fell, a female alien exited the ship and proceeded to make repairs to the hull while we watched. Much to Bucky's dismay, I took it upon myself to make contact and proceeded to hum and dance my way up to her singing "Stand by Me," by Ben E. King. I figured music was the universal language and hoped that a soft approach might win the night."

Bucky interjected, "For the record, sir, I thought this was a terrible idea and tried to stop him. But Bubble Butt has this thing he calls his 'music brain.' When that music starts playing in his head, I don't think he hears anything or anyone else!"

Ford responded, "I love that song, it's totally a universal classic, and I can picture the scene."

Chuck added, "Yeah, I dig your taste in music, BB. How about throwing a little Chuck Berry in there?"

I glanced at Chuck with a big grin on my face. "You just gave me a great idea for your nickname! Hold that thought for a while." I then refocused on the president and continued, "Well, the song and dance worked. She introduced herself as Blue Nova One and invited me to help her with the hull repairs. Her clothing was shiny, smooth and metallic, and it fit her like a glove. Her face and hands were exposed and her skin was blue, but her complexion was perfect. Other than being a bit on the thin side, she was beautiful."

Chuck, maybe getting a little too relaxed with the conversation, enquired, "Did your music brain start playing **"Devil with a Blue Dress On/Good Golly Miss Molly"** by Mitch Ryder and the Detroit Wheels?"

Chuck didn't know who he was messing with just yet; I bet I knew more about that song than he did. The song was released in September 1966 and reached number four on the Billboard Hot 100. It actually described a femme fatale in a blue dress, not a devil. "I said her skin was blue, not her outfit. You and Captain Denver here are gonna get along famously, and we'll pull both your minds out of the gutter as we go!" Bucky—who had been nicknamed Captain Denver by Peggy Sue Harding— and Chuck smiled at each other, and we all laughed.

"I understood her to be speaking English, but she said that she did not speak English. She said I heard her in English and told me that we had already met, but I did not perceive that we had met. She knew the others were hiding in the bushes, and she also claimed to know Bucky, Pumpkin, Willy's brother Goondoggy, and Bowmar."

Chuck interrupted again, half laughing, "What kind of name is *Goondoggy?*"

"Wait 'til I give you your nickname here in a few minutes," I replied. "Blue Nova One gave us valuable intel on the incoming Japanese ground forces. She admitted that their expedition to Earth did not go as planned, and we agreed to try and protect them and their spaceship until they could safely depart. We cleaned up the blue exotic matter that had spilled on the ground and she took it with her. I have to say that I enjoyed my time with her and can't seem to totally get my mind off her, but she was the only alien that we met. This brings me to the idea that I have brewing for our next White Hole Project mission."

"OK, Bubble Butt, we are all ears," the president stated.

"I know that we have an amazing space program through NASA here in the United States, and it is something that we are all incredibly proud of."

The president interjected, "Two weeks from today, on July 15th, we are launching the Apollo-Soyuz Project to test the compatibility of rendezvous and docking systems for American and Soviet spacecraft, and to open the way for international space rescue as well as future joint space missions. NASA designed a universal docking module that will serve as an airlock and transfer corridor between our Apollo capsule and the Russian Soyuz craft. Astronauts Tom Stafford, Vance Brand, and Deke Slayton are flying this upcoming mission for us. It's the first Apollo rocket mission since Apollo 17's 1972 trip to the Moon."

"Understood, sir," I replied. "What I have in mind would be off the record, and every bit as secret as both the White Hole Project and Area 51. I think that I might have figured out a way to use the White Hole Project to transport a contingent of the Bad Love Gang to Blue Nova One's planet."

"SHUUT UP!" Bowmar sang out. "How are you gonna do that?!"

I smiled and shrugged. "We'll talk it through, but Mr. President, I think we can do it. It will take some planning over the next several months, but I can tell you that time travel and space travel are intimately intertwined. Whatever happens, whether we succeed or fail, the world cannot know. This needs to stay between you, us, and that *Book of Presidents* sitting in your lap. All we need is for the White Hole Project to stay safe and secret in our hometown of Oak Ridge, Tennessee."

President Ford softly smiled and stared at us during a brief period of silence before he spoke. "I just don't even pretend to know how you and your Bad Love Gang ever came to be, but I am really glad to know you. You can proceed with planning this next mission, but we have a major problem to address regarding your safety and the safety of the White Hole Project. That is why I invited you here today, and also why Chuck is sitting here with us this morning. After I spoke with you on April 30th, we managed to apprehend much of Borya Krovopuskov's Russian spy network. However, Borya and his wife Catherine killed five of our finest FBI and CIA agents when we tried to apprehend them. They are extremely dangerous, and remain at large at this moment. We have their two children, Bobby and Natalie, in custody but probably cannot hold them much longer. Chuck here has distinguished himself with the FBI in Russian counterespionage and can work with his connections and with Bucky in his role of leading the Denver Project to stop Krovopuskov. We now know that Krovopuskov has legendary status with the KGB, but the Russian diplomatic channels disavow any knowledge of him or his actions. We are working on it through the CIA and FBI, but I want Chuck to be undercover, on site in Oak Ridge and working directly with you. There is a Russian Bear at large, and we are all going bear hunting together on this one."

Waldo spoke up, "It must have been Borya that sent two of his henchmen after us on the road here yesterday. I should have put that first bullet between his beady little eyes on New Year's Eve. Don't worry, Mr. President; the next time we face that guy, he's goin' down."

The meeting was coming to an end. Chuck sat up straight and asked me, "So, what is my nickname as part of the Bad Love Gang?"

"You're gonna be sorry you asked," Bowmar quipped.

With a smirky grin on my face, I answered, "We're calling you Chuck 'Ding-a-Ling' Brooks. Maybe just 'Ding' for short, since you mentioned that you were a Chuck Berry fan. Chuck Berry's novelty song 'My Ding-a-Ling' (needing no further explanation) hit the Billboard number one position in the US in 1972 and prevented one of my favorites, 'Burning Love' by Elvis Presley, from hitting the number one spot at the time."

Chuck responded, "But they called me 'Dick Tracy' at Quantico."

"You're in the Bad Love Gang now, Ding; get used to it," I advised.

CHAPTER FIVE:

THE DING FACTOR

"Don't let the same dog bite you twice."
—Chuck Berry

Tuesday, July 1, 1975 at 8:30 AM local time, the Lafayette Room in the Hay-Adams Hotel, Washington, DC

Our meeting with President Ford ended at 7:40 AM sharp. So as the five of us left the Oval Office, David Peterson, Chief of the Central Intelligence Agency (CIA) and Lieutenant General Brent Scowcroft, Deputy Assistant for National Security Affairs, both walked by us and into the Oval Office. Donald Rumsfeld was waiting for us outside the Oval Office. He was fully acquainted with Chuck Brooks, who did an excellent job of introducing the four of us, complete with nicknames. After we all shook hands, Rumsfeld was brief and to the point, handing us his personal contact card as he spoke. "Anytime you need to reach the president, call me at the number on this card. I set his schedule and have access to him at all times. Waldo, your car repairs will be completed sometime between now and tomorrow morning. I have been assured that it will be returned to the Hay-Adams valet parking team and ready for you by seven AM." He gave Waldo a thin smile. "The team doing the body work knows to treat that car like it's their first-born child. We have you staying tonight at the hotel and checking out tomorrow morning. Make your lunch and/or dinner reservations for today and tonight anywhere here in DC through the hotel concierge, and your meals will be paid for. Do I need to call agent Cotton to escort you back to the hotel?"

"No need to call Dan; I will escort them from here. We are all headed to the Lafayette Room for some breakfast and brainstorming," Chuck answered.

Rumsfeld responded, "I love their eggs Benedict. Now you have me a little jealous."

"Thanks for getting my Charger repaired so promptly. I didn't know the government was capable of working so fast," Waldo teased.

Rumsfeld tilted his head and shrugged as he replied. "I never said it was government work. And besides, you were never here; I don't see you anywhere on today's schedule. But thanks to all of you, for whatever you do."

As we parted ways and walked out of the White House, I thought, *Now, that is the definition of* plausible deniability *if I ever heard it!*

The five of us walked back to the Hay-Adams and to the Lafayette Room, making small talk until we were all seated together at a private corner table where we could get to know Chuck a bit better, and discuss his plan to thwart and/or apprehend Borya. Bucky got the conversation started. "So, Ding... Tell us about yourself, and how you got tapped by President Ford to be working with us."

"I guess you could say that working for the FBI runs in my family now. I understand that you guys are big fans of FDR. It was Roosevelt that established the Special Intelligence Service, which was a covert counterintelligence branch of the FBI located in South America during World War II. The FBI placed numerous undercover agents in Latin America; my dad was one of those agents assigned to La Paz,

Bolivia. While on duty in La Paz, he met and fell in love with my mom. There were more than 1.5 million expatriate Germans living in South America at that time in the 1940s, and it was an active area of Axis espionage, propaganda, and sabotage. My dad and his colleagues uncovered some crazy Nazi spy shit, the kind of stuff you might read about in spy novels or see in the movies, and a lot of it remains classified to this day. After the war ended, my parents moved to Virginia and started a family. I'm the oldest of three siblings, and I have two sisters. Growing up, I idolized my dad's career in the FBI and wanted to be like him.

"I went to Howard University here in DC, starting as an undergraduate in pre-law in 1965. I graduated from law school in 1972. I then joined the FBI and enrolled in the FBI Academy at Quantico, Virginia. I was interested in Russian history as an undergrad, became fluent in speaking Russian, and then decided to specialize in Russian counterespionage as my first career step with the FBI. I've had some success in undercover anti-KGB investigations here in DC, and got the call about helping with a covert anti-KGB mission in Tennessee. Unfortunately, one of my Quantico classmates, Dave Johnson, was among the five agents killed during the attempted apprehension of Borya Krovopuskov and his wife Catherine. Borya killed Dave and two other FBI agents, and wounded several other people, when we tried to apprehend him at the Oak Ridge National Laboratory three weeks ago. At the same time, while trying to arrest Catherine at their home in Knoxville, two CIA agents met their demise at her hands. We did get some vague snippets that the two of them may have headed to New York City, where there is much more Russian support to hide them—but nothing concrete. We detained their two college-age children, Bobby and Natalie Krovo, but there is no indication so far that either of them knows that their parents are nefarious Russian master spies. We do suspect that both Borya and Catherine are super-pissed that we are holding their two children in custody.

"The Denver Project and the Bad Love Gang may have handed the president, the FBI, and the CIA the biggest treasure trove of soviet KGB spies in the annals of US counterespionage recordkeeping. We determined that the infamous and notorious Russian spy Leonid Romanovich Kvasnikov, who organized the spy cell that stole the secrets of the Manhattan project from Los Alamos, personally trained Borya and sent him to Oak Ridge, Tennessee in 1944. Borya, working at Oak Ridge National Laboratory and Catherine, working at the University of Tennessee, Knoxville, probably headed the oldest and most extensive Soviet KGB sleeper cell network in modern Soviet/American history. We have already arrested a dozen key KGB agents in the Krovos' Southeast US network, and we have twice that many under active surveillance at this moment. Borya and Catherine Krovo sit atop the FBI's most-wanted list; they are considered not just armed and dangerous, but to be lethal weapons themselves."

Bowmar said, "Both my parents attended Howard University; that is where they met and fell in love. I'm sorry to hear about your classmate, Dave Johnson, dying at Borya's hands. Were you two close friends?"

"I wouldn't say we were close, but we were at the top of our class in pistol marksmanship, and we frequently target shot together. If I close my eyes, I can see him standing next to me at Quantico's indoor range, bragging that his shot pattern was grouped tighter than mine."

Waldo couldn't help himself. "When you get to Tennessee, I'll let you take your pick from my gun collection and we'll have a little competition right there in Oak Ridge to see if you can outgun a Korean War Vet. By the way, what have you been reading about us in those FBI files they keep on the world at large?"

Ding responded, "I figured one of you would ask, and yes, I did a little homework before I showed up in the Oval Office this morning. Starting with you, Waldo, I understand that you are a decorated US Army Korean War Medal of Honor recipient, for leading the repelling of an enemy attack. I read your file; you saved a lot of lives that day, and took a few bullets in the process. I get that you are calm and confident under fire. Your military record is spotless, but I find it...well, you might say *interesting*, that you are now identified with the Denver Project and the Bad Love Gang. I know that you're married to Mary—and basically, it looks like she's an angel, or at least a saint."

Waldo reacted with a grin. "God smiled on me for unknown reasons when it comes to Mary. Bucky here dragged me into the Denver Project in front of President Roosevelt on our most recent time-travel mission. I had to accept the assignment to keep my tough-guy image intact. But the Bad Love Gang, now that's a different story." He looked at me and Bowmar and continued, "Mary and I couldn't have children of our own and basically adopted all these little shit-faced kids in our neighborhood when they were still learning how to blow their noses and tie their own shoes. They have called themselves the Bad Love Gang since they graduated from riding tricycles. We've watched them all grow up like they belong to us. Once in a while we try to give them some advice, but mainly, Mary and I listen well, and our door is always open to them. She and I don't have any children of our own, but we know that we have the biggest family in the neighborhood. Now that they have discovered the White Hole Project and time travel, I find myself using some of my military skills to try and keep everyone safe and alive. I do have to say, after our last two time-travel missions, they've all come of age pretty well and have become fairly good at taking care of themselves. Don't let that go to your big head there, Bubble Butt, or your big brain, Bowmar. Life is never, ever boring when it comes to the Bad Love Gang. Mary and I have talked about our interesting lives with the Bad Love Gang a lot; it definitely keeps us both feeling young."

"Waldo is a retired Army Captain, but he has been posing as a USAAF two-star Major General during these last two time-travel missions," Bucky added. "After watching his ground assault tactics recently in Colorado, I think his Major General rank fits him just fine. Another thing: the guy *always* has a gun. Which reminds me, did you manage to slip into the Oval Office with a gun this morning?"

Waldo answered with a devilish sneer, "If I did, I'd never admit to it. But I will say it would have to get past the metal detectors."

Ding shrugged that comment off and continued, "I read Bucky's amazing file from the time he entered West Point until the time he went missing on an unnamed top-secret mission, was presumed dead, and subsequently buried with full military honors in Denver on March 24, 1945. But now I understand that you guys rescued him from being stuck in time and brought him back to the future with you. How's that working out for you, Bucky?"

"I'll have to agree with Waldo, it sure hasn't been boring!" Bucky exclaimed. "The Bad Love Gang saved my life, and they have become my modern family here in 1975. To tell you the truth, I feel like I have one foot in 1945 and one foot in 1975; who else can say that? My parents now know that I'm still alive, even though they buried me. Roosevelt put me in charge of the Denver Project, so for now, I'm focused on protecting the security and integrity of the White Hole Project and Area 51. I have great connections with presidents Roosevelt, Truman and Ford, in addition to Vannevar Bush and Colonel Carter Clarke of the Vennona Project. I have had top-secret clearance to Area 51 since 1942. Blue Nova One, the alien we recently met, also seems to know me. My future is somehow still coming together."

"I see you playing a pivotal role in our upcoming attempt to get back to Blue Nova One. Your future is with us, Captain Denver—Romeo of the skies," I teased.

"What's that all about?" Ding enquired.

"I won a girl's heart in high school by taking her flying, and Bubble Butt won't let it go. All you need to know is that I'm hard to kill and ready to put this Borya bastard away for good," Bucky retorted.

I clarified, "Her name is Peggy Sue Harding, and she's waiting for Bucky back in 1945. A Chinese spy named Ming Sung and an Indian secret agent named Nisha Singh also have the hots for him."

Bowmar added, "Yeah, we also call him Captain Confidence sometimes, because his self-confidence is a chick magnet."

Bucky shot back, "Captain Confidence is getting ready to step on your testicles, Bowmar, and make you a chick *period!*"

Waldo was enjoying the banter, but stepped in to shut it down with a smirk. "All right, boys, let's get back on track now."

Ding was chuckling at this point as he resumed giving us his impressions of our files. "We have a small file on Bowmar's family because his dad, John Williams, works as a nuclear physicist at Oak Ridge National Laboratory and his file is available to the FBI. Bowmar's mother Lisa works as an attorney in Knoxville. There are two children, Brianna and Nathan, aka Bowmar, who is noted in the file to be a childhood genius."

"You'll get to know Brianna too; we call her Cleopatra, because she quickly becomes the queen of any social circle she enters. Maybe she can become a queen on Blue Nova One's planet if and when we get there! Now Bowmar, on the other hand... He's orbiting up there somewhere," I pointed straight up, "and it's my job to grab his foot and bring him back down to earth just a bit."

Ding nodded. "That brings me to you, Bubble Butt. There's not much on file other than your father was an Army sergeant under

General Douglas MacArthur in the Philippines in World War II, and was honorably discharged. I understand that you like to plan the group's adventures and missions, and that you have a love for music. Based on the discussion in the Oval Office, it sounds like you are a risk taker."

"That's all fair enough, Ding. You will also discover that I don't have a shy bone in my body. I love to laugh, and try my best to find humor in various situations. You've got a good start on us, but the Bad Love Gang can be a bit unpredictable at times; there are quite a few different personalities and skill sets. We tease and verbally abuse each other to no end, but one thing is for sure: We all would go to the mat for each other, if push came to shove. We get the job done somehow, whenever we work together. Let's get back to talking more about you. How do you plan to set up shop in Oak Ridge?"

"In my alternative world, I would have been a radio announcer," Ding stated.

"I don't have a career yet, and think I want to become a doctor," I admitted. "But in my alternative world, I want to be James Bond or a rock and roll star! How about you, Waldo? What would you be?"

"I'd be happy as a country western singer or racing on the NASCAR circuit...or I'd be just fine testing firearms for a living," he said as he pointed at me using his right hand as a gun. He closed his left eye and aimed with his right, squinting and then squeezing the trigger.

Bucky chimed in, "I wanna race airplanes or test pilot some of these new jets I see flying around in 1975."

"I want to be a stand-up comedian and make people laugh 'til they cry. That's so far out of my league that it seems like a good alternative universe," Bowmar explained.

We all smiled at each other as Ding continued, "The Bureau has arranged for me to move to Oak Ridge and become a new radio announcer for WATO 1290 AM, as my cover."

This time our encyclopedic Bowmar spoke so excitedly and rapidly it was like he'd just been plugged into a wall socket. "That's our high school radio station, the voice of the Wildcats! The mighty WATO 1290 AM! The call letters ATO were chosen for the first three letters in Atomic City, as Oak Ridge was known at the time of the Manhattan Project. The station commenced broadcasting February 1, 1948 under the authority of the US Atomic Energy Commission, and was Oak Ridge's original community radio station. It was the first radio station to be established on a US military reservation. WATO, nicknamed the 'Atomic Talker,' has broadcast our Oak Ridge High School football games every year consecutively from 1948 until now in 1975. I've been in that station; the equipment inside includes several Gates Yard 80 boards and some awesome sounding RCA ribbon microphones, considered by many to be the most natural-sounding microphone ever made. The Harris transmitter has hand cranks to make phase adjustments in the three-tower array for the lower power night pattern. It's all super cool!"

I commented, "Wow, Bowmar, that was an atomic Oak Ridge radio station education! Maybe you should join Ding in the broadcasting booth this fall and provide historical fun facts on demand! Then we could say 'WATO, the talk radio station that guarantees to boost your IQ while you listen to Friday night football.'"

Bowmar frowned at me and countered, "Maybe you should go with Ding and exercise your music brain there, Bubble Rock."

Waldo added, "Ding, if you're gonna be on our local radio station, you better play some country western music. I'll give you my Johnny Cash collection, for starters."

Ding replied, "The radio station will be the perfect cover for me in Oak Ridge, and make it easy for me to set up secret communications with local field agents and the FBI network. My assignment is to work closely with you and Bucky to find this KGB devil Borya Krovopuskov, and keep your work at the White Hole Project safe."

"How do you propose that we find and capture Borya?" Bucky asked.

Ding answered, "We set a trap with some tasty cheese that the chief mice cannot resist."

"And what flavor of cheese might that be?" Bucky enquired.

"We put their two children, Bobbie and Natalie under house arrest or in some kind of protective custody at the Krovos' home in Knoxville. Between being pissed at the Bad Love Gang in Oak Ridge and wanting to get their children out of Knoxville, we might get a shot at them," Ding revealed.

Waldo couldn't help himself, "If I get another shot at them, it will be like a giant, unforgiving mousetrap from Hell slamming shut on their little, mouse-like Russian necks."

We all laughed at Waldo's bravado, and I tried to conclude the breakfast discussion on a lighter note, "So Ding, since you are a Chuck Berry fan, what song are you gonna lead off with when you start your radio show on WATO?"

"That's easy, BB," Ding responded. "Chuck 'Ding-a-Ling' Brooks will open the show with **'Johnny B. Goode.'** That should get everyone moving! Other than Elvis Presley's early hits, I think it is one of the most recognizable songs in the history of rock and roll. Here's a biographical fun fact for you: Chuck Berry was born at 2520 *Goode* Avenue, in St. Louis, Missouri."

The song immediately played in my brain as I responded, "Ding, you're OK. I think we're going to have some fun together while we try to bring Borya to justice. Besides that, I play offensive guard for the Oakridge Wildcats football team, and we think that we have a shot at the Tennessee state title this year. I block for an outstanding running back named Craig Freeman; you'll be calling out his name a lot while announcing on WATO this football season."

"I'm looking forward to it, Bubble Butt! I should be relocated to Oak Ridge in two weeks. You guys contact me if you need anything between now and then. I am glad to be working with you," Ding finished.

We all shook hands and Ding headed out of the hotel. We were all being watched and followed.

CHAPTER SIX:

A STROLL ON THE MALL

"[...] government of the people, by the people, for the people, shall not perish from the Earth."
—Abraham Lincoln

Tuesday, July 1, 1975 at 12 noon local time, the National Mall, Washington, DC

The beginnings of the Washington DC National Mall were envisioned by a French-American military engineer named Pierre Charles L'Enfant. The historic Constitution of the United States, ratified in June 1788 and officially taking effect in March 1789, gave the newly organized Congress of the United States authority to establish a federal district up to ten square miles in size. America's first president, George Washington, appointed L'Enfant in 1791 to plan the new "Federal City." It was Pierre who designed the basic plan for Washington, DC, known today as the L'Enfant Plan. Pierre proposed a garden-lined "grand avenue" approximately one mile long and four hundred feet wide, in an area that would lie between the United States Capitol and a monument honoring George Washington, placed directly south of the White House (built in 1884). The National Mall occupies the site of this planned grand avenue, but the L'Enfant Plan—like most big projects in Washington DC—went through innumerable changes over time.

In 1902, the McMillan Commission extended L'Enfant's plan and called for a radical redesign of the Mall, creating an open space with a three hundred feet wide vista containing a long, broad expanse of grass. Four rows of American elm trees planted fifty feet apart between two paths or streets would line each side of the vista. Grand museums and buildings housing cultural and educational institutions would be constructed and line each outer path or street, opposite the elms. Notable projects constructed on the National Mall during the 1900s included the Jamie L. Whitten Federal Building in 1908, the National Museum of Natural History in 1910, the Lincoln Memorial in 1922, the Lincoln Memorial Reflecting Pool in 1923, the Freer Gallery of Art in 1923, the District of Columbia War Memorial in 1931, the US Botanic Garden in 1933, the National Gallery of Art West Building in 1941, the Thomas Jefferson Memorial in 1943, the National Museum of American History in 1964, and the Hirshhorn Museum and Sculpture Garden in 1974. The National Air and Space Museum was well under construction when we visited in July 1975.

After finishing breakfast with Ding; Bucky, Waldo, Bowmar, and I decided to spend our day touring the National Mall, which was an easy walk south from the Hay-Adams Hotel. Our first stop was the Washington Monument, which is really one of the most iconic and widely recognized American landmarks on the planet. As we walked south on 17th Street past the south lawn of the White House, Bowmar asked, "Do you remember what happened on Human Kindness Day this year?"

I replied, "I know it was held here on the National Mall about six weeks ago, with Stevie Wonder as the headlining act." As I said that, one of my favorite Stevie Wonder songs started playing in my brain: **"Higher Ground,"** released in July 1973. Stevie wrote that song in the span of three hours, and it hit number one on the US Billboard Hot R&B Singles. Wonder was involved in a near-fatal accident in August 1973 that left him in a coma just after recording and releasing "Higher Ground." His cousin was driving and collided with a tractor trailer that was hauling trees and logs. One of the logs struck Stevie right in the forehead, leaving him scarred and in a coma. Early in Wonder's recovery from this terrible accident, his road manager sang the song's melody into the singer's ear; Wonder reportedly responded by moving his fingers with the music. While Stevie Wonder had said he would like to believe in reincarnation, I liked the words because it talked about starting over fresh after making too many sins or mistakes. God knows, we all need a fresh start from time to time!

"Bubble Butt, I'm trying to talk to you," I heard Bowmar say, the volume of his voice exceeding the focus threshold of my music brain in action.

"Oh, yeah... Sorry, Bowmar. What happened at Human Kindness Day?"

Bowmar continued, Waldo and Bucky listening in on our discussion. "The first Human Kindness Day was held on April 22, 1972, and was officially known as Roberta Flack Human Kindness Day. The event was designed to honor the singer, who had attended Howard University and had been a fixture singing live at Mr. Henry's nightclub here in DC. The 1972 event drew 25,000 people, while the 1973 event drew 35,000. The 1974 event drew 55,000 people. At this year's event on May 10, 1975, the crowd was huge: an estimated 125,000 people, stretching from the Washington Monument west to 17th Street NW. A deal had been struck with the event's organizers; security was to be provided by 800 armband-wearing volunteer marshals. The DC police had agreed not to interfere. Unfortunately, a mere 262 volunteer marshals actually showed up to provide security for the event.

"What happened next was an on-site, real-time crime wave that marked the end of future Human Kindness Day events. It's probably not wise to take a large crowd that size and more or less advertise that there is no police protection. There were sporadic assaults early in the day, but the real violence didn't start until after Stevie Wonder's performance. People started blindly stealing handbags, and it got to be a thing to grab a woman's blouse, rip it open, and run. A 22-year-old man from Vienna, Austria was standing at the base of the Washington Monument when a group of men snatched his wallet. He tried to chase them down, but was hit in the mouth with a club. An 18-year-old boy from Annapolis, Maryland, was jumped by a group of about 20 teenagers who beat him and threw bottles at him. The worst injury was to a guy named Steven Laine, who was stabbed in his right eye, losing that eye while innocently walking across the Mall on his way home from working at the US Agriculture Department. The National Park Service recorded 500 incidents of robbery, with some 600 people injured; 150 people were hospitalized. The Park Police considered laying down a tear gas barrage to clear the Washington Monument grounds but decided against it, fearing the rioters would spill into downtown."

Bucky commented, "Boy, things have sure changed a lot since my time of 1945! I just think that there was more respect for the general rule of law and for each other back then. We wouldn't think to need 800 police guarding an outdoor event, unless maybe if the president of the United States was going to be there."

Waldo added, "I agree, things have definitely changed since 1945...but Bowmar is right. You can't advertise 'no police' and then expect that a criminal element won't be waiting in the wings to take advantage of the situation. That is human nature. You guys need to go back and watch Clint Eastwood in *The Good, the Bad and the Ugly*."

My music brain played the theme from **"The Good the Bad and the Ugly"** by Ennio Morricone, written for the famous 1967 Clint Eastwood spaghetti western film. As the movie's theme song played, I visualized a bizarre scene with the four of us walking toward the Washington Monument in cowboy garb, getting ready to gun down the bad guys. Then my brain snapped out of it and I said, "Waldo, what the heck does that movie have to do with the breakdown of security at Human Kindness Day this year?"

Waldo replied, "Not a lot, but I was thinking they should rename it, that's all. Call it the 'Kind, the Bad, and the Ugly Day.'"

We all chuckled. I smiled and thought, *That's pretty creative for Waldo! We must be rubbing off on him in some small way.*

We enjoyed the Washington Monument, especially the spectacular views from the top floor observation deck. Bowmar pointed out that at an elaborate 4th of July event in 1848, the monument's cornerstone—containing a zinc time capsule with a portrait of George Washington, newspapers from fourteen states, and US coins, along with copies of the Declaration of Independence and the Constitution—was laid in a ceremony attended by thousands, including a then little-known US congressman from Illinois by the name of Abraham Lincoln. During the Civil War, construction came to a complete halt and the site was used for the grazing and slaughtering of government cattle, earning it the nickname "Beef Depot Monument." The completed monument was dedicated on February 21, 1885, and officially opened to the public on October 9, 1888. It was the tallest structure in the world at 555 feet 5 inches tall between 1884 and 1889, after which it was overtaken by the Eiffel Tower in Paris. There's a single elevator that takes people up to the observation deck; only 55 people could be admitted into the monument every half hour. That meant that around 500,000 people were able to enjoy the spectacular views from the top of the Washington Monument every year, including us, four members of the Bad Love Gang, on July 1, 1975.

We exited the Washington Monument and headed west along the Lincoln Memorial Reflecting Pool, where perhaps most-famously on August 28, 1963, Martin Luther King Jr. gave his historic "I Have a Dream" speech. Overlooking the Reflecting Pool with 250,000 people in attendance, he called for civil and economic rights for black Americans and an end to racism in the United States. King later paid the ultimate price for all his efforts when he was assassinated at the Lorraine Motel in Memphis, Tennessee on April 4, 1968. I mentioned this to Bowmar as we walked together, and he said, "King would have been very proud that on January 2nd 1975, Walter Washington became the first elected mayor of the District of Columbia in more than 100 years, and also the first black mayor of a major US city."

The Lincoln Memorial Reflecting Pool was the largest of any of Washington's reflecting pools at about 2,028 feet long and 167 feet wide; its deepest part in the center was only about 30 inches deep. Despite the shallowness, the pool held almost 7 million gallons, pulling its water from pipes leading to the nearby Tidal Basin—where we would walk to after visiting Lincoln. I mentally reflected about President Lincoln, who certainly ranks in the top tier of American presidents, as we approached his memorial.

He was born into poverty in an American frontier log cabin. He was self-educated, became a lawyer, and got elected to Congress from the state of Illinois before being elected as the 16th president of the United States, from 1861–1865. He led our nation through its greatest moral conflict and political crisis in the American Civil War to end slavery. He abolished slavery while preserving the Union, a miracle in its time by any measure. He advanced the Thirteenth Amendment to the United States Constitution, which outlawed slavery across the country. His life in this world was not easy or one of privilege; he suffered innumerable personal and political setbacks all along the way to get the job done, and then paid the ultimate price when he was assassinated. He was a great man.

As the four of us neared the steps from the reflecting pool leading up to the Lincoln Monument. I asked Bowmar to give us some interesting facts about this next stop. Bowmar gladly obliged, of course.

"There are eighty-seven steps from the reflecting pool to the chamber where Lincoln's statue sits. He started his famous Gettysburg Address by saying 'Four score and seven years ago, our fathers brought forth on this continent a new nation, conceived in liberty, and dedicated to the proposition that all men are created equal.' The number eighty-seven represents the four score and seven years ago. Moreover, there are fifty-eight steps leading from the plaza level up to the chamber, two steps for the number of terms he served as president, and fifty-six steps for his age when he was assassinated. The memorial design has thirty-six exterior columns to symbolize the thirty-six states in the Union at the time of Lincoln's death. You're really only seeing a little more than half of the structure. The Monument's foundation extends sixty-six feet into the earth at its deepest point to support the weight of its marble construction."

As Bowmar spoke and we climbed the steps to the Lincoln Memorial, I felt a brief sensation that we were being watched. I reasoned that maybe the FBI was keeping an eye on us at the request of agent Chuck "Ding" Brooks. I was only half right.

We read the carved inscriptions of Lincoln's Second Inaugural Address and his Gettysburg Address on the north and south side chamber walls inside the monument, and got our picture taken together standing in front of Lincoln's statue. Leaving the Lincoln Memorial, I could not help but get a strong sense of the history of our hard-fought freedoms and amazing democracy as we continued walking around the National Mall. We turned from the south side of the Lincoln Memorial Reflecting Pool across the grassy area to briefly see the District of Columbia War Memorial, then circled around the Tidal Basin to get to the Jefferson Memorial. My brain was going a hundred miles an hour as I processed mental pictures of Vietnam War protests that had been held on these grounds not so long ago. Simultaneously, I was paranoid that we were being followed and worried that somebody had a gun pointed at us. My music brain, trying to push the fear away, started to play one of the most recognized anti-war songs, **"For What It's Worth,"** written by Stephen Stills and performed by Buffalo Springfield. The song made Buffalo Springfield a one-hit wonder, and was a 1960's anthem for the political unrest that America was emerging from with war in Vietnam now in the rear-view mirror. The song's words, however, were pertinent to how I was feeling at the moment.

Franklin D. Roosevelt, who we had just time-traveled to visit, had personally contacted the Commission of Fine Arts in 1934 to create a memorial for Thomas Jefferson, whom FDR deeply admired. The day after construction started, on November 18, 1938, a group of women chained themselves to a tree at the construction site in a protest referred to as the Cherry Tree Rebellion. They were opposed to the cherry trees on site being removed for the building of the monument. The Jefferson Memorial was dedicated by President Roosevelt on a very fitting April 13, 1943. FDR chose this date because Jefferson would have been 200 years old. At the time of the dedication, the statue of Jefferson's likeness inside the memorial was made of plaster, due to wartime restrictions on the use of metal for domestic projects.

The permanent bronze statue, installed four years later after WWII had ended, weighed ten thousand pounds and stood nineteen feet tall. The Jefferson Memorial was placed in a direct line one mile due south of the White House, completing the amazing southern view from the White House, which I am certain made Roosevelt proud.

We experienced and admired the Jefferson Memorial, then talked a bit about our incredible visit with FDR at the Little White House on April 12, 1945 as we walked to the Freer Gallery of Art. That museum focused on Asian art, displaying Chinese paintings, Korean pottery, Japanese folding screens, Near Eastern ceramics, and Buddhist sculptures. The Freer also housed the impressive and famous Peacock Room, which was a masterpiece of interior decorative art and design. The room was painted and paneled in a rich, unified palette of brilliant blue-greens with over-glazing and metallic gold leaf by American artist James McNeill Whistler. I had wanted to finish the day with at least two hours to visit the National Museum of Natural History. It was 4:15 PM when we left the Freer Gallery of Art and walked to our last stop for the day—or so we thought.

CHAPTER SEVEN:

DINOSAURS AND BORYA'S THREAT

"A single death is a tragedy; a million deaths is a statistic."
—Joseph Stalin

Tuesday July 1, 1975 at 4:30 PM local time,
the National Museum of Natural History, Washington, DC

The Smithsonian's National Museum of Natural History on the National Mall was established in 1910, and is one of the most visited museums—the number one most visited natural history museum—in the world. The main building has an impressive area of 1.5 million square feet, with 325,000 square feet used for exhibition and public space. The museum's collections contained over 145 million specimens of animals, fossils, plants, human remains, human cultural artifacts, minerals, rocks, and meteorites, making it the largest natural history collection in the world. It was also home to well over a hundred professional natural history scientists, the largest group of scientists dedicated to the study of natural and cultural history in the world. Approaching and entering through the Roman-style doorway, we were impressed with the architecture of the 1910 Beaux-Arts building, its soaring rotunda and the 13-foot-tall African elephant named Henry watching over the space. Gazing at Henry, we decided as a group that we would give him the Bad Love Gang nickname "Hankster" instead.

"Let's go see the dinosaurs!" I exclaimed. "Did you guys know that the Hall of Dinosaurs exhibit was called 'The Hall of Extinct Monsters' when this museum opened in 1910? I sure wish Goondoggy was here with us; he has been fascinated with dinosaurs since we were little kids. We would play in the dirt in our yards or wherever with our toy dinosaurs and make up all sorts of dino noises as we pretended they fought for survival."

Waldo was chuckling to himself and I asked him why. He replied, "The monsters that Mary and I know are far from extinct!"

"I'm not sure that we know that dinosaurs made much noise other than the crunching of the earth under their feet," Bowmar mused. "Dinosaurs roamed the earth for 165 million years before their extinction event struck from outer space. That's a lot of years to explore with time travel, wouldn't you say?"

Bucky protested, "I have no interest in taking the risk of getting stuck in time again and trying to avoid being the next tasty meal for a T. rex—or any other carnivorous dinosaur, for that matter."

"Yeah, they would definitely have a fantastic feast with all your young, tender, soft, sweet bodies! Yum, yum!" Waldo joked. "But they would find no pleasure in my leathery, worn and torn, sour old flesh. I'd put on a caveman outfit, grab a big club, and make myself king of the dinos!"

We made our way to the Hall of Dinosaurs, and I was itching to have a discussion with Bowmar about specific dinosaurs and dino-facts. As we made our way there, we were unknowingly being spied upon by two janitors, one male and one female, who watched our every step from opposite ends of the large room and communicated with each other as we moved. They were none other than Borya Krovopuskov and his wife Catherine, disguised as museum cleaning staff. We were also being followed by two undercover FBI agents, Bill Cupp and Isaiah Jones, who had been appointed by Ding to "protect" us.

Walking amongst the exhibits together as a group, I asked Bowmar, "So, what is the latest theory about why these dinosaurs became extinct?"

Bowmar relished this opportunity to speculate; he might as well have been a professional tour guide. Several children nearby heard Bowmar speaking and collected to hover around us, listening intently. "No one knows for sure, but modern evidence points to a cataclysm called an impact event befalling our planet about 65–66 million years ago; extinction came from outer space. Imagine a comet or an asteroid five to ten miles in diameter hurtling through space, passing through our atmosphere and striking Earth at 38,000 miles per hour. The energy released by its impact would be a couple million times greater than the most potent nuclear bomb. Mile-high and higher tsunamis would have flooded the continents, drowning many forms of life. Shock waves would have triggered earthquakes and volcanic eruptions. The heat released would bake and broil the earth's surface, igniting horrendous fires worldwide. Debris, smoke and soot would fill the atmosphere, turning the sky black, blocking out the sunlight and plunging our planet into darkness, potentially lasting for months to years. The earth's temperatures would have then plunged into the freezing zone, killing plants and leaving herbivores with nothing to eat. Many dinosaurs would have died within weeks. The strongest of the carnivores who feasted on the herbivores would have died a month or two later. Only the small scavenging mammals that could burrow into the ground and eat whatever remained would have survived, along with insects, maybe some birds, and creatures of the deep seas and lakes."

I enquired, "How often does that happen? When are we due again for an impact like that? How do we even know that stuff actually happens?"

Bowmar continued, "Well...impact events have physical consequences that we can observe and have been found to regularly occur in planetary systems. For example, since we were kids, people joked that our moon looks like Swiss cheese, meaning that it's full of holes or craters. How do you think those craters got there? Those are impact craters left by large solid objects colliding with the moon, like asteroids, comets, or meteoroids. However, when large objects from outer space strike-terrestrial planets like our Earth, there can be significant environmental consequences. Unlike the moon, our dense atmosphere provides significant protection from collisions because most space objects burn up from the friction of entering our atmosphere, or at least break up into small debris before they reach Earth's surface. The 'latest' impact event to change evolution and history on Earth happened about 65–66 million years ago. Otherwise, these dinosaurs in front of us might still be roaming around.

"Think about this: every day, tons of cosmic dust and grains of sand-sized particles shower the Earth. Roughly once per year, an automobile-sized asteroid passes through our atmosphere, causing an extraordinary fireball, and burns up before reaching the surface. These are typically witnessed by many observers, and sometimes caught on film. All space rocks smaller than about 80 feet in diameter will most likely burn up as they enter the Earth's atmosphere and cause little or no damage. However, every 2,000 years or so, a space object the size of a football field strikes the Earth and causes measurable damage to a specific and limited geographic area. In fact, any solid object less than one-half mile in diameter hitting the earth will likely only cause local damage to the impact area. We believe anything larger than that could have worldwide effects. It's only once every several million years, more or less, that an object large enough to threaten Earth's civilization comes along—and those objects are numerous out there. Take for example the asteroid belt located between Mars and Jupiter, discovered in 1801 by Giuseppe Piazzi when he identified Ceres, a dwarf planet asteroid. Over the next few decades, more objects were found between Mars and Jupiter; by the 1850s, astronomers began calling the region 'the asteroid belt.' The asteroids that populate the asteroid belt between Mars and Jupiter are irregularly shaped and solid, made of rock and metal. They are generally held in their current orbits by planetary gravitational forces and pose no threat to Earth, but they range in size from dust particles to as big 583 miles in diameter."

As Bowmar spoke and the group of children standing around us were mesmerized by his knowledge, my music brain started playing **"Rocket Man"** by Elton John, loud and clear! Released in March 1972, it was a global hit, reaching as high as number two on the UK Singles Chart. I knew the words by heart and when Bowmar mentioned the asteroid belt between Mars and Pluto, that's all it took for my brain to play the song. It described a Mars-bound astronaut's mixed emotions about leaving his family in order to do his job. I guess by 1972 we were starting to think that being an astronaut was like having a regular job, although I had always thought of astronauts as being brave and willing to take extraordinary risks in the line of duty. The song also reminded me of all the science that I did not understand, but wanted to. I mused about how life is not nearly long enough to learn it all. I silently vowed to myself to always keep learning as a way of life.

I came back to reality as one of the young girls listening to Bowmar asked, "What was the most dangerous dinosaur, and what was the smartest dinosaur?" We were all standing in front of the *Tyrannosaurus rex* exhibit. I was curious to hear Bowmar's thoughts about this, as he was totally tuned in to his young audience but not often (ever) inclined to give standard answers.

"This dino guy standing before us was also known as the 'tyrant lizard' and had a record-holding, phenomenal bite force that was three times more powerful than a great white shark: stronger than any land animal that has ever lived. Its bone-splintering jaws chomped down with a force almost as huge as its own body weight, bringing to bear all sixty of its saw-edged conical teeth, some of which were twelve inches long. *T. rex* was capable of delivering bites that could crush stones. Other dinosaurs had to bite their prey multiple times to bring it down; *T. rex* only had to bite once. In general, it fed on plant-eating dinosaurs."

Everyone standing around us was completely captivated as Bowmar went on, speaking animatedly and passionately about the subject matter. "However, contrary to popular opinion, *T. rex* may have had some competition for the title of the most-dangerous dinosaur. *Spinosaurus aegyptiacus* was likely the largest meat-eating dinosaur that ever lived. Measuring over fifty feet long and standing three stories tall, he was twelve feet longer than *T. rex*, weighed in at twenty tons, and was one of the few dinosaurs known to be able to swim. Its vertebrae were twenty percent larger than those of *T. rex*. It had a gigantic sail made of skin, supported by six and a half feet long spines protruding from its back. *Spinosaurus* and *Tyrannosaurus* both had great depth perception due to binocular vision. However, *Spinosaurus* had a definite size and weight advantage over *T. rex*. When it did not get its tummy filled by eating prey from the waters, this adaptable predator took to the land and hunted there for its meals. Spinosaurus was fast, strong, and possessed a punishing set of claws that could hold its prey. Its crocodile-like jaws were full of smooth, conical, pointed teeth that were well adapted to spearing its victims, rather than ripping flesh from bone."

I enjoyed the variety of expressions on the children's faces, wide-eyed amazement evident along with their oohs and aahs. Some were even holding their cheeks in their hands. A few more joined the group listening to Bowmar speak.

"The smartest dinosaur may have been the *Troodon*. It had behaviors in common with both crocodiles and birds, stood about five to eleven feet tall, and weighed about seventy-five to one hundred ten pounds. This dinosaur was an opportunistic omnivore, feeding on fruits, plants, and nuts as well as smaller animals—including mammals, birds, and other dinosaurs. The most notable feature of *Troodon* was its unusually large brain, or *encephalization quotient*, which is the size of the brain in proportion to the size of the rest of the body; this made it the 'Albert Einstein' of the Cretaceous period. It was also noted for its huge, orb-like eyes that were set toward the front rather than the sides of its face, giving it superior binocular vision and enabling nighttime hunting. Processing more visual information necessarily entailed having a larger brain, which also helps to explain *Troodon's* relatively high IQ. *Troodons* were fast on their feet, too. While smaller than many of the carnivorous dinosaurs, a group of highly intelligent *Troodons* hunting as a large, coordinated pack could easily have brought down much bigger animals, making it potentially very dangerous as well. Another fun fact about *Troodons*: they were famous for their parenting routines. *Troodon* females laid two eggs per day over the course of a week or so, resulting in circular clutches of sixteen to twenty-four eggs. It's possible that these eggs were brooded by the male of the species."

Bowmar then grinned at the group of kids attentively assembled around us and said, "I'll take one more question before this class is over."

One of the boys, cute and apparently about age seven, softly enquired, "Which dinosaur would make the best pet?"

Bowmar warmly smiled at the boy. "I've thought about that question myself. There are several possibilities, depending on what kind of pet you are looking for—such as a bird, a dog, or a reptile. One possibility was the *Psittacosaurus*, which meant 'parrot lizard.' It was a small plant-eater that had a narrow, horny beak with no teeth. *Psittacosaurus* had a head sort of like a parrot's, along with a lizard-type body and four long fingers on each hand. Its arms were shorter than its legs, but it could walk on its hind legs or on all fours. *Psittacosaurus* was about two and a half to six and a half feet long from snout to tail, but only about four feet tall with a slender build; various species weighed anywhere from forty-four to two hundred twenty pounds. One may have been brightly colored like canary yellow with a spotted pattern. It had a life span much like a typical dog, at least ten or eleven years. *Psittacosaurus* may have lived in herds, and had an intermediate encephalization quotient, or intelligence, among dinosaurs."

One of the girls who looked about eleven years old announced, "I want a bright yellow parrot lizard pet like that! All my friends would be *soo* jealous!" The rest of the children giggled and agreed. Bowmar had moved in front of the Triceratops exhibit.

"The other one I like for a pet is Protoceratops whose name meant 'first horned face' and was a relative of larger horned dinosaurs, a bit like a miniature *Triceratops* that we see here. It walked on four legs instead of two, and had a bony frill that protected its neck (males had larger frills than females) but retained its sharp beak for chomping on plants. Where *Psittacosaurus* was mostly slender, *Protoceratops* was robust and a bit portly, built more like a large modern sheep—one approximately six feet long and weighing four hundred pounds. You definitely wouldn't want it to sit on you, because some fully grown adults could weigh as much as nine hundred pounds. It also may have been a herding animal and had an intermediate encephalization quotient. It would be easy to imagine having a pet *Protoceratops* trotting along on the end of a leash, like a big, chunky prehistoric puppy." All the children giggled again and stood there admiring Bowmar, hoping for more.

Bucky was a bit of a party pooper when he announced, "I'm sorry to break up this party, kids, but we need to take *Brontosaurus* Bowmar away from you to continue our museum tour." Then he looked at the three of us and whispered, "I have to piss like a prehistoric racehorse! Any of you need to go?"

I responded, "I'll think I'll join you to drain my *Spinosaurus*." I looked at Waldo and enquired, "That giant *Prostate*-osaurus of yours in need of relief?"

Waldo replied, "Go screw yourself, *Bubblebutt*-osaurus! I can wait 'til later. Go do some work on your encephalization quotient while you try to find that tiny prehistoric lizard of yours."

The men's restroom was tucked away behind the far corner, and Boris saw us making our initial move in that direction. He quietly radioed to Catherine, "Bubble Butt and Bucky are on their way to the men's room; I'll get there ahead of them. You follow behind them to put the barriers up in front of the door—and stick to the plan." She instantly acknowledged and both of them were swiftly in motion, but hidden in plain sight dressed as museum janitors. Boris made haste getting to the men's room well ahead of us. When he arrived, there was only one man standing there, washing his hands at the sink and getting ready to leave. Boris went into one of the stalls, locked the door, sat on the toilet, and quickly readied his Italian Beretta 9mm M1951 semi-automatic pistol fed from an 8-round clip. He attached his custom-made silencer and chambered the first bullet, then took off the safety and put two more full clips in his deep right pocket. If the situation demanded, he would shoot left-handed; his right hand was not fully recovered from the wound he suffered from the shootout with Waldo on New Year's Eve. He heard the man at the sink exit the rest-room and radioed Catherine. "We're set, and I'm the only one here."

Catherine, pushing her janitor's cart of tools, supplies, and yellow warning signs also reached the location of the men's room before us, hiding just around the corner. She was right-handed and made certain that the two loaded syringes were in her right pocket and ready to go. The syringes both contained sodium thiopental, an ultra-short-acting barbiturate that was commonly used during the induction phase of general anesthesia in order to get people asleep and intubated. Following intravenous injection, the drug rapidly reaches the brain and renders the patient—or victim, in this situation—unconscious within 30-45 seconds. At one minute, the drug reaches its peak concentration of about 60% of the total dose in the brain. Thereafter, the drug distributes to the rest of the body; in about 5-10 minutes, the concentration is low enough in the brain that consciousness returns. That's all the time they would need to execute their bold plan. Catherine also had a Beretta pistol with silencer prepared to fire and in the pocket of her cart. The cart was large enough to carry two adults.

The undercover FBI agent, Bill Cupp, did notice Catherine pushing her cart a bit faster than what might be considered normal. *That is one helluva shapely janitor pushing that cart*, he thought. He radioed his FBI counterpart, Isaiah Jones, and said, "Bubble Butt and Bucky are headed to the men's room; I think I'll keep an eye on them while you watch Bowmar and Waldo."

Jones radioed back, "Ten-four, Bill; just shout out if you need me."

At the time of that radio exchange, Bucky and I entered the men's room and walked up to two of the urinals to relieve ourselves. The second we touched the door to enter, Catherine was on the move to place the yellow CAUTION: WET FLOOR warning signs around the entrance to the men's room. I can safely say there is nothing like standing at a urinal to piss and in mid-stream have a man with a gun unexpectedly come from behind and threaten to kill you point blank.

Bucky and I both immediately recognized Boris's voice as he snuck up behind us and announced, "Both of you put your hands on the wall in front of you where I can see them. If either of you makes a move at this moment, you're dead; it's that simple."

I asked, "Can I pull up my zipper?"

"Only if you can pull it up with your time-traveling mind, Bubble Butt," Borya replied. Bucky and I remained frozen while Borya spoke again, "Nobody is safe until our children, Bobby and Natalie, are released. That means both of you, your Bad Love Gang comrades, and even your families. How would you like your sisters Kathy and Denise to disappear, Bubble Butt?" Despite my fear, I could also feel my blood start to boil.

As Borya was speaking, his wife Catherine entered the men's room pushing her cart, and we got our first-ever look at her. Catherine was seven years younger than Boris at age forty-seven, but she looked younger than that. She was about five foot seven inches tall with long, wavy blonde hair extending below her shoulders, pulled back into a ponytail. She was obviously attractive, but also athletic. It made sense, knowing Borya's athleticism from the New Year's ambush encounter at the White Hole Project. She looked and sounded totally American. Borya looked at her said, "Make it quick, my love."

Catherine dumped the contents of her cart on the bathroom floor and then pushed the cart behind us. She stood directly behind Bucky and took out the first syringe. "Bucky, I'm pulling your left arm behind your back. The second you struggle or fail to cooperate, Borya's first bullet goes directly into the back of Bubble Butt's brain. Understand?" she demanded.

Bucky angrily replied, "I understand."

It was July, and Bucky had a short-sleeved sport shirt on. Catherine pulled his left arm back and effortlessly inserted her needle into one of his prominent forearm veins, injecting the sodium thiopental. Bucky's legs gave way as he slipped into unconsciousness; he asked "What's that?" on his way down. Catherine knew exactly what she was doing, as she had positioned the cart behind him, guiding him backwards into it as he fell.

Oh, holy shit! They're kidnapping us, and I'm next!

FBI Agent Bill Cupp was approaching the men's room and radioed Agent Jones. "Something's fishy here. The men's room is blocked off, but I thought I saw Bucky and Bubble Butt go in there. I'm going to check it out. Stand by one."

Jones replied, "Copy that."

Catherine said, "You're next, Bubble Butt. Give me your left arm."

I ran what seemed like a thousand scenarios through my brain, adrenaline surging and my heart racing like a cheetah. I couldn't seem to visualize an escape plan as I felt Catherine yank my left arm behind my back. In the next split second, the scenario changed.

Bill Cupp came through the door, pushing it open with his left hand and holding his .45 ACP Colt M1911A1 pistol in his right. He saw the mop and broom handles laying on the bathroom floor as the door cracked open and was instantaneously on high alert. He thought he was prepared. Catherine was holding my left arm getting ready to inject me as the door came open. The cart containing Bucky was positioned behind her, and Borya was on the other side of the cart with his gun pointed at the back of my head. The row of bathroom stalls was directly behind him.

The moment the door started to open, I thought it was some unsuspecting soul—or even worse, a young boy—coming through the door.

Borya had a straight view to the door; he could see Agent Cupp leading with a gun in his right hand. Borya swung his silenced pistol away from the back of my head to aim at the incoming man holding a gun.

In the next instant, seeing and sensing Borya's shift of focus, I knew it was now or never to try and make a difference in what happened next. I yelled, "NO!" as loud as I could, forcefully yanked my left arm away from Catherine, and pushed myself back away from the wall and urinal with all my adrenaline-enhanced might.

As I made my desperate move, Bill Cupp's exposed body became visible to Borya. Borya opened fire with his silenced Beretta, expending five of the eight bullets in his first clip. Bill was blown back, struck in the torso, shoulder, and the side of his neck; his bullet-proof vest was not enough to save him. He got three shots off: one hit the back wall of the restroom and the other two hit the ceiling. Everyone in the museum heard Bill's three shots. With his dying breath, Bill yelled into his mic, "Nine-ninety-nine, nine-ninety-nine!" This is the police code that means urgent help needed/officer down.

My violent push away from the wall and the urinal did not save Bill Cupp, but it did force Catherine to fall backwards into the cart on top of the sleeping Bucky. The cart rolled, with both of them riding in it, to smash into Borya and knock him back into the toilet stall behind him. I regained my balance and ran for the door. Borya fired his last three rounds blindly through the thin steel wall of the bathroom stall, hoping to hit me. One round did strike the door frame next to my right shoulder as I bolted out of the bathroom. As I exited the bathroom, I saw Bill Cupp's lifeless-appearing body on the floor. As I ran, I yelled at the top of my lungs, "EVERYBODY DOWN! GET DOWN, HE'S GOT A GUN!"

Agent Isaiah Jones heard the shots fired and Agent Bill Cupp's dying words, "nine-ninety-nine," knowing that his partner had been shot. He drew his gun and ran toward the men's room, radioing for backup as he ran. It was pure pandemonium in the museum, with panicked people running everywhere and screaming uncontrollably. Waldo told Bowmar to take cover with the group of kids he had just spoken to, helping get them down on the floor. Waldo then started running toward the shots fired.

As Borya reflexively loaded his next clip, he yelled at Catherine, "We have to leave Bucky and get the hell out of here NOW!" The two of them regained their footing and sprinted out of the men's room, heading for the closest exit. Agent Jones was closing in and saw me running towards him; I could see Waldo in the distance running towards the two of us. Jones thought he had a shot at the two janitors running for the exit. "Get down, Bubble Butt!" I hit the deck at full stride and slid on the floor toward Jones. As soon as I was down, he fired three rounds at Borya and Catherine, who were both sprinting toward the stairs going down to the Constitution Avenue exit. Jones' shots hit the wall, a window, and a pillar—but missed the rapidly moving targets.

I watched as Jones took his shots and saw Borya's and Catherine's backs as they made it out the museum exit. Waldo arrived and automatically asked me if I was OK. I was super pissed and full of adrenaline when I looked Waldo in the eyes and barked, "Bucky's been drugged and is in the janitor's cart in the men's room. Give me your gun."

Waldo, knowing what I was thinking and not wanting to put me in danger by complying, said, "I don't have a gun."

My whole body and face turned red. I stomped my right foot hard and roared, "GIVE ME THE GODDAMMED GUN, WALDO!"

He knew I was dead serious, and not handing over the weapon would be risking a physical confrontation with me. "OK, Bubble Butt, don't get yourself killed today." He bent over and reached into his ankle holster, then handed me the same .32 ACP Walther PPK that he had used against Borya on New Year's Eve; it was his favorite ankle holster firearm. He also handed me an extra clip. "You've got seven shots with each clip, Bubble Butt. Good luck."

As Waldo handed me the Walther PPK, I looked him in the eyes and said, "The end of our motto says 'don't die.' I'm not dying today, Waldo."

I turned and asked Jones, "Are you FBI?"

He answered. "Hell yes, assigned to keep an eye on you."

I replied, "Call Ding, tell him what I'm wearing, tell him that I'm chasing Borya and Catherine Krovopuskov out the Constitution Avenue exit, and tell him to send help fast! Do it now. I'm sorry, but I think your partner is dead." I turned and sprinted to the same stairway exit used by Borya and Catherine.

CHAPTER EIGHT:
BUBBLE BUTT IS DOWN

"Boy, there's nothing more thrilling than a chase.
I'd often thought, over the years, that someone should
do a whole film where it's nothing but a chase."
—Mel Gibson

*Tuesday, July 1, 1975 at 5:45 PM local time, outside the
Constitution Avenue entrance to the National Museum of
Natural History, Washington, DC*

The hippie counter-culture movement blossomed throughout the United States from the mid-1960s and began to lose steam in the mid-1970s after the end of the Vietnam War. The movement largely originated on college campuses in the United States and spread to other countries, including Canada and Britain. No longer wanting to keep up with the Joneses, it rejected the white picket fence mores of mainstream American life and Puritanical sexual norms. I remember seeing hippies protesting violence and war while promoting their pacifist cause by placing flowers in the barrels of guns held by soldiers or police officers while others made daisy flower chains. This earned them the nickname "flower children." The Flower Power movement advocated nonviolence and love, a popular phrase being "Make love, not war." The movement advocated a counterculture narrative that pushed peace, drugs, and free love across the United States. Recreational use of drugs, particularly marijuana and hallucinogenic LSD, was practiced as a way of expanding consciousness.

Hippies promoted openness and tolerance as opposed to the excessive restrictiveness, regulation, and regimentation that they perceived in middle-class Western society. They often practiced open sexual relationships and lived in communes. Many sought spiritual guidance outside the Judeo-Christian tradition such as Buddhism, Hinduism, Confucianism, and other Eastern religions, sometimes in various combinations. Astrology was also popular, and the hippie era was often referred to as the Age of Aquarius. The song **"Aquarius/Let the Sunshine In"** by The Fifth Dimension epitomized the mood of the times, and became an anthem of the movement. It was actually a medley of two songs that was released in March of 1969 and spent six weeks at number one on the US Billboard Hot 100 pop singles chart. It also hit number one in Canada. The song was recorded in two cities, Los Angeles and Las Vegas, and then mixed together in the studio which was unusual. It won the Grammy Award for Record of the Year.

Hippies developed their own distinctive dress and appearance style that generally included the men having long hair, beards, and beads along with other necklaces, often including peace-sign pendants. Headbands and hats were in play for both sexes. Long flowing granny dresses as well as tunics or sundresses and loose, flowy skirts were popular with women. Rimless granny glasses were favorites of both men and women. The preferred colors were a psychedelic mix of bright shades (hence the birth of tie-dye shirts), or anything with a wild assortment of flowers. Women wore bell-sleeve tops, and both women and men wore bell bottoms in various fabrics—the bigger the flare the better. Hippie men loved wearing vests, usually open and without a shirt; buckskin vests were especially coveted. The 1960s/1970s fashions bled over into mainstream styles and even trendy designer house fashions. Growing up in the middle of this era and being surrounded by its stylish nuances probably prepared me for what happened next.

Borya and Catherine had turned right outside the Constitution Avenue exit, ducked behind a row of hedges near the building, and unzipped their janitor jumpsuits, leaving them behind in the bushes. Underneath, they were both dressed like hippies and had accessories to embellish their disguises. Borya wore frayed bell-bottom jeans and a weathered buckskin vest. He was bare-chested, accessorized with a thick silver peace-sign necklace, a long wig, and a psychedelic headband. He finished the look off with round wire-rim glasses. Catherine had on a flowy, crazy bright flower-power dress that hit just below the knees and she wore mid-calf calfskin boots that tied up in the front. She let her long, wavy blonde hair down, put on a flower power headband and wore a large, white peace-sign necklace. She finished her look with large, circular, wire-rim glasses with a soft pink tint. The two of them looked like they belonged together, in a hippie sort of way. After making the quick change of appearance, they calmly headed across Constitution Avenue and briefly stood at the northeast corner of 10th Street NW and Constitution Avenue, waiting for their escape vehicle to arrive.

I bolted out of the National Museum of Natural History Constitution Avenue exit, stopped, and looked both east and west across the grassy areas. The museum was not that crowded late on a Tuesday afternoon, but frightened people were running out of the exit and randomly scattering in all directions. Nothing immediately caught my eye, but I was still full of adrenaline and on high alert. I had tucked the Walther PPK in my waistband at the small of my back. Running straight ahead to the edge of Constitution, I could hear police sirens closing in from all directions. I gazed west and east up and down Constitution Avenue, then north up 10th Street NW. Just as I looked up 10th Street, a yellow convertible Volkswagen Beetle, covered in flowers painted with outrageous, wild psychedelic colors, was coming west on Constitution rather fast. It suddenly skidded to a stop at 10th Street. A guy riding a gold Honda CL-350 Scrambler directly behind the VW bug fishtailed and had to lay his bike down to avoid a major collision with the Beetle. The motorcycle rider was pissed; he stood up and started yelling at the driver of the VW. As the VW came to a stop, I saw two hippies—a man and an attractive, longish blonde-haired woman—hurry from the sidewalk over to the convertible. The woman got in the back seat while the bare-chested man with long hair in a buckskin vest walked directly up to the motorcyclist, who had yanked his helmet off and continued to yell profanities at the VW driver. Without saying a word, the hippie karate chopped the motorcyclist in the neck, silencing him, then kicked him back. The man fell backwards over the Honda Scrambler onto the street. No real hippie acts that way. It wasn't exactly, "Hey man, sorry about the bad stop, peace and love to you, we'll send some smoke up and ask for healing." I knew the pair had to be Borya and Catherine dressed as hippies.

There was traffic going east on my side of the road as I pulled the Walther PPK from my waistband, then pointed it across the road at the VW and Borya, who was getting in the passenger side. I screamed at the top of my lungs, "HEY! BEATNIK BORYA! PUT *THIS* IN YOUR PEACE PIPE AND SMOKE IT!" I did not have much of a shot, having to aim between the bidirectional traffic, but I fired a single round that missed Borya to his right and drilled through the passenger side of the windshield as he was getting into the car.

Borya slammed the VW's passenger door shut and yelled at the driver, "GO, GO, GO!" The Beetle took off north on 10th Street NW, oddly enough moving directly past the US Department of Justice as it left the corner of Tenth and Constitution.

I wasted no time running across Constitution directly to the downed motorcyclist. He was dazed, having trouble getting his breath from the karate chop to the neck. I rapidly pulled him up on the curb, grabbed his sparkly gold helmet, pulled it on and fastened it. "I'm a government agent, and I'm borrowing your bike," I declared. He still couldn't speak, but nodded and held his open palms in the air in obvious pain and frustration.

I knew Honda motorcycles like the back of my hand. I had grown up riding dirt bikes with the Bad Love Gang in Oak Ridge, Tennessee. We'd all had dirt bikes since we were eleven or twelve years old and almost to a person, we were all fans of the Honda motorcycle brand. At home, I was currently riding a 1973 Honda SL 125 with raised fenders, an upswept exhaust system, 21-inch front wheel, 18-inch rear wheel, and universal knobby tires; it was rated at 12 horsepower. With a few minor engine/exhaust tweaks, it could reach a top speed of 65 mph, but it was a bit heavy (weighing about 238 pounds) for the serious off-road theatrics that our gang loved to perform—or in many cases, *attempted* to perform.

The Honda CL-350 Scrambler that I was "borrowing" was actually more of a street bike, but it had a higher rear fender, a braced handlebar, and a high-mount exhaust, all of which supposedly gave it some off-road capability and hence the *Scrambler* designation. It came with a 19-inch front wheel, an 18-inch rear wheel, and was rated at 32 horsepower. This bike weighed in at 346 pounds and had a top speed of nearly 100 mph. I made haste, knowing I had no time to lose. The Scrambler was lying on its side with a bent rearview mirror and some scratches, but had taken no serious damage. I jumped on and touched the electric start button, and it reliably fired right up. Traffic behind me was stopped and I popped a short wheelie as I took off and raced north on 10th Street NW to catch the yellow VW convertible Super Beetle covered in psychedelic flowers that I was mentally calling the Hippie Beetle.

Borya and Catherine had been picked up by a professional Russian KGB driver named Alek Baranov. Alek had turbocharged the innocent looking Hippie Beetle and beefed up the suspension; it was no slouch. They had sped past the US Department of Justice, but were forced to momentarily stop in front of the heavier traffic pattern going both directions on Pennsylvania Avenue NW. That brief pause allowed me to spot them again. As I approached Pennsylvania Avenue, I could see them make the decision to continue north on 10th Street against one-way traffic on the other side of Pennsylvania, probably trying to make following them or catching up to them more difficult. I had to get across Pennsylvania fast despite the traffic to stay in the chase. I could see a sliver of an opening and decided to take a chance. I hoped the drivers would see me better while pulling a wheelie, so I gunned it hard and rode the wheelie across Pennsylvania, making the bike look taller and more noticeable. As I rode across Pennsylvania Avenue, it created quite the scene of chaotic wreckage. A large delivery truck skidded sideways in the eastbound lane of Pennsylvania trying to avoid me; several cars skidded and swerved in the westbound lane, causing numerous rear-end collisions behind them. Somehow, I made it across unscathed and gained ground on the Hippie Beetle.

Alek, Borya, and Catherine were driving the wrong way on one-way 10th Street directly past the Federal Bureau of Investigation (FBI) Head-quarters. Stunned bystanders probably assumed they were hippies and stoned out of their minds. In my mind, it took a lot of balls for them to drive right by FBI Headquarters going the wrong way on a one-way street, all the while being at the top of the FBI and CIA most-wanted lists! As they came into view more clearly ahead of me, I swear I saw Catherine in the back seat, blowing people kisses and waving her fingers in the V peace sign. Her long, wavy hair was blowing like a blonde flag in the breeze from the speeding convertible as they passed the west side of the FBI building.

They crossed E Street NW, staying on 10th Street, and came to a stand-still traffic jam directly in front of Ford's Theatre. On April 9, 1865 the Confederate Army's General Robert E. Lee surrendered to Union Commander Ulysses S. Grant, effectively ending the American Civil War. On April 14, 1865—five days after General Lee's surrender at Appomattox Court House in Virginia—President Lincoln and his wife attended a performance of the play *Our American Cousin* at Ford's Theatre. The infamous actor John Wilkes Booth made his way into the presidential box and shot Lincoln in the back of the head with a .44-caliber bullet fired from a Derringer at close range. Booth then jumped down to the stage and escaped through a door in the rear of the theater. After Lincoln was shot, doctors beckoned soldiers to carry the mortally-wounded president into the street in search of a house where they could make him more comfortable and attend to him. Directly across the street, a man on the steps of a home owned by tailor William Petersen signaled to them. They took Lincoln into the first-floor bedroom and laid him diagonally on the bed; he was six foot, four inches tall and would not otherwise fit. Many people came to visit him throughout the night, before he died the next morning at 7:22 AM. The Petersen House was acquired by the US government in 1896 as the "House Where Lincoln Died," and was the federal government's first purchase of a historic home.

The Hippie Beetle swerved to the left of the traffic snarl, bumping up on the sidewalk in front of the Petersen House. I went to the right of the traffic jam, on the sidewalk directly in front of Ford's Theatre.

Borya saw me catching up to them from across the street, and rose up to try and get a shot. Wild-eyed crazy, he pulled his Beretta 9mm M1951 semi-automatic pistol up and took several shots that whizzed by me and fortunately struck the front doors of Ford's Theatre, rather than hitting any innocent bystanders. One of the arched windows above the entrance was struck by a bullet and shattered. *Holy shit, that's insane! Bullets fired at the Ford Theater 110 years after Lincoln's assassination, and I'm in the middle of it!*" I thought. I found temporary cover beside a panel van stuck in traffic as the Hippie Beetle sped up the opposite sidewalk, forcing pedestrians to scatter, run, and dive in all directions. When the Hippie Beetle cleared the traffic jam, Alek the driver made his way back onto the street. Once the coast was clear, I continued my pursuit.

Up ahead, the Beetle made a left turn on F Street NW, then made the next right heading north on 11th Street NW. I had been wondering where the hell all the police were, because I wasn't pretending that I could bring the three experienced Russian KGB agents down by myself. Just as the thought crossed my mind, two squad cars with sirens blaring arrived a half-block behind me—and were forced to stop because of the traffic jam on 10th Street and the absolute mayhem left in the wake of the wild chase and gunshots fired. At least I knew that they were actively engaged in the chase, and that emboldened me to continue.

When I turned north on 11th Street, I had to make up some ground to stay in the hunt. There was construction going on, activity on both sides of the street affecting the flow of traffic. Despite the time of day on a Tuesday, workers were jackhammering the streets and sidewalks and there was scaffolding everywhere, with cranes and lots of workers in hardhats scattered about. The temperature was in the mid to high eighties, and there had been a rain shower earlier in the day. It was hot and humid in Washington DC, and I saw construction workers pouring water on their heads and wiping sweat off their faces as I drove the Honda 350 Scrambler past them like I was racing through an obstacle course of traffic congestion and construction sites. It was July and hot in the city, so my zany music brain started to play **"Summer in the City,"** by The Lovin' Spoonful. I loved this song, and purposely played it every hot Tennessee summer so it was not a shocker that it popped up in my brain. Released on the Fourth of July 1966, it hit number one on the Billboard Hot 100 in August 1966 and stayed there for three consecutive weeks, eventually going gold. The song uniquely featured the sound effects of jackhammers and cars honking to represent noisy city streets. I'm certain the melody playing in my brain made me ride faster, with new rhythm in my twists and turns. Soon I was back on the tail of the Hippie Beetle.

The hot pursuit continued north on 11th Street, and I saw the Hippie Beetle turn left on I Street NW; this time, they were going the correct direction on a one-way street. I closed the distance as we neared to Franklin Square Park on our right. Named after Benjamin Franklin, the 4.8-acre land parcel was originally the site of natural springs, purchased by the federal government in 1832 and turned into a park. During the Civil War, it served as an encampment for resting, wounded, and dying Union soldiers. The park remained largely unchanged until the 1870s, when landscaping, benches, and paths were added. A bronze statue of Commodore John Barry was dedicated on May 16, 1914; he was an Irish-American officer in the Continental Navy during the American Revolutionary War, and was appointed a captain in the Continental Navy on December 7, 1775. He was the first captain placed in command of a US warship commissioned for service under the Continental flag. He shares the moniker "The Father of the American Navy" along with John Paul Jones and

John Adams. In 1935, the Public Works Administration gave the city $75,000 to further improve Franklin Square. The fountain, a flagstone plaza, a geometric system of concrete pathways, and new trees were all added. Interestingly, the park is also at the site of Alexander Graham Bell's first wireless message transmitted on his newly invented photophone, a device that allowed for the transmission of sound on a beam of light. The message was sent from the east side of the park square at the historic Franklin School to a window in a building on L Street on June 3, 1880.

At the southwest corner of Franklin Square Park, where I Street NW intersects with 14th Street NW, more road construction stalled traffic. Alek Baranov, driving the Hippie Beetle, made the decision to take the car off-road, going north through Franklin Square Park to K Street NW then continuing west, bypassing the snarled traffic. The park was partially terraced and sloped uphill from I Street to K Street with many large trees, large grassy areas, concrete pathways, many benches, the fountain in the middle of the park, and the statue of Commodore John Barry on the west side of the park. I could see him making his move to drive north through the park, mostly trying to follow the concrete pathways. I thought this would be an opportune time to try and stop them without getting myself caught or killed.

I plotted a course to pass in front of them, intending to try a left-handed shot with the Walther PPK, keeping my right hand on the throttle. It was a wild and reckless plan, I admit. I weaved and sped northwest across the park, attempting to strategically intersect with the three KGB agents heading north in the Hippie Beetle. People were screaming, dogs were pulling their leashes free from the hands of their owners, panicked birds were flying in every direction... It was chaos and confusion throughout the park. My trajectory and timing worked, and because of the many trees and obstacles in the park, they did not see me coming until I was passing in front of them. I squeezed off two shots with the Walther PPK, using my left hand as best I could. The first shot hit the front of the Beetle in the cargo area, but the second shot struck Alek Baranov's right earlobe and stunned the living shit out of him. Borya tried his best to take a shot back at me, but Baranov was momentarily disoriented and grabbed his ear with his right hand, resulting in the steering wheel being pulled to the left by his left hand. He had to hit the brakes or crash. The Hippie Beetle spun out and Borya's single shot of return fire went aimlessly off into space.

I nearly hit a tree directly ahead of me as I had momentarily focused on taking the shots. Regaining the forward field of view, I had to veer to my left, barely missing the tree as I fumbled my left hand back into place. For a millisecond, I thought that I was going to pull out of the temporary danger and perceived loss of control—but then my luck ran out. I missed the tree, but my revised course had me staring directly at a young mother rushing to push her baby carriage away from the scene of havoc. I had to swerve back right to miss them, putting me on an unavoidable collision course with the back side of a park bench. I had ridden dirt bikes and motorcycles since I was a kid, and knew every trick in the book, but I only had 12–15 feet ahead of me to react and was going roughly 30–35 MPH on a 346-pound bike. I couldn't steer around the bench, and I was afraid to lay the bike down and slide into the bench going that fast. I elected to fully engage the front and rear brakes and try to slow down a bit, while trying to make the impact with the back of the bench at a perfect ninety-degree angle.

At the time of impact, my front wheel must have been tilted just a tiny bit back to the left rather than at the ninety-degree right angle I had hoped. The impact turned the front wheel of the motorcycle violently to the left as I flew forward off the bike. The left handlebar jammed precisely into my groin with such physical force as to partially tear a hole in my left femoral artery, without ripping the skin open. I was catapulted into space, flying over the unforgivingly stationary park bench. At that moment, I had a closed-wound hole in my left femoral artery; unbeknown to me, a large hematoma was rapidly growing in my left groin area and vital oxygenated blood was not being effectively delivered to my left leg and left foot. I hit the ground at least a dozen feet on the other side of the bench and didn't know how badly I was injured until I stood up to see what had happened to the Hippie Beetle and its occupants.

They had spun out to a stop and Alek Baranov's mangled right earlobe was bleeding profusely. The sounds of police sirens approaching the park from the east and the south filled the air and were growing louder. I could see flashing lights approaching the southeast corner of the park. Both Borya and Catherine were able to partially witness my misfortune through the park trees and were amazed but also angered by my persistence. Although he was dazed and confused, Baranov screamed at Borya and Catherine, "Let's go! *Kill* him! Finish off that crazy Bubble Butt son of bitch right here and now!" Borya knew they were out of time with the police closing in and needed to take control of the situation. He physically yanked Baranov out of the driver's seat and shoved him awkwardly into the back seat; Catherine reading his moves and helping. Borya then slid into the driver's seat and drove directly north out of the park onto K Street, heading west. He drove to a rendezvous location in Georgetown, where he ditched the Hippie Beetle. The three of them were picked up by a nondescript black sedan as planned, but their getaway was nearly foiled by my attempted heroics.

When I stood up and saw the psychedelic yellow Hippie Beetle getting away, I waved my right fist and yelled at them as loud as I could, "*Go back to Russia, shitheads!*" At the same time, my music brain started playing **"Back in the U.S.S.R."** by the Beatles. The moment I yelled,

I knew something was wrong. I felt intense pain in my groin and the world started spinning, hard to see with all the stars in my eyes. I knew that I was beginning to faint and crumpled to the ground in a semi-controlled fashion. I felt clammy and chilled all over, and my heart was pounding and racing in my chest. I settled cautiously on my back, but the world did not stop spinning. It had all started to feel like I was in a dream when I saw Ding appear in my field of vision. He yelled into his radio, "Bubble Butt's down! *Bubble Butt's down!*" The music faded, and my world went dark.

CHAPTER NINE:

MODERN MEDICINE

"Do as much as possible for the patient,
and as little as possible to the patient."
—Dr. Bernard Lown

Tuesday, July 1, 1975 at 9:00 PM local time,
Georgetown University Hospital, Washington, DC

F BI Agent Isaiah Jones notified Ding the minute I started chasing
Borya and Catherine Krovopuskov from the National Museum
of Natural History. He was working at his desk at FBI Headquarters
when Isaiah's call came in, and couldn't believe his ears that the Krovopuskovs were brazen enough to be conducting business in his backyard of Washington DC, especially after recently being placed on the
most-wanted lists of both the FBI and CIA. Ding ran to his car and
monitored the police radio channel, which was filled with chatter
about the status of the chase with shots fired at 10th Street and Constitution, and on 10th Street in front of the Ford Theatre. For this
new assignment, Ding had been given a brand new, unmarked, 1975,
silver Chevrolet Nova 9C1 sedan with black interior. The 1975 police
package Nova was a collaborative effort between the Chevy Camaro
and Nova engineers. The Nova had a 350 cubic inch V-8 with a

four-barrel carburetor mated to a three-speed automatic transmission. The engineers took the brakes from the larger Chevy Impala sedan and suspension components from the high-performance Camaro. The police Nova sedan was a 1970s high-performance wolf in sheep's clothing. Ding wasted no time using his high-performance Nova with siren blasting, dashboard-mounted light and front grill lights flashing to get to the scene of the real-time pursuit.

He caught up with the chase at the southeast corner of Franklin Square Park just in time to see me in the middle of my race to intersect with the Hippie Beetle. He watched as events unfolded, then turned his Nova north into the park off I Street, following the general path of the Hippie Beetle. When he saw me strike the back of the park bench and fly through the air, he astutely drove directly to me, thinking to rescue me and/or protect me in case the Russians came for me.

When Ding got to me, I was moaning about the pain in my groin before I passed out. He couldn't see any blood, but could feel a soft-ball-sized lump. He quickly took his knife out and cut my blue jeans open over the wound to get a better look. There was a large, reddish-blue hematoma on the left side of my groin that was pulsating with my heartbeat. He then took the tennis shoe and sock off my left foot, alarmed to see the foot was pale with a light blue tint and cold to the touch. *Shit, this is bad; he is bleeding internally and his leg is cold. I can't wait for an ambulance,* he thought.

A small crowd of people had gathered around us. Ding reflexively showed his badge as he announced that he was an FBI agent. He requested help to move me to the back seat of his Chevy Nova Sedan. Several bystanders helped gently carry me to the car and placed me across the back seat. Ding again turned on his siren and flashing lights, radioing dispatch. Speaking with authority, he said, "This is agent Brooks. I am headed to Georgetown University Hospital Emergency

Room with a high-priority government asset who has a severe vascular injury to his left upper leg. I need vascular trauma surgeons on standby at the ER door *now*. I'll be there in minutes, over."

The dispatcher assigned to Ding's special task force replied, "Understood; they will be waiting for you. Take K Street to Canal Road, to Foxhall Road, to Reservoir Road. That is your fastest route, over."

Ding replied, "I know that route well; anything you can do to clear the way will help. I'm putting this new Nova to the test! Patch Chief of Staff Rumsfeld through to me ASAP." I slipped in and out of consciousness in the back seat as Ding raced to the Georgetown University Hospital Emergency Room in a record time of just under ten minutes.

Ding knew that he was taking me to a center of excellence for vascular surgery. Georgetown University Hospital was one of our nation capital's oldest academic teaching hospitals, founded in 1898 as part of Georgetown University. The facility originally opened with 33 beds and was staffed by the Sisters of St. Francis. The Hospital moved to its current location on Reservoir Road NW in 1930. Through its birth and long-term relationship with Georgetown University, the hospital trained students from both the School of Medicine and the School of Nursing. The Main Hospital was built in 1947, the first building erected in the Georgetown University Hospital complex. Of historic interest, John Fitzgerald Kennedy Jr. was born at Georgetown University Hospital on November 25, 1960, two weeks after his father, Massachusetts senator John F. Kennedy (JFK), was elected president of the United States. The younger brother of Carolyn Kennedy was nicknamed "John-John" by the press. The nickname, used by the media but not by the Kennedy family, originated from a reporter who misheard JFK calling him John twice in quick succession.

Three minutes before arriving at the emergency room, Rumsfeld was on the radio with Ding. "What happened, and what do you need?"

"The Krovopuskovs are at large here in DC, and Bubble Butt was injured on a motorcycle while trying to stop them. He nearly succeeded. He needs the best vascular surgeon at Georgetown, right now. I'm nearly there; he's in the back seat, slipping in and out of consciousness."

Rumsfeld calmly replied, "I'm on it," and hung up.

Five minutes later, President Gerald Ford was on the phone with Charles A. Hufnagel, MD. The American surgeon had invented the first artificial heart valve in the early 1950s, and later made significant contributions to the development of the modern heart-lung machine. He was the chairman of the Georgetown Department of Surgery, and had served in that capacity since 1969. In 1974, Dr. Hufnagel served as chairman of a three-member medical panel that evaluated the medical condition of President Richard Nixon. President Nixon had undergone pelvic surgery for a chronic vascular condition, phlebitis. The evaluation was ordered by Federal Judge John J. Sirica, who was presiding at the trial of Nixon aides accused of covering up the Watergate break-in. The lawyers representing Nixon asserted that he was physically too weak to testify. The medical panel did determine that Mr. Nixon was too ill to testify for at least six weeks. The doctors made it a point to protect the confidentiality of Nixon's medical records and refused to cite a reason for recommending against his testifying; Nixon never did testify.

Dr. Hufnagel answered President Ford's call. "Good evening, Mr. President. What can I do for you?"

"A young man named Kevin Schafer is being admitted to your emergency room at this very moment with a traumatic vascular injury to his left leg," President Ford explained. "We consider him to be a very high-priority government asset, and will be providing security for him while he recovers in the hospital. Our agent in charge, Chuck Brooks, is there with him now. Schafer needs your best."

Hufnagel replied, "I'm offsite at this time, but our best attending vascular limb surgeon, Dr. Aram Shahbazian, is there. I'll see to it that he personally takes the case."

"I appreciate that, Dr. Hufnagel. One more thing: Schafer's nickname is 'Bubble Butt,' and he has a lot of friends with crazy nicknames. You might want to let Dr. Shahbazian know that. Thanks again," Ford concluded.

Hufnagel smiled to himself about the patient's nickname and immediately contacted Dr. Shahbazian through the hospital switchboard. Dr. Shahbazian was making late rounds with his surgical residents and two vascular surgical fellows when he took the urgent call from his boss, Chairman Hufnagel. Shahbazian got off the phone and dismissed the residents, then took the two vascular fellows with him and assumed control of the team that had met Ding (and me) at the emergency room entrance. The team swiftly moved me to a private trauma bay in the emergency room, where they immediately started IVs in both arms, put an oxygen mask on my face, cut my clothes off, put a catheter in my bladder, hooked me up to the cardiac monitor, drew multiple tubes of blood for tests including type and cross blood to order from the blood bank, injected me with some IV Demerol, and assessed my injuries. Other than some superficial cuts and scratches and the deeper bruises on my arms, legs, and hips from the landing on the hard ground, my most-threatening injury was a presumed closed wound rupture of my left femoral artery. I was in and out of consciousness, but was able to respond reasonably lucidly when I met Dr. Shahbazian. He was calm and reassuring as he told me that I would need surgery to save my leg, and that he needed an x-ray of my blood vessels to know exactly where to operate and what to expect once he got there.

I think I responded with something like, "Call my parents. Tell them I'm OK, and make sure that you save my leg!"

They were already wheeling me to Radiology. Dr. Shahbazian smiled at me and said, "Sounds like a plan, Bubble Butt. I'll see you in the operating room real soon."

As they wheeled me into the Radiology Department, my brain was starting to somewhat function again. I prayed to God to help me, and save my life and left leg. I kept feeling like I was taking part in some sort of a dream. Then my unrepentant music brain started playing **"Dream On"** by Aerosmith. Totally in my brain, I laughed at myself. *My brain is experiencing IV narcotics for the first time,* I thought. Written by lead singer Steven Tyler, the classic rock ballad appeared on their debut 1973 album recorded in Boston, Massachusetts. The song was their first major hit and became a classic rock radio staple. It only peaked at number 59 on the Billboard Hot 100, but hit bigtime in the band's native Boston, where it was the number one single of the year on Boston radio station WBZ-FM, "Rockin' Stereo 106.7." One of my all-time favorite rock ballads, the song was about dreaming until your dreams come true. I knew all the words by heart and was thinking about how I'd lost the battle that day, but knew I had to lose a few times in order to win. *Maybe tomorrow the good Lord will take me away, but that's not happening today,* I mused, *just like I told Waldo when I took his Walther PPK and ran after Borya and Catherine.* Anyway, the song seemed perfect, considering my predicament. I briefly dreamed about using the White Hole Project to travel to another planet, the Demerol making it extra vivid.

The last thing I remembered before going to surgery was someone in Radiology telling me "this might burn a little bit." They injected me with contrast and my lower body and left leg felt like they were on fire, burning from the inside out. It was excruciating; they must have given me some more pain medicine, putting me under. I think I experienced what the fires of hell must be like, and I'd prefer not to go back!

I came to at 9:00 PM, or at least that was my first post-surgical recollection. I was on a stretcher, being wheeled into a private room on the hospital surgical floor. Bowmar, Bucky, Waldo, and Ding were all there as they transferred me from the stretcher to the bed. I immediately noticed that my left leg was still attached. I looked at Waldo, and my first words were a bit rough because my mouth was dry and my sticky tongue felt entirely too heavy. I said, "I told you I wouldn't die today. Did you call my parents?"

"You made a good effort to die today, Bubble Butt!" Waldo exclaimed.

I weakly responded, "Now I can officially say that I'm hard to kill, just like Bucky."

Bucky chimed in with a grin. "You have a few more close calls to make it through before you can claim that one, BB."

"Shit," I growled. "I thought one big one would earn me the honors."

Bowmar spoke next. "Your surgeon came out to talk to us when he was done and said you were singing Steven Tyler's high notes of "Dream On" like you had inhaled helium right before they put you to sleep. He said the whole operating room team started singing with you, and kept going even after you were asleep! He said, 'That was the most fun emergency vascular repair I ever did.' He told us your leg will be fine, but it will take you a few months to fully recover."

"I don't have a few months; football practice starts next month," I countered. I looked at Ding and enquired, "How did you find me? I remember you were the first person I saw after my wreck."

"I'm FBI, that's how," Ding retorted. "With regards to football, you *were* the football today! I saw you hit the park bench and take to the air; I think you could have cleared the goal posts for an extra point."

"You mean *three* points, for the winning field goal with one second remaining on the game clock," I corrected him with a smirk. "I guess I owe you my life, Ding, or at least my leg. Thanks for being there for me today." I reached out and shook Ding's hand.

"You drove that motorcycle directly in front of three highly-trained and deadly KGB agents trying to escape in that jacked-up psychedelic VW Super Beetle, and took your best shot at them with the Walther PPK in your left hand while driving the bike with your right. One of your bullets hit the driver in his right ear and they nearly bought it. Then, you avoided hitting a baby being pushed in a carriage by its mother, and sacrificed yourself against the back of a park bench. I'd say that you have a bright future with the FBI, Bubble Butt."

I paused for a moment and came back with, "No; no, *you* have a bright future with the Bad Love Gang, Ding."

Waldo interrupted, "I spoke to your parents...and then President Ford called them."

A small surge of adrenaline went through my body and I exclaimed, "President Ford called my parents?! What the heck?!"

Waldo reverted to his role of surrogate parent. "You needed surgery emergently, and you are underage: unable to consent. Larry and Gloria were out to dinner and not immediately available. President Ford spoke directly to Dr. Shahbazian and approved your surgery. Once the local authorities in Oak Ridge located your parents, they put them on the phone with the president. They were flabbergasted, nearly speechless to say the least, and of course consented for your surgery while you were in the operating room."

"I get that, but how did President Ford explain how he knew me or why I was riding a motorcycle here in DC?"

"The president plans to call you tomorrow morning. He will let you know what he said to your folks. I told them that you rented a motorcycle and accidently collided with the tail end of the presidential motorcade, so it didn't make the news. The president liked that excuse, and said that he could somehow work with that. I guess one of your sisters bellowed, 'That sounds like something my little Bubble Butt brother would do!' Anyway, your family and most, if not all, of the Bad Love Gang are driving here tomorrow in a caravan. Rumsfeld has made arrangements for all of them that show up to stay at the Hay-Adams Hotel."

"What happened to Borya, Catherine, and their driver?" I enquired.

Ding answered that one. "They managed to drive to Georgetown, parking the VW on a quiet neighborhood street. Then two eyewitnesses we interviewed saw them get into a black sedan and drive off. Neither of the eyewitnesses got a license plate number, though, and there are a gazillion black sedans driving the streets of this town. We are tracing the Beetle's history, but for the moment, it looks like they got away cleanly. We do have a bulletin out looking for someone with a significant right ear injury who seeks medical care."

I was beginning to fade out again but got a few last words in. "Ding, your idea to use Bobbie and Natalie Krovopuskov as bait to lure Borya and Catherine is sound. They were going to kidnap Bucky and me today at the museum and use us as collateral to get Bobbie and Natalie released. You need to start thinking about how to set that trap in Knoxville with some tasty cheese that the chief mice cannot resist." I drifted off, barely finishing my sentence.

CHAPTER TEN:

THE DRAKE EQUATION

"Only by doing the best we can with the very best that an era offers, do we find the way to do better in the future."
—Frank Drake

Saturday, September 6, 1975 at 9:00 PM local time, the White Hole Project, Oak Ridge, Tennessee

Two months had passed since I was discharged from Georgetown University Hospital after having the tear in my left femoral artery repaired. I played right offensive guard for the Oak Ridge Wildcat High School football team, and it was my senior year; there was no way that I was going to miss my senior year of football. Besides, we had a hell of a team going into this fall 1975 season. I blocked for an outstanding all-purpose running back named Craig Freeman. He was part of a two running back option offense. On ninety-five percent of the plays, the eventual ball carrier would not be known until after the ball was snapped. I was a pulling guard because of my "bubble butt" speed, and would pull from my guard position to lead the blocking around the ends for the ball carriers. I loved it. I was fast, and also bench pressing 300 pounds by my senior year. There was nothing else like barreling into and through defensive bodies in the acceleration of a successful running play, and then watching your running back go for extra yards! My music brain would play our fight song throughout the game: *Roll, Wildcats, roll. The fight is on; let's take it across the goal. Let's roll, Wildcats, roll.* As a team, we all knew that we had a decent shot at getting to the playoffs—and maybe another Tennessee state football title. The Wildcats had won three prior state championship titles in 1956, 1958, and 1962. We were due again my senior year, I was sure.

I had spent the last half of July and the entire month of August focusing on doing everything possible to recover from surgery from the top of my head to the bottoms of my feet. My local doctor pleaded with me to take it slow, but as soon as Dr. Shahbazian said I could work out using my left leg, all bets were off. I was going for it nonstop with weight training, isometrics, and running: hills, sprints, and distance. My offensive line coach, Harry Stocker, was one rough and tough son of a bitch, but he liked me and knew I was coming back. Stocker was always drinking a cup of coffee and chomping on an unlit stubby cigar while he gruffly barked out of the other corner of his mouth at us to work harder in practice. I worked with the offensive line non-contact until the last week of August and missed the first game, but was back in the lineup for the first game in September. I had played the night before, and felt fine. On one play I had pulled around the right end to block for Freeman and "buried" an outside defensive linebacker near our sideline. Ding was announcing the game in his new undercover role as the voice of the Wildcats, live on the Mighty WATO 1290 AM. He enthusiastically proclaimed, "That punishing outside block by Kevin Bubble Butt Schafer paved the way for Freeman to dance another ten yards down the sideline!" I got the wind knocked out of me going down on the play and was slow to get up. Coach Harry Stocker was standing near me on the sideline and had seen the whole play up close. Rather than act worried that I had somehow reinjured myself, he yelled at me as he chomped on his ugly stub of a cigar: "Get up, you big pussy! Get back in the game! Rub a little dirt in that groin of yours; that'll take care of it! Get back in the huddle and learn how to block!" Half our sideline was dying laughing at Stocker's theatrics directed at me.

FBI Special Agent Chuck "Ding" Brooks, appointed by President Ford to head the task force assigned to apprehend Borya and Catherine Krovopuskov—and now part of the Bad Love Gang—had moved to Oak Ridge in late July and assumed his role working at local radio station WATO 1290 AM. After Borya killed FBI Agent Bill Cupp in cold blood at the National Museum of Natural History on July 1st and shot his way across downtown Washington DC during his madcap getaway in the Hippie Beetle, the FBI had kept the two Krovopuskov children (Bobby and Natalie) in custody. Ding had assembled a hand-picked team of undercover FBI agents and established a local office/command center in Knoxville. The CIA was also covertly involved in the effort to apprehend the Krovopuskovs.

Ding was busy setting the stage to bring Bobby and Natalie Krovopuskov back to their family home in Knoxville under protective custody. Ding and the FBI had convinced their Aunt, Nancy Royer, who was Catherine's older sister, to cooperate in the effort to apprehend Borya and Catherine alive in return for a more lenient treatment of Catherine. Nancy had been close to her nephew Bobby and her niece Natalie since they were born. She and the rest of Catherine's family were horrified to learn that Catherine (born and raised in Tennessee) had been living a double life as a professor at the University of Tennessee and as a KGB agent recruited by Borya. Nancy had agreed to live at the family home with Bobby and Natalie when they arrived in Knoxville and supervise their activities. Ding and his team would leave enough crumbs of information lying around so Borya's spy network would know Bobby and Natalie's whereabouts. The plan hinged on the assumption and hope that the parents would take the calculated risk to get to their children. Nancy loved her "KGB brainwashed sister," and hoped to somehow bring her back into the family fold. Ding's timetable aimed to have all the players in place and bring Bobby and Natalie to Knoxville on October 1, 1975.

In the meantime, Ding had grown closer to me, Bowmar, Bucky, and Waldo. He was getting to know the rest of the Bad Love Gang just by hanging out at Waldo and Mary's house and spending time with everyone as they would come and go during the week and/or weekends. He was living out his fantasy alternative life as a radio announcer on Oak Ridge WATO 1290 AM, and he was an instant hit with the listeners! He was not only continuing the long-standing tradition of announcing Oak Ridge Wildcat football games and talking sports, he was also playing music with a wide-ranging selection of contemporary rock, R&B, soul, and even threw in some country-western here and there, which made Waldo happy.

Ding had amazing energy and wit. The rumor was out that many times he could be seen dancing away in the D.J. booth at the station, or on site at the high school broadcasts, when the music was playing. Bowmar and I even managed to go on the air with him once a week, billed as "Music and Trivia with Bubble Butt and Bowmar." I would pick a few songs to play with some fun facts and people would call in and ask Bowmar about any topic under the sun. Amazingly for the audience, but of no surprise to me and Ding, Bowmar knew all the answers. It was getting to the point where callers were purposely trying to stump Bowmar, but to no avail.

The week before, while hanging out together, Ding had asked me a casual question. "What current top-forty song would get everyone on their feet and dancing at half-time?"

I reflexively answered, "If you want to get our high school dancing, then all you gotta play is **"Get Down Tonight"** by KC and the Sunshine Band. It's their first number one hit, it's number one on the Billboard Hot 100 and number one on the Billboard hot soul singles. I'll be in the locker room at half-time, but I'd get down to that music if I were out there in the stands. Whether you know how to dance or not, your body just involuntarily starts jiving to that song. You can't help yourself!"

The night before, Ding waited for the high school band to complete their half-time number and then announced over the outdoor speaker system, "I have a special request from senior Wildcat offensive guard, Kevin 'Bubble Butt' Schafer, who is back in the lineup tonight for his first game as a senior. He asked me to play this song to get you psyched for the second half of tonight's game." He then played **"Get Down Tonight"** by KC and the Sunshine Band over the speaker system. The school bands, cheerleaders, and entire student body watching on both sides of the field went wild. Everyone was dancing and singing the refrain at the tops of their lungs. We could hear the ruckus and singing from inside the locker room; people at home could probably hear it from a mile away. I thought, *Ding is all right! We are gonna have some fun this football season.*

I had invited Bowmar and Bucky to spend the night with me and our Bad Love Gang pet golden hamster, Rasputin, at the White Hole Project on Saturday night. Along with my vigorous rehab efforts, I had been researching my idea about using the White Hole for the possibility of space travel. Bowmar, to his credit, had been patiently waiting for this moment, curious to find out what I had in mind since I had mentioned it in front of President Ford. I had them come into the lab in the exotic matter containment room, where I had arranged for what amounted to a small classroom setting for our discussion. I had written the Drake Equation on a portable blackboard, which was facing the wall. Bowmar and Bucky got comfortable in their chairs with some ice-cold sweet tea while I stood and talked.

"Two and a half months ago, Bucky, Pumpkin, Willy and I met the alien woman, Blue Nova One, in the forests of southern China. Other than the Bad Love Gang and a very small circle of people in the know, humanity is still only aware of one intelligent civilization in the Universe: our own. However, some very smart scientists have been pondering about the likelihood of other advanced alien civilizations for quite some time. That's where the famous Drake Equation, named after astrophysicist Dr. Frank Drake, comes into play. In 1961, the scientist J.P.T. Pearman of the National Academy of Sciences approached Drake to convene the first scientific meeting on the search for extraterrestrial intelligence, or SETI, conference at the National Radio Astronomy Observatory's Green Bank location in West Virginia. Besides Drake and Pearman, three Nobel laureates attended the meeting, along with physicist Philip Morrison and a dark-haired, brilliant, 27-year-old astronomy postdoctoral fellow named Carl Sagan. The conference opened on the morning of November 1, 1961. After the guests were comfortably seated and sipping coffee, Drake wrote what became his famous equation on a chalkboard. I am showing it to you now, but bear in mind, this pertained only to our own Milky Way Galaxy when Drake conceived it. I am going to give you very conservative numbers for all the assumed values."

I turned the chalkboard around and continued my impromptu lecture, reading out the equation and explaining the variables.

"$N = R* \cdot fp \cdot ne \cdot fl \cdot fi \cdot fc \cdot L$.

"N = The calculated number of intelligent alien civilizations in our galaxy.

"R* = The average rate of star formation in our galaxy which we will say is a conservative one per year over the life of the galaxy.

"fp = The fraction of those stars that have planets, and here we'll use 0.2 to 0.5.

"ne = The average number of planets that can potentially support life per star that has planets; here we'll use a range of one to five.

"fl = The fraction of planets that could support life that actually *develop* life at some point. Here we will use 100%, or one. One thing we know about this, the planet has to have water.

"fi = The fraction of planets with life that actually go on to develop intelligent life and alien civilizations. We will use 100%, or one.

"fc = The fraction of civilizations that develop technologies to release detectable signs of their existence into space. We will assume 10-20%, or 0.1-0.2.

"L = the length of time for which such civilizations release detectable signals into space. This could be very highly variable, but we'll say 1,000 to 100,000,000 years.

"Inserting the above minimum numbers into the equation gives a minimum N of 20, and inserting the maximum numbers gives a maximum N of 50,000,000. At the original meeting in 1961, they concluded that N ≈ L, and there were probably between 1,000 and 100,000,000 planets with civilizations in the Milky Way. I took an unscientific average of the scientific papers analyzing the original Drake Equation to estimate the number of intelligent alien civilizations in our galaxy and came up with 3,500."

Bowmar interrupted, "That number even seems a bit high to me."

I smiled, "Patience, my bosom Brainiac buddy. But I agree with you, and I will explain why. First let me say that looking at these Drake equation factors, it becomes clear that none of them can be precisely determined by modern science. Moreover, as we move from the left to right in this equation, estimating each factor becomes more controversial. The later terms are highly speculative; assigning values might betray our personal biases more than representing tested and proven scientific facts."

"That's one of the problems that always bothered me about my first test launch in the White Hole Project," Bucky interposed. "I would ask questions, and many times the answers from these supposedly brilliant scientists would be, 'That is what the data suggests.' How would you feel stepping into this time machine in 1945 to be transported back in time based on suggestive data?"

I continued, "I want to broaden the scope of our discussion by at least two different variables: time and distance, or size of the universe as a whole. First the universe is billions of years old; let's just say it's about fourteen billion years old. Our ancestors have been around this planet for about five million years, give or take, but most advances in our civilization have occurred in the last ten thousand years. What if we get into World War III and nuke ourselves into extinction? Or another extinction level event from outer space comes our way sometime in the next ten thousand years? In other words, civilizations come and go over the course of that giant time frame of fourteen billion years that we are considering. Let me pose a different question; are we earthlings the first intelligent civilization in the entire universe, somewhere in the middle, or the latest civilization to evolve? My point is that there is a time limit that intelligent civilizations have to potentially contact each other or visit each other. In other words, maybe timing is everything.

"If that is not mind-boggling enough, then let's consider the scope of the universe. The original Drake Equation pertained just to our own Milky Way Galaxy. The famous American astronomer, Edwin Hubble, who died in 1953, greatly helped us begin to understand the size and increasing size of the universe. In the early 1920s, Hubble was using the 100-inch Hooker Telescope at Mount Wilson Observatory in California, which was the world's largest at the time. At that time, the prevailing view of the cosmos was that the universe consisted entirely of the Milky Way. Using the Hooker Telescope at Mt. Wilson, Hubble was able to take measurements using a particular type of star that changes its brightness, which are called Cepheid variables. These stars were in so-called spiral nebulae, or interstellar clouds, including the Andromeda Nebula and Triangulum Nebula. His measurements, made in 1924, proved conclusively that these nebulae were much too distant to be part of the Milky Way and were, in fact, entire galaxies outside our own Milky Way. Hubble had discovered that the universe was far larger than anyone had believed, and that spiral nebulae like Andromeda and Triangulum were actually distant galaxies.

"If you look through your telescope tonight at light coming from the Andromeda Galaxy, it took those photons of light 2.5 million years to hit your eye because they started their journey 2.5 million light years away—and that Andromeda Galaxy is basically on our cosmic doorstep. The number of stars contained in the Andromeda Galaxy is estimated at one trillion, or roughly twice the number estimated for the Milky Way. Think about how many potential planets that one additional galaxy represents. Now we believe there could be billions of galaxies, but every time we get bigger, better telescopes, that number grows. Think of this: Even if the minimum number of alien planets having intelligent life in our own Milky Way Galaxy is off by a factor of ten, and there are just two such planets in our galaxy and an average of one or two in other galaxies, that still means there are *billions* of other planets in the whole of the universe capable of harboring intelligent alien life. How mind-blowing is that?"

Bowmar chimed in, "I like where you are going with this. If we would have accepted that there were 3,500 intelligent alien planets in just our own Milky Way Galaxy, with some having had the time opportunity to evolve to their maximum potential, then it makes me wonder why we are not routinely interacting with aliens every day. But if we accept, as you suggest, one to ten such planets per galaxy, then it might be much more of a random chance event for intelligent alien life forms to interact with each other, in their own galaxy or across galaxies."

"I actually said one to two intelligent alien planets per galaxy trying to be super, super conservative. But even so, the number of possibilities for intelligent life in the whole of the Universe elsewhere is still astronomical...no pun intended. But let's also talk briefly about raw distance across this Universe of billions of galaxies. Again, I go back to Edwin Hubble's observation published in 1929, which showed that galaxies are receding or moving away from Earth with a velocity that is proportional to their distance from us; more distant galaxies recede faster than nearby galaxies. Think of an expanding raisin cake with each of the raisins it contains representing a galaxy, with the Earth raisin at the center. The outer raisins are moving away from center Earth raisin faster than the raisins that are close to Earth as the cake expands. Thus, more distant objects move relatively faster than nearby ones. This relationship became known as is Hubble's Law, and it indicates a constant expansion of the universe. The slope of the relationship is called the Hubble Constant; it represents the constant rate of cosmic expansion caused by the stretching of spacetime continuum itself. Although the expansion rate is constant in all directions at any given time, this rate changes with time throughout the life of the universe.

"So just how big is the universe in actual size? Based on the estimated age of the universe and the rate of cosmic expansion, astrophysicists have estimated that the observable Universe is a sphere measuring about ninety-three *billion* light-years across. However, beyond that, the universe likely extends much farther and could even be infinite. Who really knows? For the sake of a brief argument about effective space travel, let's say that Earth is somewhere near the middle of that sphere, even though we don't know the position of Earth relative to the 'edge' of the Universe as a whole. OK, if we are in the center, it will take us 46.5 billion years to get to a planet near the edge of the known Universe, traveling in a spaceship at the speed of light. Even if we could exceed the speed of light traveling with Captain Kirk and the crew of the starship Enterprise from *Star Trek*, we couldn't get that far in the Universe. Warp speed is a multiple of the speed of light. Let's say that warp factor one is the speed of light, warp factor five is 200 times the speed of light, and warp factor nine is 1,500 times the speed of light. Even if we travel at 1,500 times the speed of light, it would still take us 31 million years to get to a planet at the edge of the known Universe. I don't know about you guys, but I'd be happy to make it beyond my ninetieth birthday, aging gracefully so long as my brain is working well and I'm mobile. We don't have the time in our lives to travel that far, even if we did have warp drive technology."

"My Uncle Barney says, 'Aging gracefully is like the nice way of saying you're gradually looking worse,'" Bucky teased.

Bowmar quipped, "Old age isn't so bad, when you consider the alternative."

I joined in the banter too, of course. "I like that George Burns line where he says, 'That guy is so old that when he orders a three-minute egg, they ask for his money up front!'"

I resumed, "So what I am telling the two of you here and now is that current science fiction doesn't hold water about traveling from one side of the Universe to the other. We're not going to get into a spaceship with hyperdrive or warp speed, slam the pedal to the metal and travel billions of light years away to visit a distant planet. That's not how we are going to get there. But now, I can tell you how we *are* going to get there!"

CHAPTER ELEVEN:

BAD LOVE BEYOND

"I don't think the human race will survive the next thousand years, unless we spread into space. There are too many accidents that can befall life on a single planet. But I'm an optimist. We will reach out to the stars." —Stephen Hawking

"All civilizations become either spacefaring or extinct." —Carl Sagan

"The exploration of space will go ahead, whether we join in it or not, and it is one of the great adventures of all time, and no nation which expects to be the leader of other nations can expect to stay behind in the race for space." —John F. Kennedy

Saturday, September 6, 1975 at 11:00 PM local time, the White Hole Project, Oak Ridge, Tennessee

We all took a brief bathroom break, got fresh refills of sweet tea, and then reconvened to continue the discussion that I was leading. "Before we get into my idea for deep space travel, I want to remind you of something that happened yesterday in Sacramento, California. Our friend, President Gerald Ford, dodged a bullet—and by extension, you might say that the Bad Love Gang also dodged a bullet." I then shared the story from the news about the assassination attempt on Ford's life that had occurred the morning before, on September 5, 1975.

President Ford was scheduled to meet with California Governor Jerry Brown at the California State Capital in Sacramento. Ford had decided to walk from the Senator Hotel where he was staying. He crossed L Street and as he walked through Capitol Park, he began shaking hands with a crowd of people who had gathered there. Moving along the paved walkway toward an entrance of the state capitol building, Ford saw a woman in a brightly colored red frock, and stopped approximately halfway to the state Capitol. People on either side of Ford wanted to shake hands with him or talk a moment, and Ford assumed that the woman in red wanted the same. The woman was none other than Lynette "Squeaky" Fromme, an ardent follower of the cult group leader Charles Manson, who was convicted of murdering actress Sharon Tate and six others in Los Angeles, California, in 1969. Fromme was one of Manson's earliest and most devoted followers. In 1971, she served 90 days in jail for attempting to feed a hamburger laced with the psychedelic drug LSD to Barbara Hoyt, a witness to the Sharon Tate murder, to keep Hoyt from testifying in Manson's murder trial.

The 26-year-old Fromme managed to get within two feet of the president. She drew a Colt M1911 .45-caliber pistol (just like we had used in our WWII time travels) from her leg holster, raised her gun-wielding right arm towards Ford through the row of people standing directly in front of her, and aimed the gun at Ford's midsection. Several people then heard a metallic clicking sound. Fromme shouted, "It won't go off!" Secret Service Agent Larry Buendorf grabbed the gun, forced it from Fromme's hand, and brought her down. On the ground, Fromme reportedly said, "It didn't go off. Can you believe it? It didn't go off!" The pistol's magazine was loaded with four rounds, but there was no round in the chamber when she pulled the trigger. Secret Service agents then half-dragged Ford away from Fromme, pulling him towards the east entrance of the Capitol until Ford yelled in protest, "Put me down!" He then continued his walk to the California state house and met with Governor Jerry Brown for 30 minutes, without mentioning the assassination attempt until they were done talking business.

Bowmar responded, "I saw it all yesterday; it dominated the news channels. That sent shivers through me, since we just met with him a little over two months ago. What would we have done if he had been assassinated?"

"We could take the White Hole back to Naval Air Station (NAS), Glenview, Illinois, on Sunday, April 15, 1945, when we first met with Lieutenant Ford in Commander Staples' office," Bucky suggested. "Bubble Butt could add a warning about avoiding the woman in red in Sacramento in early September 1975 to what he told Ford about his future."

"Bucky, are you out of your mind?!" I exclaimed. We can't go around changing history like that. We have no idea how big of a ripple in time and history that would cause. If we were gonna do that, we might as well go back and find a way to assassinate Hitler before he had a chance to get started."

Bowmar rejoined, "That doesn't sound like such a bad idea, but you're right; every act of history has certain subsequent consequences, both good and bad. We could find ourselves constantly chasing after new and unexpected consequences if we tried to change history like that."

Bucky sighed. "You guys are right, but one of these days our time-travel adventures will force us to make some very hard decisions about this very topic."

"Understood, and I concur," I replied. "Fortunately, Captain Bucky, we still have President Ford alive and on our side. Now let's talk about deep space travel. Let me ask a question: If current science fiction does not allow for a spaceship to travel fast enough getting from one side of the Universe to the other, then how are we going to do it?"

Bowmar was itching to answer this question. "We take a wormhole. That's how the White Hole Project functions to connect us to different points in time."

I took a blank sheet of paper, held it up horizontally against the blackboard, and with a black felt-tip pen drew a circle labeled *Earth* on one side and another marked *Planet X* on the other. I then connected the two circles with a line and labeled it *ten billion light-years*, indicating the distance separating Earth from Planet X. "We are not going to get from Earth to Planet X in a super-fast spaceship traveling along this line; we've already covered why that is not feasible." Taking the sheet of paper from the blackboard, I held it in front of Bowmar and Bucky and folded it so the two circles representing Earth and Planet-X were on top of one another. "Now look at how relatively close Earth is to Planet X. We connect the two with a wormhole, take the short cut, and trim tens of millions of years off our travel time."

Bucky was scratching his head a bit, so Bowmar shared some of his brain power. "A wormhole, or Einstein-Rosen bridge, links different points in spacetime and is based on a special solution of the Einstein field equations. Wormholes are totally consistent with Einstein's general theory of relativity. As BB has indicated, it can be visualized as a tunnel, with the ends at separate locations in the spacetime continuum. A wormhole could connect extremely long distances, such as a billion light years or more, joining different galaxies in the Universe and especially different points in time—as our current White Hole Project was especially designed to accomplish. The main reason Bubble

Butt and I think it works is because of the discovery of exotic matter from the alien spaceship in Area 51. Exotic matter is what holds the wormhole tunnel open long enough for us or aliens to pass through it and safely travel to the other side."

I then continued, "This is why the alien spaceship hidden in Area 51 is constructed as two flying saucers connected by a telescoping funnel containing high concentrations of exotic matter. Blue Nova One and her alien civilization have managed to construct what I am calling an Intergalactic Transport Drive, or ITD. The ITD gets their spaceship quickly from one distant galaxy to the next through well-designed wormholes—or white holes, as we call them—while their spaceship also has a more 'standard' light speed propulsion unit used to drive around and explore various planets in whatever galaxy they are visiting or investigating."

"Did you come up with all this when they injected you with pain drugs and gassed you with anesthesia two months ago?" Bucky quipped.

"Oh, yes! And I dreamed that the Bad Love Gang had become the symbolic rulers of a distant galaxy, each one of us with a planet named in our honor. Planet Goondoggy had people with no fear taking wild chances at every turn, and Planet Pud had average aliens doing average things," I joked.

We all laughed and Bowmar enquired, "What about Planet Bowmar?"

"They were always trying to outsmart each other—until one of the females outsmarted Bowmar, and he realized she was his queen. They lived happily ever after."

Bucky caved in and got us back on track. "I don't want to know about Planet Bucky, smartass; save it for later. So, how do you think we are going to use this White Hole Project for deep space travel? It is only designed to send us from now back to the World War II years, January 1, 1942 through December 31, 1945. How can you make it work for deep space travel?"

This was the moment that I had been waiting for. I walked up close to Bucky, looked him directly in the eyes with all seriousness, and enquired, "What did you *really* see the night of June 17, 1942 as you stood on the balcony of the alien spaceship, looking down on the six alien beings seated in the eye of the racetrack before they vanished?"

Bucky froze, staring back at me as his face turned a paler shade. Bowmar interjected, "I've thought a lot about this since you first floated the idea to us in Washington DC. I'd have to spend a lot of time trying to reverse engineer components from the alien spaceship, and use newer 1975 computer components to modernize the White Hole Project—or maybe take some of the components from the alien ship and bring them here. Alternatively, I thought maybe we just try to learn how to use the alien ship in Area 51."

Continuing to stare into Bucky's eyes I countered, "Why don't we just hitch a ride? Wouldn't that be simpler?"

Bowmar responded, "I don't understand. What do you mean by suggesting that we 'hitch a ride?'"

With my eyes still squarely fixed on Bucky, I responded, "Bucky is going to explain what I mean, aren't you Bucky?"

Bucky gulped and said, "I don't know how you figured this out, BB, but here's what he means. On June 17, 1942, when I came to the edge of the balcony and looked down on the racetrack, I did see six alien beings, just as I outlined in my official report. That was true. But I also saw myself get on that racetrack with them, along with eight other people. There were fifteen bodies on that racetrack, six aliens, me, and eight other humans: five white males, one black female, one black male, and one white female. One of the white males was about nine or ten years old. I closed my eyes and shook my head because I saw myself down there. When I opened my eyes, they were all vanishing into space. I convinced myself that I'd seen some kind of mirage or optical illusion, and could not bring myself to report it out of fear that I would be declared mentally unfit for duty. It has haunted me continuously until this moment. Now I have it off my chest. How did you know, BB?"

Bowmar interrupted, "Oh, holy shit! That was me, Cleopatra, Crisco, Bucky, Bubble Butt, Ben, and three other Bad Love Gang members on that racetrack stage!"

I added, "Based on what Blue Nova One said on that fateful night in the south China forest, Goondoggy and Pumpkin were definitely with us. We'll have to decide who else is going; who is the ninth person?"

Bucky rather humbly implored, "Please explain the rest to me, BB, because I'm still feeling a bit uncertain about all this. And I am sorry for not telling you until tonight."

"Don't beat yourself up over it any longer. What you did was totally understandable. When Blue Nova One said we had already met and then said that she knew you, Pumpkin, Goondoggy, and Bowmar, I was dumbfounded. It started me thinking about it day and night. I know that the White Hole Project is not currently designed to transport us to other planets, so I started to think about how it could be used for us to have met Blue Nova One before the time travel mission to China. We met her on June 22, 1942 in China. You saw the aliens and yourself, plus a group of us, depart on June 17, 1942 from Nevada. The White Hole Project can send us back in time any time between 1/1/1942 and 12/31/1945. My brain finally connected all the dots. We use the White Hole Project to send nine of us back to the site of the Nevada alien ship crash site on the night of Wednesday, June 17, 1942. We know how to get on board the ship using one of the alternative entrances, and we know our way around the inside of the ship, now that we've had a chance to examine the spaceship in Nevada before going to China on our last mission. We are using Global Cosmic Positioning Devices, GCPDs, made with the same blue exotic matter unique to that alien spaceship in Nevada. The nine of us get on the stage along with the six aliens at the exact right moment and we hitch a ride to Blue Nova One's planet. If I think like Bowmar thinks, I can say that it has already happened, since Bucky saw it happen on June 17, 1942."

Bowmar enquired, "How do we get back?"

"We will have to assume that when Willy hits the recall button here at the White Hole Project, it will recall us not just through time, but through space as well."

Bucky retorted, "There's that 'we have to assume' mentality again. What if the recall button doesn't work, with us being located in some distant galaxy?"

I answered, "We would have to ask Blue Nova One for help to get back. Unless we all decide that we want to stay on her planet."

"Why do you want to do this?" Bowmar asked.

"Blue Nova One made it sound like a matter of course that we had previously met and would meet again. There is some reason that we need to go; I'm just not privy to it yet. Or maybe I need more time to figure it out. In some ways, I feel like we have already gone and come back, but I don't have any memories of it. Besides, we have the unique opportunity to expand our knowledge that we are not alone in the Universe. As Captain James T. Kirk would say, 'To boldly go where no man has gone before.' I am sure that I'll be afraid when we execute the plan for this mission, but right now I am more excited to go than afraid."

Bucky queried, "When do you want to go?"

"Semester break in December or spring break in March; I don't want us to be missing in action during our senior year of high school.

Let's the three of us agree to get a plan put together to make this happen, and then talk with the rest of the Bad Love Gang when we're ready." We all high-fived with each other and made a pact to start plotting and planning.

CHAPTER TWELVE:

THE THRILLA IN MANILA

"I'm young; I'm handsome; I'm fast. I can't possibly be beat."
—Muhammad Ali

Tuesday, September 30, 1975 at 11:00 PM local time,
the Krovo/Krovopuskov family home in Knoxville, Tennessee

It was 11:00 PM eastern time Tuesday night in Knoxville, and 8:00 PM on the US west coast. With the global time zone changes, it was 11:00 AM Wednesday morning October 1, 1975 in Manila at the Araneta Coliseum in Cubao, Quezon City, Philippines. The greatest boxing match in history and one of the greatest sporting events in history was underway in front of a record global television audience of 1 billion, including 100 million viewers watching the fight on closed-circuit theatre television and 500,000 pay-per-view buys on HBO. That night in America, HBO became the first television network in history to deliver a continuous signal via satellite by broadcasting the third and final Mohammed Ali versus Joe Frazier bout for the world championship. They had split their first two contests, with Frazier beating the previously undefeated Ali in March 1971 and Ali beating Frazier in the second match in January 1974. Prior to the third and greatest fight in recorded history, Ali, using his classic rhyming boastfulness, said that the determining fight with Joe Frazier in the Philippines would "be a killa and a thrilla and a chilla, when I get that gorilla in Manila." As was the standard expectation with Ali championship fights, this served to raise the stakes while pissing off and emboldening his heavyweight opponent, Smokin' Joe Frazier.

The entire Bad Love Gang was gathered to watch the fight on pay-for-view HBO at Waldo and Mary's house in Oak Ridge. Ding had assembled his hand-picked FBI team to watch the match at the Krovo/Krovopuskov home twenty-two miles to the east, in the Sequoyah Hills neighborhood of Knoxville. Ding's team had been diligently working to wire the Krovos' home for sound, install hidden cameras inside and outside, and bug all the phones. Ding had met with his team earlier in the evening, and they were running slightly behind schedule with all their preparations. His team had convinced Ding to wait two or three additional weeks before bringing Bobby and Natalie Krovo to live in the home with their Aunt Royer as bait for Borya and Catherine Krovopuskov.

When the two fighters met at the center of the ring for the referee's instructions, Ali continued to verbally taunt Joe Frazier. "You don't have it, Joe, you don't have it! I'm going to put you away!" Frazier smiled back and said, "We'll see." The conditions inside the aluminum-roofed Philippine Coliseum were unbelievably hot and humid as the historic fight got underway; some likened it to being in a steam cooker. Frazier estimated the temperature in the ring under the lighting used for televising the match at roughly 120 degrees Fahrenheit. Ali later said that he lost five pounds of sweat during the fight. But the energy inside the Coliseum was undeniably electrified and magnified, if not close to a nuclear chain reaction! The Filipinos had been in love with the sport of boxing since the 1960s, and the country adored

Mohammed Ali. The 25,000 fans that were crammed into the Coliseum to witness history rose to their feet and cheered for Ali, the reigning world champion. From the ring of the first bell, it was all fast and furious action as Ali dominated the first four rounds, hoping to knock out Frazier in the early going. But Frazier, and especially his chin, survived the opening punishment. He found his mojo in the middle rounds as he forced Ali to the ropes and landed vicious, unrelenting left hooks to Ali's body and head. By round ten, the match was even. Both men had trained to their physical limits for this third encounter; what happened next was the stuff of professional boxing legend.

In round eleven, Frazier began to wear down, while Ali mythically and inexplicably, found some deep inner reserve of stored energy and seized control of the fight in round twelve. In rounds thirteen and especially fourteen, Ali methodically imposed his will upon Frazier, pummeling away at Frazier's face and head. Despite the brutality of professional boxing, watching the heavyweight champion Ali dance and punch was almost like watching an opera. The 25,000-strong crowd were on their feet, jumping and screaming "Ali, Ali, Ali!" The noise was exhilarating and deafening. The same chant was occurring in Waldo's great room from the Bad Love Gang, in the Krovopuskovs' home from Ding and his FBI team, and across much of the rest of the world. Both fighters gave their very hearts and souls to the sport of boxing in those waning moments as Ali punched well beyond human limits and Frazier miraculously absorbed the unremitting, grueling punishment to somehow remain standing and then blindly find the way to his corner at the end of round fourteen.

Sitting down in his corner at the end of round fourteen, Smokin' Joe Frazier was done. Frazier's trainer, Eddie Futch, knew that Joe had been badly hurt in the last two rounds. The swelling around Joe's eyes was forcing him to raise his head in order to see his opponent, making him excessively vulnerable. In Futch's sober judgement, a victory was now out of reach, and another three minutes of punishment was too much of a risk to undertake. Futch and Frazier briefly argued in their corner, but Futch told Frazier, "It's all over. No one will forget what you did here today." He threw in the towel and stopped the fight before round fifteen could get underway. After the fight, Joe Frazier said, "Man, I hit him with punches that'd bring down the walls of a city. Lawdy, lawdy, he's a great champion." Ali was quoted as saying, "It was like death. Closest thing to dying that I know of." One thing is for certain, it was boxing history—and we all watched it on television thanks to a record-setting night on HBO.

The Krovo home was located in the Sequoyah Hills neighborhood of Knoxville, Tennessee. Borya Krovopuskov had trained directly under the tutelage of the infamous and notorious Russian KGB spy Leonid Romanovich Kvasnikov in New York City, then moved to the Knoxville/Oak Ridge area in October of 1944. With his impressive academic credentials in advanced chemical engineering, and going by his new American identity as Russ Krovo, Borya had landed a job working at the K-25 plant in Oak Ridge, Tennessee. K-25 was the code name given by the Manhattan Project for the program to produce enriched uranium for the atomic bomb using the gaseous diffusion method in which gaseous Uranium-235 (the fissionable uranium isotope for the atomic bomb) was separated from naturally occurring uranium-238 through an incredibly fine mesh. This separation process was extremely space intensive, requiring a very large building. When it was finished in 1944, the K-25 building covered 44 acres enclosing over 1,640,000 square feet, making it the world's largest building under one roof at the time. The ultra-top-secret White Hole Project time-travel machine had been built deep below ground and adjacent to K-25 during the K-25 construction.

When Borya Krovopuskov, aka Russ Krovo, moved to area, he was well funded by the KGB. Knowing not to flaunt his wealth, Borya used it to gradually build respect for Russ as a solid local citizen. He had rented a home for two years and then bought the house in Sequoyah Hills in late 1946, knowing that it would serve as the future headquarters for his KGB sleeper cell. The house was in a neighborhood that should bring respect, not suspicion, his way. Initially developed in the 1920s, Sequoyah Hills was one of Knoxville's first suburbs, located between the city's downtown area and West Knoxville with Oak Ridge located 22 miles further to the west. Sequoyah Hills was located on a peninsula created by a bend of the Tennessee River known as Looney's Bend. The neighborhood was surrounded by the river on three sides—east, south, and west—and Kingston Pike Highway on the north. The area was generally hilly, with a bluff rising above the river shore, bestowing many houses with sweeping views of the river and downtown Knoxville in the distance. Cherokee Boulevard ran in a U-shape around the edge of the peninsula, while the other main road, Scenic Drive, traveled north to south across the center of the peninsula.

The Krovopuskov home, built in 1928, was located off Cherokee Boulevard on the northeast side of the bend with backyard views of the Tennessee River and the old city of Knoxville. The two-story, four-bedroom house was an interesting combination of architecture: mainly English Tudor, but with a twist of Victorian, having a turret entryway and another turret at the north corner containing an elegant dining room surrounded by windows and marvelous views. A covered veranda wrapped around connecting the two turrets. The exterior used brick, stone, and stucco walls enhanced by the classic Tudor exterior framing, along with tall ornamental brick chimneys. The home had four thousand square feet above ground and a large finished basement. The driveway to the home from the street was long, and the front yard was beautifully manicured. It was an elegant home with three acres of property, but it was not a mansion.

Borya/Russ married Catherine Royer in 1950; her sister Nancy was the maid of honor at the wedding. The Krovos subsequently had two children: Robert, or Bobbie, in early 1955, and Natalie in late 1956. In the summer of 1962, they built a pool in the back yard for the growing family and Borya secretly constructed an underground escape tunnel leading out of their basement, around the pool, and out to the bluff overlooking the Tennessee River. The tunnel entrance from the basement was well concealed behind a false wall and the exit was covered with earth and sod; it was only to be used in the event of a dire emergency to escape the house, and the river would be used for egress away from the area. Through the years, Borya had planned many routes to leave the house and Sequoyah Hills in a hurry, but soon he would be planning how to get back in unnoticed.

Robert or Bobbie Krovo, age 20, had been a star cross-country runner since high school and was a junior on the cross-country team at the University of North Carolina at Chapel Hill. The University of North Carolina at Chapel Hill (aka UNC-Chapel Hill) was considered to be the flagship of the University of the North Carolina system. Strong in both academics and National Collegiate Athletic Association (NCAA) Division I level sports, it was considered to be a "Public Ivy," or a public college offering an academic experience equivalent to an Ivy League school. Chartered in 1789, the university enrolled its first students in 1795, making it one of the oldest public universities in the United States. The University of North Carolina at Chapel Hill made the claim to have been the only public university that graduated students in the eighteenth century. The university's sports teams were nicknamed the Tar Heels in reference to North Carolina's eighteenth-century prominence as a tar and pitch producer. The school mascot was a live British breed domestic sheep, a Dorset Horn ram named Rameses; the tradition dated back to 1924. The school was especially known for its prowess in basketball. The basketball coach Dean Smith who started at UNC Chapel Hill in 1961 was widely known for his original idea of "The Carolina Way," in which he challenged his players to "Play hard, play smart, play together." In other words, he told them to be smart and mentally strong in the classroom and excel in sports.

Bobbie was six feet tall with the thin, muscular, and graceful build of a long-distance runner. He had a quiet demeanor but was not overtly shy. As a junior at UNC Chapel Hill, he carried a respectable cumulative grade point average (GPA) of 3.53, and was majoring in political science with an eye towards law school. His life, as well as that of his sister, Natalie, had been turned upside down in the summer of 1975, when they were both detained by the FBI and informed that their parents were at the top of FBI's most-wanted list for foreign espionage and domestic terrorism. Both he and his sister were essentially forced to delay college and take their fall 1975 semesters off while the FBI was evaluating both of them and deciding how to proceed.

Natalie was 18 years old and would be turning 19 in December 1975. She had just graduated from high school and was scheduled to enter her freshman year of college at the University of Tennessee, Knoxville (UTK) where her mother, Cathy Krovo, who held a PhD in political science, taught international studies along with Russian and Chinese language classes. UT Knoxville, founded in 1794—two years before Tennessee became the 16th state—functioned as the flagship campus for the University of Tennessee system. Academically and professionally, UTK students benefited from the fact that the university had historically great relationships with various Tennessee businesses and governmental institutions, most notably the Oak Ridge National Lab (ORNL) and the Tennessee Valley Authority (TVA). The university helped co-manage the Oak Ridge National Laboratory, the US Department of Energy's largest science and energy lab. Students and faculty could tackle research projects there and had unparalleled access to some of the world's greatest scientific minds and facilities. Natalie's dad (Borya) had worked at the ORNL since 1944.

The UT sports teams competed in the NCAA Division I Southeastern Conference, and were known as the Vols and the Lady Vols, short for Volunteers. The teams had gone by that name since 1902. Tennessee was known as the Volunteer State for the large number of Tennesseans who volunteered for duty in the War of 1812, the Mexican-American War, and the American Civil War. The school had nearly 40 fraternities and sororities for students to join, and Natalie had planned to go through sorority rush with two of her best friends from high school who were also planning to go to UTK. Like her mom, Natalie was a five-foot-seven inch, slender, attractive, 18-year-old blonde who had an A average in high school and enjoyed playing both softball and volleyball. Although UTK did not yet have a women's softball team, they had first fielded a women's varsity volleyball team in the fall of 1958 and had started to keep game records in 1973. Natalie was excited to try out for the women's volleyball team at UTK. She was not yet certain of her collegiate academic track, but excelled in math and science and had always been interested in her dad's work at ORNL. All of her freshman year college plans had been put on hold with the revelation of her parents' FBI most-wanted status.

Both Bobbie and Natalie had been grilled by trained FBI interrogators for what seemed like endless hours regarding what they knew about their parents coordinated KGB espionage activities. Neither of them gave any indication that they knew anything about such felonious activity. Other than typical teenager resentments about not always getting what they wanted and deserved, both Krovo children generally expressed praise and love for their parents, and shock and dismay about the espionage and domestic terrorism charges. They were both told in no uncertain terms that if they cooperated with the FBI in the effort to apprehend their parents, they would be allowed to continue their futures with clean records and their parents would be treated fairly. They both expressed love and affection for their Aunt Nancy Royer (Cathy Krovo's sister) and the willingness to submit to her guidance while the three of them lived together at the Krovos' Sequoyah Hills family home as bait, hoping for the parents to return for their two "children."

Cathy and Nancy Royer had grown up together in Johnson City, Tennessee, where their parents—John and Darlene—had met while going to school at East Tennessee State Normal School, training to become teachers. John and Darlene had married young, as was typical in that era, and started their family. Nancy was born in late 1924 and Cathy in 1927. Their parents stayed in Johnson City and grew with the college. East Tennessee State officially became a college in 1925 when it changed its name to East Tennessee State Teachers College. In 1930, the school changed its name to East Tennessee State Teachers College, Johnson City. By 1943, East Tennessee State Teachers College expanded into a liberal arts college becoming East Tennessee State College. Finally, the college became East Tennessee State University in 1963. John and Darlene both retired in 1969 with distinguished careers as life-long educators at ETSU. Both Nancy and Cathy had followed in their parents' footsteps and attended the University of Tennessee, Knoxville (UTK). Nancy elected to get a bachelor's degree, get married, have three children, and teach elementary school in Knoxville. Cathy got her PhD and joined the teaching staff at UTK.

Catherine (Cathy) Royer was 23 years old when she married Russ Krovo in 1950. Russ was charming, smart, athletic and full of positive energy. He held an important career position at ORNL and had "family wealth," which was in reality KGB wealth. Coming from a not-so-wealthy family of life-long educators, she was swept off her feet and felt like a princess when she saw her new home in Sequoyah Hills. Between 1950 and early 1955, before their first child, Bobby, was born, Russ successfully indoctrinated Cathy into the KGB philosophy and way of life. They became a married, covert KGB team and their secret activities together actually created an even more exciting marital bond that made their lives anything but boring. Cathy was like the proverbial frog, being gradually heated in the water; she was totally cooked before she could jump out of the pot.

Cathy's conversion to the KGB had gone undetected by Nancy and the rest of the Royer family, save for one thing. After marrying Russ, Cathy had furthered her education to become fluent in speaking both Russian and Mandarin Chinese, and subsequently taught both Russian and Chinese language classes at UTK. Nancy had also learned over time that her brother-in-law Russ was fluent in English, Russian, Mandarin Chinese, German, French, and Spanish. When approached by Ding and his FBI team, informed of the espionage and terrorism charges against her brother-in-law and sister, Nancy told them she was always a bit curious about all the languages that Russ spoke, and how her sister had taken up the Russian and Chinese languages. Nancy loved her sister dearly and was not afraid of her brother-in-law (although she should have been); she volunteered to help with the FBI plan.

Monday, October 20, 1975 at 1:00 PM local time, the Krovo/ Krovopuskov family home, Sequoyah Hills neighborhood, Knoxville, Tennessee

Ding and his team helped Bobbie and Natalie Krovo, along with their Aunt Nancy Royer, return to the Krovo family home in Sequoya

Hills. Although both Bobbie and Natalie were somewhat relieved to finally be home, they were apprehensive and intimidated to learn about the various surveillance devices installed throughout their beloved childhood home, along with the panic buttons strategically placed in every room. It was not going to be life as normal and this bait and trap FBI plan would take some getting used to. The bait was in place, and now it was a wait and watch game with all FBI hands on deck around the clock.

CHAPTER THIRTEEN:

HANNAH HAS CANCER AND THE WILDCATS WIN

"What lies behind us and what lies before us are tiny matters
compared to what lies within us."
—Ralph Waldo Emerson

Friday, November 28, 1975 at 10:00 AM local time,
the White Hole Project, Oak Ridge, Tennessee

One year prior, in November 1974, the Bad Love Gang had taken our first White Hole Project time-travel mission to save Jews and Gypsies from the Holocaust in November of 1944. We had successfully rescued thirteen souls from certain death in the Holocaust at Chelmno, Poland using the famous WWII B-17 Flying Fortress known in the history books as the Phantom Fortress as our rescue vehicle. After our safe return in time, we had agreed to try and keep track of anyone that we rescued, to build a database in case our time travels ever created anything more than a slight wrinkle in time. Bowmar especially had done a great job of learning how to track our rescued Holocaust victims.

During our rescue mission to Chelmno, Meatball had fallen head over heels in love with the eighteen-year-old Jewish girl we rescued named Hannah Lieb. We had to literally pry the two of them apart at the Chièvres Airfield in Belgium for Meatball to get back on the plane with us to stay on schedule. A year had passed for Meatball and the rest of us, but 31 years had passed for Hannah and her family. Two weeks prior we had just discovered that Hannah and her family were living in Jerusalem, Israel. She was 49 years old and dying of breast cancer that had metastasized, spreading throughout her body. She was on a lot of pain medications, and her level of consciousness had been fading in and out. She had been crying out, "Bad Love come back!" and "Meatball!" We sent Meatball to Jerusalem to see Hannah, and Waldo graciously paid for the trip. Meatball had returned home from Israel just in time to spend Thanksgiving with his family. We were all anxious to hear about his trip.

As Meatball was reuniting with Hannah in Jerusalem, I was at home in Oak Ridge lying on my bed. About to doze off for a nap, I was startled by music playing. I rolled over in bed and standing three feet away was a sixty-two-year-old man with a familiar face: my own. My older self had traveled back in time to try and give the teenage version of me some words of wisdom: not to tell me what would happen in the future, but to give me some principles to guide me better as I tackled it.

On Friday, November 28, 1975, the morning after Thanksgiving Day, the entire Bad Love Gang was coming together at the White Hole Project. We planned to discuss Meatball's return from Jerusalem and my crazy encounter with my sixty-two-year-old self. It was an amazing day for another reason as well. Our own Oak Ridge High School Wildcats football team was scheduled to play the Maplewood High School Panthers for the Tennessee State Class AAA championship at 7:30 PM. We had handily beat Sullivan Central High School on November 14th by a score of 35–0, and had won a thriller the week before against McMinn County High School on November 21st with a score of 28–14. Tonight's game was for all the glory and was thirteen years in the making; our three prior Tennessee State football titles had been earned back in 1962, 1958, and 1956.

After everyone arrived, the entire group gathered together sitting on the comfy, padded central stage of the lower White Hole Project racetrack. Meatball filled us all in on his trip to Jerusalem with intermittent tears in his eyes as he spoke. "Hannah Lieb, whom I fell in love with during our rescue mission to Poland, moved with her family to Jerusalem, Israel in late 1946 and has lived there since then. She got pregnant the day before we flew them all out of Poland, when she and I went to that idyllic pond together near the country cottage where we were all hiding. That moment in time was magical; nothing could have stopped the intense passion that we were feeling for each other. I have a thirty-year-old son with her named Elijah. He's a stud, an Israeli Special Defense Forces commando, just a chip off the old block!" Meatball smiled through the tears and we all laughed. "Hannah is now forty-nine years old and has terminal breast cancer. She never got married, this whole time. She is too young to die!" His tears were flowing freely down his cheeks, as Meatball sobbed. "She doesn't have long to live. We have to figure out a way to save her!"

The group was silent as Crisco, Cleopatra, and Ben all tried to support and comfort Meatball. I looked at Bucky and Bowmar; they both knew exactly what I was thinking and nodded in agreement. At a time like this, I couldn't believe how strong my brotherly bond was with the two of them. How lucky I was to have them and the Bad Love Gang as my extended family! Thanksgiving Day 1975 had been extended into the Friday after.

I stood up to address Meatball and the group. "Although I can't promise a miracle, we may have a way to save Hannah. Bowmar, Bucky, and I have been discussing and planning the details of our next time-travel mission over the past couple of months. We would have to move our timetable up a bit, but it's doable."

Meatball, now sitting on the floor with his head down, looked up at me with anticipation and a sense of relief. "Whatever you've got in mind, if we can rescue Hannah, I am with you all the way!"

Goondoggy exclaimed, "You know me; I'm ready to go! Let's do it!"

Everyone yelled, "*Goondoggy!*"

Willy shook his head and said, "There he goes again. That's my brother! Always ready and raring to rush into the waiting jaws of death at a moment's notice!" We all laughed, overwhelmed with relief and hope. "So, Bubble Butt, tell us what your older self said to you when he—you—paid you a visit."

"That was an intriguing conversation, Willy," I responded. "He—I—was trying to give me some wisdom for the future without giving the future away. However, he slipped a little bit...and maybe that has something to do with us trying to rescue Hannah. I'll try to paraphrase some of what 62-year-old me said.

"Change and challenge are normal in life; you get to choose how you react. Don't shrink away, but grow from these things.

"Most things that happen in life are beyond our control. Control yourself and your own response; you can't control others.

"Peace is the opposite of fear.

"Learn from the past, plan for the future, live in the moment.

"Always seek God's face, not just his hand.

"The truth is, the more difficult your situation, the more treasure there is to discover in it.

"Life is too short to live it negative.

"Know that your best days are ahead."

Willy enquired, "You said that he or the older you slipped a little bit. What was said that was a slip?"

"At the end of our ten minutes together, he—or I—said, 'You and the Bad Love Gang will make history in 1975. Don't blow it, Bubble Butt!'"

The Runt butted in at that point. "Oh, I see that glimmer of a glint in your eyes again! You get that way every single time you come up with some grand, crazy plan for us to undertake, Bubble Butt... only this time, I don't see us going back to China for the cure to Hannah's cancer. And you sure as hell better not be taking a motorcycle to wherever you're planning to go." Everyone giggled at that last comment.

"Very funny, Runt," I replied. "Although where we are going, I can't wait to try out one of their motorcycles!"

Cleopatra, sitting with her right arm around Meatball, joined the conversation. "I'd like to go back to the Broadmoor Hotel and stay a little longer this time. I hope that you have a nice hotel and resort picked out for us to stay at and enjoy while you do your fighter pilot shit to rescue the world."

Crisco, sitting opposite of Cleopatra with her left arm wrapped around Meatball, added, "I want to go to some exotic destination this time, like some idyllic island in the south Pacific: aquamarine, crystal-clear water, beautiful flowers, colorful birds, powdery white sand beaches, and lazy, sunny days."

Goondoggy added, with a mischievous smirk, "Wherever we go, I want some new, exciting adventure. You know me, I want to try something I've never done before: maybe something electrifying and death defying!"

The Pud sarcastically retorted, "I guess shooting a WWII flame thrower at the Colorado Vodka Cowboy KGB agents wasn't exciting enough for you, huh, Goondoggy? Maybe we need to get you a tank to play with, so you can run over shit and flatten it into pancakes."

Everyone was laughing at this point. Even Meatball was starting to recover. Crazy Ike chimed in with his prototypical shit-eating grin, "I want to go where the golf courses are a tougher challenge to my Arnold Palmer drives and Bobby Jones putts. Other than making a baby, I'm jealous of Meatball for finding love during our time travels. I want to find love on this next trip: you know, like a sailor having a girl at every port of call."

The laughter and giggles continued unabated and at this point, I was going with the flow and couldn't help myself. I grabbed a cassette and plugged it into our new high-end Sony cassette player with Marantz components and Klipsch Heresy speakers that filled the White Hole Project vault with incredible sound. The song **"Brandy (You're a Fine Girl)"** by Looking Glass played as Crazy Ike agreed, "That's what I'm talking about!" The song was a number one hit in the US and Canada, telling the story of Brandy, a barmaid in a busy seaport harbor town. Brandy pined for the sailor she loved, but he left her because his love of the sea was greater. It was a dreamy, soft rock song of our generation, and the Bad Love Gang knew all the words and sang along as the music played.

As the music faded, Benzion "Ben" Kaplan, the now nine-year-old Jewish orphan boy who had been on the run from the Nazis during the Holocaust when we rescued him, declared, "I've been sitting here for a year while you guys have been time traveling, so I want to go on this mission. Whatever it is, I want to go!"

Pumpkin, who had joined the Bad Love Gang at the same time as Ben and had then adopted Ben, spoke up in in his crisp British accent. "That's an absolutely lovely idea, my son, but it gives me the collywobbles. You can go so long as I am going, and then we can have a smashing time together."

I responded and said, "Oh, for sure *you* are time-traveling with us, Pumpkin. Where we're going, we will need your unearthly navigational skills in case we somehow get lost."

Tater, who had been very busy with his extended family visiting for Thanksgiving, had held back a bit. He finally joined the conversation and injected his southern wit. "I've been busier than a cat covering crap on a marble floor, but I'd like to keep running with the big dogs and go on this here mission. I enjoyed using that bazooka against the bad guys on our last mission, but I think I'd like to pursue some peace this time around."

We were all chuckling at Tater as I answered, "I think you just hit the nail on the proverbial head there, Tater. We are going to want to pursue peace on this mission, for sure."

Waldo, sitting with his arm around Mary, asked, "Since when does this group manage to find peace in its time travels? I'm the one carrying the peacemaker here. We all know how that works." He patted his ankle holster, and we knew he was packing.

I smiled big at Waldo and replied, "You're not going on this mission, Waldo. You're staying right here and guarding the White Hole along with Ding and his team, in case our 'friend' Borya comes a-calling in some fashion. Willy is going to be running the controls here at the White Hole, and we need him to do his job safe and sound."

Spaghetti Head in his usual Italian mafia-style accent joked, "Yep, I don't know much about making peace. I am always explaining to my friends that my family isn't fighting, that's just how they talk to each other. Then we eat a big meal and go see a *Godfather* movie and everything is OK. So, what is this time travel mission of peace that you are planning, Bubble Butt?"

"Thanks, Spaghetti Head; you made me hungry for lunch, thinking about your amazing family meals! OK, first let me say that we need a strong contingent of our group to stay here, working with Waldo and Ding to protect the White Hole in case Borya comes a-knockin' while a group of us are away and rockin'. I'll explain later, but because of the mission parameters, only nine of us can possibly go. The nine that are going are Bowmar, Bucky, Cleopatra, Crisco, Goondoggy, the Pud, Pumpkin, Ben, and me. Crazy Ike, I need you, Tater, Spaghetti Head, and Meatball working with Waldo and Ding's team to protect this place. Meatball, you need to stay safe and healthy and be ready to go when we come back.

"The nine of us that are going on this mission are taking the White Hole back to June 17, 1942. That's the night the alien space-ship first crashed at Area 51 in the southwestern Nevada desert, and when Bucky witnessed the six aliens being transported away. Our group of nine will sneak aboard the alien ship and join the six aliens just before they escape back to their planet. We will, in effect, hitch a ride along with them back to their planet. The alien Blue Nova One, whom we met in the south China forest in late June, said that she already knew me, Bucky, Bowmar, Pumpkin, and Goondoggy.

"I've known or had the sense that we were destined to do this ever since meeting and talking to Blue Nova One that night in June. It took me a while to put the pieces of the puzzle together, with Bow-mar's and Bucky's help. Then, my sixty-two-year-old self came back to talk to me and said we'll make history in 1975, and not to blow it. There's not much time left in 1975; December is almost here."

Meatball smartly enquired, "How do you know that getting on that stage with the aliens when they're transported will work for you, and how does this picture get Hannah cured of cancer?"

I replied, "Our GCPD's are using the exact same blue exotic matter they are using. Unbeknown to all of you until now, Bucky saw nine other people—including himself—get on that stage the night of June 17, 1942 and then watched them all disappear together. In Bucky's defense, he never told anyone the full extent of that story because he thought he saw a mirage or an optical illusion, and did not want to be declared mentally unfit for duty. Blue Nova One's planet is quite obviously more advanced than we are. I'm not sure what we have to offer them, but they did come to our planet for some reason. Whatever it was did not work out for them, but we did help them get safely away, and we have met. I am making the assumption that because they are so advanced; they may either have the cure for cancer—or at least the cure for Hannah's cancer. Provided we get that treatment while we are there, we will bring it back with us and then get it to Hannah."

"What if Hannah dies before we can get to her with the treatment?" Meatball almost whispered.

I swallowed hard and answered, "Then we use the White Hole, travel back to 1944, find Hannah, and get the treatment to her at that time."

Bowmar looked cross-eyed at me, "That goes against everything that we have discussed using this machine for! You really are changing history if you do that!"

I knew that I was on thin ice and softly said, "I know that, Bowmar. I didn't know the full extent of Hannah's situation until here and now, and I haven't had time to think and process every detail through. God knows my brain doesn't work as quickly as yours, but my heart works just as fast. We have to save Hannah if we can. This is one dilemma that we can review with Blue Nova One and get her advice. They must have faced a similar situation at some point, given their advanced technologies."

There was a pause of complete silence in the room and then the Pud asked, "When do we leave?"

I tried to recover and get us back in sync as a group. "First we have a state championship football game to win tonight." I yelled, "Let's roll, Wildcats, roll!"

Most of the others joined in, chanting, "Let's roll, Wildcats, roll!"

I finished the group discussion by answering the Pud's question. "We leave in two weeks, at the start of semester break."

Friday, November 28, 1975 at 8:15 PM local time,
the Tennessee Class AAA State Championship game:
the Oakridge Wildcats versus the Maplewood Panthers

The 1975 Tennessee Class AAA State Championship football game was underway. It was cold and icy for Tennessee that night, and we were 21-point underdogs. Our defensive linebackers were all over the field demolishing the Panther's offensive bids. The offensive line was paving the way for Craig Freeman to run rampant (during the 3-game championship run, he ran for over 300 yards and scored 8 touchdowns) while our offensive line coach Harry Stocker chewed his way through at least a dozen unlit stogies and yelled at us until his vocal cords wore out. Ding was having the time of his life announcing the state championship football game on Oak Ridge WATO 1290 AM radio. All his broadcasting fantasies were being fulfilled.

Lurking amongst the crowd, disguised in long winter coats with hoods and scarves concealing their faces, Borya and Catherine Krovopuskov listened to Ding on their transistor radio and watched me play and block through binoculars. They easily went unnoticed as the 1975 Wildcat football team beat the odds that night, winning their fourth Tennessee state high school championship with a final score of Oak Ridge 46, Maplewood 22.

CHAPTER FOURTEEN:
WORMHOLE TO PLANET AZUR

"The Earth is the cradle of humanity,
but mankind cannot stay in the cradle forever."
—Konstantin Tsiolkovsky

*Saturday, December 13, 1975 at 11:55 PM local time,
the White Hole Project, Oak Ridge, Tennessee*

The entire Bad Love Gang had gathered at the White Hole Project for this historic launch. Bucky, Bowmar, Waldo, and I had spoken to President Ford the night before by phone and explained our plan for intergalactic space travel. Ford mentioned that he had spoken to James Fletcher, the Administrator of NASA, earlier that day and told us he wished he could share what was secretly happening behind the scenes. We reassured him that we were quite content to keep this entire endeavor totally top secret, but looked forward to disclosing our exploits to him when we returned. He did say that as soon as we hung up, he was writing about our planned space travel in the *Book of Presidents*. He would follow up to complete the story once we were back. He offered to throw a *very* private celebration for us at the White House when we successfully returned. I reassured him that we were definitely coming back and looked forward to a clandestine Bad

Love Gang, White House Gala of extraterrestrial proportions; we all laughed at that concept. As we hung up, he said, "Make me proud, gentlemen. I have admired your work for more than thirty years." I looked at Bowmar and commented, "So weird to hear him say that. You and I have a ways to go just to *be* thirty years old!"

There were nine of us positioned together in a circle on the soft central floor of the lower White Hole time machine racetrack, with the black box in the middle of our circle. Bucky was dressed exactly the same way that he had been on Wednesday, June 17, 1942 as Second Lieutenant Jack Smith of the US Eighth Air Force. He had to appear that way in case we had any unforeseen issues on site; he had been the ranking officer in the remote southwestern desert of Nevada that fateful night of the alien spaceship crash. Bowmar, Cleopatra, Crisco, Goondoggy, the Pud, Pumpkin, Ben, and I were all wearing our best hiking shoes, blue jeans, comfortable shirts, light jackets, and backpacks with extra clothing, tennis shoes, and gear. The black box contained walkie talkies, the Pud's VHF base unit, ropes, camping and climbing gear, Swiss Army knives, hunting knives, and of course my newest Marantz Superscope Boombox and cassette music collection. What was conspicuously missing, much to Waldo's chagrin, were guns and ammunition. When I had first met Blue Nova One at the alien spaceship crash site in the south China forest nearly six months earlier, I had stripped the guns away from my body before approaching her. I insisted with the group as a whole that it would be a mistake to take guns on an intergalactic space mission of peace. Save for Waldo and to a lesser degree Bucky, I met with little resistance.

Willy was manning the controls of the White Hole Project time machine and dialed in to send us out at exactly 11:55 PM local time. He, Bucky, and Bowmar had carefully programmed the global geographic coordinates for the alien spaceship crash site at Groom Dry

Lake, Area 51, and had aligned the upper racetrack to June 17, 1942. We would arrive at 8:55 PM local time in Nevada, which would give us roughly an hour to prepare and position ourselves at a safe but traversable distance on foot to the crash site. We planned to access the spaceship at an alternate entryway on the side opposite the oncoming military ground crews racing to the scene. We would need to move quickly, because it did not take long for the younger version of Bucky and his ground crews to race to the crash site that night.

Waldo, Mary, Ding, Crazy Ike, Tater, the Runt, and Spaghetti Head were all watching from the second floor White Hole balcony, with a bird's-eye view of the nine of us positioned on the lower racetrack. With T-minus two minutes, Meatball yelled down to us, "Thank you for taking this mission for Hannah; get that cure for her and I will be forever grateful!"

I answered, "We are going for it big, Meatball. You be ready to go when we come back."

Tater couldn't help but get his two cents in. "Y'all get that cure for Hannah, and Meatball is gonna be happy as a dead pig in the sunshine."

For the first time in a large group setting, Ben responded to Tater, imitating his southern drawl reasonably well. "If you can't run with the big dogs, Tater, then you better just stay under the porch for a while longer 'til we get back!"

We all laughed at that surprise response and display of wit from the nine-year-old Ben. Tater retorted, "There might be some hope for that young man somewhere on God's green creation!"

"I gotta feeling he's gonna get his first shot at Bad Love stardom on some barmy blue creation," Pumpkin remarked.

It was T-minus one minute, and my music brain took the word *blue* and started playing Elvis Presley's **"Blue Suede Shoes."** I stood up and started doing my best Elvis impersonation, singing into my make-believe microphone and dancing in place on the soft lower racetrack floor while pointing at my imaginary blue suede shoes. Everyone was just flabbergasted and laughing at the same time, losing track of the countdown to launch and the significance of our mission. Cleopatra and Crisco joined in the routine, standing up to dance together, humming the song and swooning at "Elvis" as I sang and danced.

In addition to country western music, Waldo also loved Elvis Presley. He bellowed, "Go Elvis, go!"

I glanced at my watch, saw that the launch was seconds away, and shouted back in my Elvis drawl, "Elvis has left the building; thank you very much!" At that moment, Willy hit the *SEND* button on the control panel and poof, we were gone.

Mary looked at Waldo and said, "That Bubble Butt is just as crazy as they come. Where does that kid get all his energy?"

"I don't know, but Blue Nova One and her planet are in for some kind of music revival, if Bubble Butt has his way when they get there. We need to be watching for some star to start twinkling up there later this week," Ding commented.

Wednesday, June 17, 1942 at 8:55 PM local time, Area 51, southwestern Nevada desert

The nine of us landed in a circular pattern on the salt flat desert floor of Groom Dry Lake. It was one hour after sunset, one hour before history would change and the secrets of Area 51 would be born with the crash of the alien spaceship that so few knew even existed. Bucky knew the approximate crash site because it had occurred adjacent to a new runway under construction. He led the way through the darkness to get us situated, in position to safely view the crash site and be ready to then make our way to the alien ship. Bucky, Pumpkin, Willy, and I had all been aboard the alien ship on Saturday, April 28, 1945 prior to our time-travel mission to volunteer for the AVG Flying Tigers in China. In addition to studying all the external hatches to exit and enter the ship, we had also examined what appeared to be very sophisticated drilling equipment located in some of the lower containment rooms. We would be entering through that area of the lower hull.

At about 9:25 PM, we could hear and see the lights in the distance of the B17-F Flying Fortress, piloted by the younger version of Bucky and coming in for a trial night landing. Bucky looked at all of us. "That's *me* flying that plane...how weird is *that?!*" he marveled. "The show starts soon; watch the lights go out in five minutes."

Several of us were watching through binoculars and could see the Indian Springs Airfield runway lights as well as the various building and hanger lights of the six-month-old airbase in the distance. Thinking about what we were witnessing, it made me remember something. "Hey, Bucky, I just remembered that this night in history was your twenty-fourth birthday. So, happy birthday, buddy."

"Yeah; thanks, BB. This wasn't quite what I was expecting on this night, but it does end with quite a bang here in a few minutes. After the lights go out and then come back on, the alien ship will be coming our way. The sky will get bright as day. Be prepared for the ground to shake like an earthquake when the ship crashes. If any of you want to look up at the incoming alien ship about to crash, put your sunglasses on."

At 9:30 PM, all the lights on the entire Indian Springs Airfield and airbase went dark. The lights on the B17-F Flying Fortress on its final landing approach went dark. We could hear the drone of the four powerful Wright Cyclone engines, but the total darkness of the area was eerie. Quite suddenly, the lights came back on. We all grabbed sunglasses out of our backpacks and started to watch the sky above. At about 9:45 PM, we could see what first looked like a shooting star, coming towards us and very rapidly getting larger. At 9:47 PM it was like the sun was coming up right over our heads, and we could see the ship's engines firing. It became as bright as high noon as the alien ship came screaming in before our eyes and the ground around us rippled and shook with a booming crash and thunderous rumbles like a high magnitude earthquake. Then darkness fell again. The alien spaceship had crash landed between us and the airbase; Bucky's positioning sense for our location to watch the crash was spot-on. The ship was a glowing white, with blue exotic matter leaking from several cracks in the damaged lower hull.

The alien space vehicle was comprised of two glowing saucer-shaped white hulls, one on top of the other. The lower hull was 150 feet in diameter and connected to the smaller upper hull, which was about 100 feet in diameter, by a bluish, glowing hour-glass shaped central core. We all knew this central core was lined with blue exotic matter, similar to the connected upper and lower racetracks at the White Hole Project. We were enraptured by the sight before us, but Bucky got our attention by shouting, "Move it! Everyone, we have to go now! We have to move fast, because twenty-four-year-old me is on the way here with the airbase soldiers in Jeeps and trucks. You can't see them because the ship is blocking the view toward the base. Everyone follow me!"

We ran to the edge of the glowing lower hull. The ship had crashed at a slight angle. The way it was canted toward the airbase, our planned entrance site on the opposite side was elevated off the ground. Somehow, we had to wave a hand or something in front of the entrance control pad next to the hatch above. We were in a big hurry and starting to feel a bit panicked as I asked, "Anyone here have any great ideas about how to get up there to reach the control panel to open the hatch?"

The group was stumped for a few precious seconds. Then the street-smart Crisco came through with the solution. "This is why you brought us women to the party tonight. I am woman, I'm invincible, I can do anything!" My music brain connected with Crisco in the heat of the moment and started to play **"I Am Woman"** by Helen Reddy. The 1972 song celebrated female empowerment and equality, quickly becoming an ongoing anthem for the women's liberation movement while hitting number one in the US and Canada. In my mind's eye, I could totally see Crisco singing it to herself.

Crisco continued, "We'll make a human ladder. Bucky, you stand directly under the control panel. Goondoggy, you bend over behind Bucky so I can step on your back to get up on Bucky's shoulders. BB, you and the Pud help me balance in the front and hold my legs steady when I stand on Bucky's shoulders. Pumpkin, you hold me steady from the back. Cleo, you and Ben open the black box and be ready in case I need something from in there." We all played our roles and standing on Bucky's shoulders, Crisco was about two feet shy with her arms outstretched to wave her hand in front of the entryway control panel. "Cleo, grab the army shovel from the box. Open the blade up and give it to me!" Crisco ordered.

Cleo responded, "You bet your cute booty, baby! You go girl, go!" Cleo handed the army shovel up to Crisco, and she was able to wave the blade of the shovel directly over the control panel. The entryway hatch flew open, bright interior bright lights of the alien spaceship shining out to illuminate the desert floor and darkness of the night around us.

As a group, we then moved slightly to the right. Crisco was able to reach the lower ledge of the open hatch and pull herself up. Bucky pushed her up by her feet, and Crisco was on board the alien ship. She looked down at us and teased, "And that's how it's done! Any of you boys down there want to take a ride tonight to some distant galaxy?" One by one, we quickly climbed the human ladder, and I took the rope from the black box so that we could pull Bucky and the box up last. By the time our entire group was on board, we could hear the army trucks approaching our side of the ship. With the wave of a hand in front of the inside control panel, the outer door closed in a flash.

We gathered ourselves and for a brief moment I had to pinch myself. *Here we are, on an alien spaceship in the middle of the southwestern Nevada desert in June of 1942,* I thought. I could feel the pinch of reality and knew we had to keep moving, but it was a moment in life that felt totally surreal. Bucky, Pumpkin, and I were the only ones in the group who knew our way around the interior of the ship so we took the lead, heading counterclockwise down the hallway and around the circumference of the lower hull, past the doorways that we knew contained sophisticated drilling equipment. We could hear the intensifying, whirring noise of the funnel containing exotic matter and connecting the lower and upper hulls. As it extended, the funnel further separated the lower and upper hulls, getting ready to transport the alien crew back to their home planet.

We were roughly halfway to the doorway we had planned to use when an entryway hatch in front of us and to our left suddenly flew open. A blue alien male stepped through the doorway and faced us, stopping five feet away. He was six feet tall with a thin build, and wearing the same type of attire that Blue Nova One had been wearing. His clothing was made of a shiny, metallic, silvery-white material, fitting snugly to his body with only his blue hands and face showing. Judging by Earth years, he looked like he was in his mid to late thirties. The nine of us froze in place, staring at him, and he stared right back at us. All of our hearts were pounding; I could feel the adrenaline surging though my veins. What seemed like a long time took only seconds.

"My name is Blue Max Ten. I am the captain of this ship and I understand your intentions for being here tonight. This ship is damaged beyond immediate repair and your military is surrounding us. Bucky, it is good to see you again with your Bad Love Gang in tow this time. You all need to follow me; we do not have long, and our white hole transport drive is nearly ready to fire." He motioned for us to follow him, and continued to talk as we walked closely behind him. "This will be a slightly longer trip than what you are used to, with your time travels here on Earth. The wormhole that we are traveling through will connect us to our home planet Azur in the Danica Galaxy, 11.5 billion light years away from our present location here on Earth. Your GCPDs contain the same blue exotic matter that we use on Azur, so you and your box of belongings will travel right along with us. Blue Nova One, whom you met, made minor adjustments in her timeline returning to Azur. Just so you know, she is the Prime Princess of Azur and is second in line to the queen. She will be waiting for us there when we land. Do you have any questions?"

Cleopatra, trying to lighten the moment with a mischievous grin, enquired, "Hey, Blue Max...I'm Cleopatra and I like to be the queen wherever I go. Do you think I could jump in there behind Blue Nova One and be third in line to the queen?" We nervously giggled at Cleo's ice-breaker.

Blue Max Ten, not really fully understanding Cleopatra's attempt to tease, responded, "I'm not sure, but I do know that Blue Nova One is always looking for new talent to make the royal court more productive."

Bowmar, a little embarrassed by his sister's antics, commented, "My sister is a bit confused by boundaries, so try not to take her too seriously. I'm curious, is Azur a sister planet to Earth, or a lot like Earth?"

Blue Max responded, "We will have a lot to talk about once we reconnect with Blue Nova One. Azur gets its name for how beautifully blue it is, from the deep blue seas covering the planet to the light blue skies and the blue exotic matter essential to our way of life. Water covers just over seventy percent of your Earth. Water covers ninety percent of Azur; the inhabitants of our planet live on islands formed by ancient volcanoes. Some islands are larger than others, but we do not have the very large, connected land masses that you have here on Earth. The island we are landing on is Queen's Island; it is generous in size, but not the largest. I believe you will like it, and there is purpose in your visit that we hope will be of mutual benefit. We must keep moving now."

He led us into the control room. Looking up in the center opening of the vessel, we could see the bluish, glowing, hourglass structure connecting the larger, lower saucer hull to the upper, smaller saucer hull. The shape and functionality reminded me of a more modern version of the White Hole Project. The wide mouth opening of the lower part of the hourglass was closing in from above to dock with the lower racetrack, and the exotic matter in the middle of the hourglass was telescoping upward, glowing a vivid blue. The whirring noise was growing ever louder and higher pitched, like it was coming to a crescendo. The computers lining the circular walls of the room had multicolored lights flashing everywhere. The scene exceeded anything of movie science fiction that we had witnessed, but it was hyperreal while overloading our senses. Goondoggy nudged me and commented, "This is totally awesome, Bubble Butt! I am *so* ready to go! Let's *light* this candle!" I smiled briefly, feeling relief because that was a perfect snapshot of Goondoggy's adventurous, fearless personality.

Slapping Goondoggy on the shoulder, I smiled and said, "You got it, Goondoggy!" The rest of the group were, to a person, wide-eyed with looks of wonder and amazement. I enquired, "Is everyone ready to go?"

Everyone except Bucky nodded. His eyes were transfixed by something above and to the left. The Pud was the only other one who managed to get words out, with his typically cynical sense of humor. "I'm just an average guy, on an average trip, to another average galaxy. What else can I say?" We couldn't help but giggle at the Pud.

I looked up and to the left to see what Bucky was staring at as we entered the lower racetrack with Blue Max. It was so completely bizarre; Bucky was staring directly at his younger self, looking down at us from the balcony above.

Seated in the eye of the racetrack were five other blue aliens, all dressed in the same clothing as Blue Max. There were two children, two adult females, and one adult male. Ben immediately went and sat down next to the two children, starting with an introduction. "I'm Benzion, or 'Ben' Kaplan. Who are you?" The male blue child introduced himself as Blue Badar Ten, and the female blue child introduced herself as Blue Bellatrix Ten. Ben responded, "Your names are so cool! We can call ourselves the three Bs." Badar exclaimed, "I can't wait to show you my flying motorcycle!"

We were all getting seated in a circle around the five blue aliens when Blue Max Ten announced, "It is time." The last thing I noticed before the world went white was the alien child Blue Badar Ten, waving goodbye to the younger Bucky standing on the balcony above us.

Traveling through the wormhole of space to Azur was perceivably longer than our white hole time travels on Earth. I found myself thinking about Goondoggy's last comment to me, and had what seemed like a dream of him and me as little boys playing together in his backyard sandbox with our toy dinosaurs. I was attacking him with the "invincible" *T. rex*, while he was surrounding my *T. rex* with smaller *Troodons* and saying, "I'm not afraid of you; you are stupid, and we are smart!" I laughed to myself, thinking of us playing in his sandbox all those years ago.

I shook my head and looked around. It was quite a sight: whirling whiteness, with occasional silent incandescent white lightning flashes and bright silvery stars sparkling in the darker background beyond... and then I witnessed the oddest thing, if for only a moment. I thought I saw a WWII-era Grumman TBF/TBM Avenger, rotating in the outer rim of the wormhole. I knew the plane because Willy and I had built models of it when we were kids. It was the most widely-used torpedo bomber of World War II. The longer trip seemed hypnotic, as I dozed again and my brain connected various random dots. I had another vision of flying the Avenger above a moonlit, simmering volcano at night with the double decker alien flying saucers parked on the side of the hill, and dinosaurs roaming in the jungle below as big waves splashed up on the beach.

I think I briefly woke again, then drifted off dreaming about Coach Harry Stocker yelling at me. "Get up off your big ass, Bubble Butt, and block like a *man*, goddammit!" I was just about to throw a cross body block on the next play when I hit the ground with a thud. On a space/time machine racetrack on planet Azur, I opened my eyes.

CHAPTER FIFTEEN:
BLUE NOVA ONE AND THE AZURIANS

"To my mathematical brain, the numbers alone make thinking about aliens perfectly rational. The real challenge is to work out what aliens might actually be like."
—Stephen Hawking

Late day one on planet Azur in the Danica Galaxy,
11.5 billion light years away from planet Earth,
at the Queen's Island Space Center

The fifteen of us, six blue aliens and nine Bad Love Gang members (along with our black box) landed together on a circular racetrack in a large, white circular room lined with computers. I immediately noticed a very tall, vertical row of windows to the outside along one of the walls. It was night outside, and I could see three moons of different sizes brightly shining through the windows. As we all looked around to get our bearings, Blue Max Ten was already standing and started to speak.

"Bad Love Gang, I want to be the first to welcome you to planet Azur. Ben and my two children have already exchanged introductions. Please meet our Co-Captain Blue Electra Seven and her husband, our navigator, Blue Izar Seven. Last but not least is my sister, Blue Zaniah Ten, who is our systems engineer."

The nine of us then introduced ourselves by first name, last name and Bad Love Gang nickname. In the midst of our introductions, Blue Nova One, whom Bucky, Pumpkin and I immediately recognized, walked on to the racetrack to join us. "Bubble Butt, Bucky, and Pumpkin, it is so nice to see you again. I look forward to getting to know all of you during your stay here. Captain Blue Max Ten, whom you have met, is the husband of Queen Azur, the supreme ruler of our planet. Blue Bellatrix Ten and Blue Badar Ten are their children. While you are here, you will be staying together in the palace guest quarters. As you all would say on Earth, I am the queen's 'right hand,' and second in command to her as the prime princess. My home is within the same royal compound, adjacent to your guest quarters. We will meet together at my home for breakfast in the morning, to discuss our failed mission to Earth and your current mission here. We have much to talk about and consider in the morning, so I recommend that you all get a good night's sleep tonight."

Cleopatra, with a warm smile, asked what many of us had been wondering. "I love all your names. I think I'm going to have a large family back on Earth so I can use some of your names for my children! What do your names mean? What do the numbers mean?"

Blue Max answered, "Azur is known as the Blue Planet because it is mostly covered by water and is also heavily influenced by blue exotic matter. All our names start with *Blue*. The middle name is really our main name used every day, and has special meaning. For example, we call my daughter Bellatrix, Bella, but *Bellatrix* means 'female warrior.' My son is named Badar, a strong name meaning 'full moon,' and our planet has three moons. The number following the middle name is the generation number of our tribe of origin."

My unrestrainable music brain couldn't help itself. When Blue Max talked about their tribe of origin, my music brain started playing

"Indian Reservation (The Lament of the Cherokee Reservation Indian)," by Paul Revere and the Raiders. I just loved that song. It went to number one in the US in July of 1971 and spent a total of 22 weeks on the Billboard Hot 100 chart. The song became certified platinum, selling over two million copies. While the song was a sad commentary regarding the mistreatment of native American Indians (in this case the Cherokee), the ending was strong, predicting their return to standing and status. Bucky could tell my mind was drifting on music and nudged me back to reality.

Blue Nova One then said, "Max, Bella, Badar, and Zaniah are all returning to the palace. They will take the nine of you and your black box to your guest quarters now. I have more work to complete tonight, but I will send for you in the morning. Enjoy the rest of your evening."

We all said goodnight to Blue Nova One as she departed. Blue Max Ten announced, "Grab all your gear and follow Zaniah and me." At this point in time, we had grown accustomed to following Max, only now it was much more relaxed. Ben walked with Bella and Badar, the children busy getting to know each other. Max and Zaniah led us out of the space/time transport room and down a long, sterile-looking white hall with windows to the outside. Looking outside as we walked, we were all mesmerized by the three bright moons of different sizes lighting the night sky. Even the stars appeared brighter and more luminescent than what we were used to. Bowmar then enquired, "Max, if planet Azur is ninety percent water and there are three moons up above, how do you deal with the movement of the tides?"

Max replied, "They are all in different orbits, but the largest of our three moons is the closest to Azur. It has the biggest effect on our tides, overshadowing the gravitational effects of other two moons and keeping our tides generally tame and predictable. However, when two or all three of our moons align, then we have tidal issues. Those three moons also tend to keep our planet's volcanoes a bit more active, with all the gravitational pulling—sometimes in a tug of war, pulling in opposite directions at the same time."

Crisco commented, "I feel like I have more pep in my step walking down this hall."

"Me too," Goondoggy agreed. "I feel like I'm ready to go for a run."

Zaniah responded, "Yes, of course. You will discover tomorrow in your visit with Blue Nova One that Azur is a sister planet to Earth, but factoring in our size, mass and density, our gravity is about ten percent less than Earth's. You will feel ten percent lighter here."

In his British slang, Pumpkin interjected, "I guess I won't be so slumped on this trip, then."

That caught Ben's ear. He looked at Pumpkin and blurted, "We'd have to be operating in 0.3 G environment for you to not be slumped, Dad." That made Ben, Bella, and Badar all giggle at once. Pumpkin's face turned its customary shade of orange, making us all laugh.

We approached a set of sleek polished doors, similar to those on the alien ship, at the end of the hall. Max waved the palm of his right hand and the doors flew open. We entered a gigantic flight bay, where three of the alien double-decker spaceships were parked side by side. The two on the ends were the same size as the ship we had left behind on Earth, but the one in the middle was impressively larger. There were many blue Azurians working various jobs throughout the flight bay, and I noticed a few of them standing and chatting at the ramp to the largest spaceship. Many of the workers who noticed our group following Max stopped what they were doing and stared at us. All the Azurians were wearing the same snugly fitting clothing made of that shiny, metallic silvery-white material. The outer flight bay doors were open to the outside, and I could tell we were embedded high on a hillside or mountain. Looking outside, I saw the moonlight reflecting off large waves in the sea below in the distance.

We walked to a separate hanger behind the largest Azurian spaceship and saw there were rows of bright, glistening, chrome, almond-shaped vehicles of various sizes, but similar design. The rear of the vehicles was wider, and the design aerodynamically tapered forward. The sleekly-shaped vehicles came to a sharp point in the front. The construction was amazingly smooth, polished and seamless. The top was a crystal clear, thick canopy providing unlimited visibility in every direction. The bottom had a slight aerodynamic curvature, and the vehicles rested on three shiny skid runners, two in the back and one in front. There was a driver's seat/cockpit with controls inside the middle of the front third, and a comfy-looking padded seating area for passengers with individual safety harnesses. The seating area wrapped around the interior circumference of the sides and rear, but not in front of the driver's field of view. The canopy was hinged at the front and when opened, steps leading up custom grooved entryways automatically lowered from the hull on both sides behind the driver's cockpit to allow for easy boarding.

Max picked one of the vehicles large enough to comfortably seat all thirteen of us. I looked at Bucky and Bowmar and said, "Wow, this is the chrome Ferrari of the future! I want to sit by Max and see how this thing works." As we boarded the Azurian "Ferrari," I was so dang excited my music brain started playing **"Going Mobile"** by The Who. The song was written by Pete Townshend and released by The Who on their epic 1971 album *Who's Next*. Townshend provided the vocals for "Going Mobile," but it was Keith Moon who was insanely amazing on the drums with this particular song. I was rockin' in my head, thinking we could take this vehicle anywhere. I wasn't too far off track.

After we were all seated, I asked Max, "What's this thing called?"

Max replied, "Translating to your language, you would call these vehicles Azurian Flashbacks. They are fast like a flash, and rather uniquely, they can flash back thirty seconds in time, in the event of a dire emergency." He pointed to a blue dashboard button. "That is the emergency reset button. Let's say something catastrophic happens, like an impending collision. If you can hit the reset button in time, the vehicle and its occupants are reset to thirty seconds earlier, so you will have time to avoid disaster."

Bowmar enquired, "Why just thirty seconds? Why not longer?"

"We determined that a thirty-second flashback does not cause too big of a ripple in the spacetime continuum, despite changing or avoiding some otherwise devastating accidents or catastrophes. It isn't perfect, but it has saved countless lives since we implemented it."

"What else can this Flashback do?" Bucky asked. "I noticed a change in pressure after the canopy closed and sealed. I also detected discreet sliding doors in the rear of the vehicle as I circled around back."

Max responded, "That was very observant, Bucky. As you now know, Azur is mostly covered by water. You will discover that our weather patterns here can change suddenly, dramatically, and violently. We needed vehicles that could fly from island to island, but also safely travel submerged under the sea in the event of fierce storms making air travel hazardous. Those rear sliding hatches you noticed are for hydroplanes and rudders, extending from the top, bottom, and sides when needed. There are ballast tanks underneath as well, to make submersible travel seamless."

"That explains the sea, but what about the air travel?" Bowmar asked. "I don't see wings or propulsion engines."

Max answered, "We have learned to harness exotic matter, and that has much to do with your mission here and your discussion with Blue Nova One tomorrow. Exotic matter has antigravity properties, and we use those properties to hover and fly in this vehicle. It is time that we go, but we can keep talking as we travel to the queen's compound." Max started the vehicle with the push of a button. At once, the three landing skids rapidly retracted while the vehicle hovered in place. Then he pushed a throttle lever slightly forward and we slowly moved ahead, steering around the large, double-decker spaceship and towards the open outer bay doors. The steering wheel was also polished chrome, and I estimated about fifteen inches in diameter. Max adjusted the steering wheel low, tilting it towards his lap. A clear panel heads-up display, which I had only read about and seen described in modern aviation journals, was lit up directly in front of Max at eye level. It displayed real-time flight data, the geography and terrain in front of and around us, plus a flight pattern to follow to the queen's compound. Bucky glanced at me and simply said, "Wow!"

"How much blue exotic matter does it take to make this puppy fly?" Bowmar asked.

Max looked confused. "Puppy? I don't understand..."

"It's just Earth slang, a term for this vehicle."

I smiled and winked at Bowmar as Max then answered, "It only takes a tiny amount compared to what you and your Bad Love Gang have witnessed that is required for our intergalactic space and time travels. The use of blue exotic matter permeates our society, its technology, and our entire way of life. We are now facing a critical shortage of blue exotic matter for the first time in our existence. When we discovered our sister planet, your home planet Earth, we determined that you have ample blue exotic matter. We had planned to covertly visit Earth, discreetly collect the blue exotic matter that we needed, and depart unnoticed."

The Pud, known by us for his unbridled cynicism was listening carefully and calmly stated, "You mean that you planned to come to Earth and steal some of our blue exotic matter out from under us."

Oh, shit... This could go sideways quick! I thought, then looked at the Pud cross-eyed. I held my index fingers up toward him, like a cross aimed at a vampire.

Zaniah, sitting next to the Pud, gently fielded that hot potato, "You're right, Pud. We debated about whether or not to get the blue exotic matter from Earth, and how to do that in a manner that would be fair and acceptable to both parties. Blue Nova One will be telling you what happened the last time we tried that approach here on our own planet."

The Pud got the picture from my gestures. Responding to Zaniah, he backed off. "I'm sure we'll get the whole story tomorrow morning."

Cleopatra quickly added, "Yeah, Pud! Don't be a turd in the punch-bowl, OK?" Zaniah looked at Cleopatra, confused, as we giggled. Cleo tried to clarify what she meant for Zaniah. "I'm telling him to mind his Ps and Qs—or, in other words, to shut up and don't be a dickhead." We all just busted our guts laughing.

Zaniah thinly smiled and said, "I think I understand most of that; I am glad you all are enjoying yourselves."

"Zaniah, you'll discover that we never seem to lack in words for each other, or have much trouble finding little ways to have fun at each other's expense." As I spoke, I noticed we had left the flight bay. Looking behind us, I saw the Queen's Island Space Center was liter-ally built into the side of a mountain, which was actually a massive ancient volcano. The night was brightly lit by the shining three moons, and I could see we were on a large island surrounded by ocean. Max increased the speed and gradually banked to the left. Directly below us, I could see dense tropical jungle. There were a series of towers topped with poles rising high above the treetops and also situated on the hill-sides of the expansive hilly terrain. The tips of the poles had blinking lights, I assumed so they could be avoided by flying Flashbacks.

As I scanned below us, I saw a flock of avians with three-foot wing-spans soaring over the treetops. Staring hard, the moonlit outlines looked to me like those of *Pterodactylus*. The name *Pterodactylus* came from the Greek word *pterodaktulos*, meaning "winged finger," which was a suitable description of its flying apparatus. The wings of *Pterodactylus* and other pterosaurs were made up of a skin and muscle membrane that stretched from the animals' highly elongated fourth fingers to their hind limbs. The bright moonlight reflected off their wings and heads. I unintentionally screeched, "*PTERODACTYLUS!*"

Goondoggy immediately asked, "Where?"

I pointed below, and Goondoggy confirmed my suspicions, thrilled with the sight of ancient flying reptiles. I turned to Max and enquired, "Max, are those what we think they are? And how can that be, with your modern society? What are all those towers and poles tipped with blinking lights?"

Max responded, "Azur has evolved over the millions of years like Earth, only unlike Earth, we have not suffered a planetary extinction event like you did during that evolutionary process. We have learned to coexist with the dinosaurs that evolved here. We allow them to live in their natural habitat, but we do limit their boundaries. The towers and poles create a network of electronic fencing above and around the jungles and forests where our dinosaurs roam. The animals are nearly vaporized if they try to traverse the canopy of fencing; they have learned their boundaries, although occasionally they try to push beyond their limits. We have a small network of what you would call forest rangers who live within the canopy to do research and dwell amongst the dinosaurs. We give those researchers a lot of flexibility about how they share that space with the dinosaurs, provided they let the animals live without threats from our species."

Goondoggy, bursting at the seams with excitement, exclaimed, "Holy Cretaceous *Pteranodon*, Batman! How do I get in there without being zapped like a fly?"

Max answered, "I don't know who Batman is, but only the few authorized researchers are allowed in there because it is far too dangerous for anyone not trained to know what to expect from that environment. Our clothing automatically disengages the electronic fencing coming and going so that none of us get 'zapped like a bug' as you say, if we accidently cross the line. But everyone knows not to go in there. That reminds me; we will be providing our clothing to each of you in the morning to wear while you are here, and teaching you its benefits."

Cleopatra looked at Crisco and said, "I wish we could get a picture of this, because we are going to look *so* hot in those body suits! We gotta get pictures of that, baby!"

"You won't get too hot; the clothing automatically senses your body temperature and depending on the external temperature, it either cools or warms your body perfectly," Zaniah explained.

Cleo smiled. "Oh, honey, we have so much to teach you while we're here."

Max pointed up ahead. "We are approaching the queen's compound. That is the palace, high in the center."

We had circled around the Queen's Island volcano, and the queen's compound was beautifully built into the side of the volcano, with breathtaking views of the island and out to the sea. Multiple waterfalls coursed down the side of the mountain amongst the various buildings and parklike areas. The architecture was classic with columns, archways, dramatically carved walls, and terraces all built with a variety of stonework and stucco-like materials—but also employing a mixture of selected metals, such as ironwork, steel, titanium, copper, and polished chrome. There were lush gardens galore, and I couldn't wait to see it all in the light of day.

Max landed the Flashback on an inlaid stone pad in the front yard of the palace guest quarters, which looked like a small palace in its own right. All the lights were on, warm glows emanating from the windows. As Max raised the Flashback's canopy, we noticed a somewhat younger and attractive female Azurian who had walked from the guest quarters to our landing pad. "I am Blue Kamaria Twelve from the queen's court. I will show you your rooms for your stay here, and get you all settled in. I will get your holographic measurements inside and have your clothing ready for you in the morning, before you go to meet with Blue Nova One. I live here, and it is my role to take care of your needs while you stay here."

To a person, the nine of us were all literally exhausted. Max, Zaniah, Bella, and Badar bid us goodnight and left in the Flashback. Kamaria took us for a tour of the guest quarters and showed us to our rooms. The beds were plush and inviting, and I made haste to unpack my backpack, brush my teeth, and climb in bed. Fifteen minutes later, already half-asleep, I heard three knocks on my door. It was Crisco. She slipped into the room and said, "I know we're both worn out, but we are on an alien planet billions of light-years from Earth. I want to cuddle with you tonight."

I replied, "Sure; that sounds good to me." We turned out the lights and got in bed with me on my side and Crisco cuddled up behind me. I softly enquired, "Did you notice anything different about the Azurians tonight? I mean, different in the way they act?"

Crisco answered, "They were all super-nice, and I did not feel threatened in any way. They seem to be telling the truth so far. But I did feel like we were at my Mom's hospital in the one of the operating rooms, trying to get or stay sterile."

I responded, "That is a good way of describing it. There were no handshakes or hugs, no physical contact—even between them. They smile when we laugh, but they don't laugh like we do; at least, we haven't seen it so far. I feel like they have lost touch with their emotions, driven by intellect and to some degree by their ambitions. Not that those things are wrong, it's just lacking a sense of balance or harmony. It will be interesting to see how Bowmar fits in here. He might perceive this as a good fit, until I bring him back down to proverbial Earth." I could feel Crisco's body twitching behind me, and then her breathing became slow and deep. I let my thoughts drift and soon joined her, sound asleep...

CHAPTER SIXTEEN:

TROUBLE IN PARADISE

"Trouble is the common denominator of living.
It is the great equalizer."
—Soren Kierkegaard

Day two, middle of the night on planet Azur,
Danica Galaxy, 11.5 billion light-years away from Earth,
in the palace guest quarters

In the middle of the night, Crisco and I were awakened by strong winds, lightening, thunder, and pouring rain beating against the windows from a powerful storm. We looked out the window together and could see lightning bolts in a multitude of patterns sparking across the sky, dancing through the darkness and lighting up the ocean in the distance, illuminating giant waves and whitecaps in the sea. Beyond the thick jungle below us, there were clear flatlands that ended at the shore; the huge crashing waves reflected the bright lights from the sky above. Despite the ferocity of the storm, our home away from home felt rock solid, safe and sound, built to withstand the raging weather outside. I commented, "Now I can see why the Flashback is also made to travel underwater. You wouldn't want to fly in this weather and, despite the storm; the ocean is safe and calm at depth."

Crisco opened the black box, sitting in the corner. She got her Canon F-1 out of the box, returned to the window, and asked me to hold back the drapes while she took some time-delayed photos of the impressive lightning show. As she finished her photo shoot, she said, "This is so incredibly surreal, to be taking pictures like this from another planet in a distant galaxy. How is it that you could even imagine us traveling through space? I just don't grasp how you do it, and I have to admit that I get scared."

I hugged her from behind as we continued to look out the window at the raging storm. "With the exception of Goondoggy, who just doesn't seem to ever connect with the emotion of fear, I think we all get scared from time to time. Feeling fear is a normal part of life, but *living* in fear is paranoia...and that's not good. Since Bowmar and I discovered the White Hole Project, our lives have changed dramatically. What used to seem like pure science fiction is now a reality for us, and we are living it. As a group, the Bad Love Gang are truly blessed to have stumbled across the destiny of time travel and now space travel—the two of which are actually closely intertwined. We have secrets that the rest of the world can only dream about. I still want to go to college and probably become a doctor, but what amount of schooling or training could ever come close to comparing with this experience? I see my parents and their generation boxed in by so many preconceived ideas and life experiences, and yet here we are breaking about every boundary known to man. I keep trying to reset my expectations and not let fear of the unknown get in the way. Just think: if we had stayed home, we wouldn't have experienced flying in the Flashback or seeing flying dinosaurs, and you wouldn't have taken those pictures of this insane lightning storm."

"I like how you put it in perspective, Bubble Butt. I think I'll try a little harder to embrace the experiences and changes that we see on our adventures, rather than trying to make them fit in some way with what I already know to be true. What do you think will happen with Blue Nova One when we meet with her later this morning?"

The storm outside was starting to relent, dissipating as fast as it blew in. I thought for a minute and then replied, "I was the first to meet and visit with Blue Nova One in the forests of southern China, back in June of this year. It was clear from our discussion then that she already knew me, Bucky, Bowmar, Pumpkin, and Goondoggy. She knew we would be coming here, and I can only conclude that has to do with her understanding of manipulating time and space travel in some fashion. That said, I am all but certain that she has something planned for us, or sees potential value in our trip here to Azur. We are not here to simply take an Azurian vacation, get a cure for Hannah, and then head back to Earth. Max spilled the beans a bit on the way here tonight. The Azurians are having issues with a shortage of blue exotic matter, so I suspect that will be a topic of discussion when we meet."

Crisco, starting to fade again, yawned and said, "OK, BB. Let's get back to bed and get some sleep, and we'll see what happens." As we lay down to go back to sleep, I pondered the day ahead and thought about a song to play in the morning to get everyone singing and dancing before our meeting with Blue Nova One.

Day two, mid-morning on planet Azur in the palace guest quarters

Crisco snuck back to her room before anyone else was awake and slept another two hours. Blue Kamaria Twelve, charged with seeing after us, let us all sleep in to our hearts' content. She had juice, Azurian coffee, and light pastries set out in a kitchen area as we made our way downstairs from our bedrooms. The kitchen was open to a great room with two-and-a-half-story arched windows having amazing views out across the jungle below and out to the sea. When we had arrived the night before, Kamaria had us each stand in a clear circular booth with our arms up above our heads. The machine had a thin vertical "wand" from top to bottom that rotated twice around our bodies, once clockwise and once counterclockwise. It took less than thirty seconds to take precise holographic measurements of our bodies, sending those measurements in real-time to an on-site, automated clothing fabrication center. Nine custom body suits made of the ubiquitous shiny, form-fitting, metallic silvery-white Azurian material were 3-D printed to perfectly fit our bodies. As each of us reached the kitchen, Kamaria handed us our outfits and asked us to try them on for size.

There were a few hushed, negative murmurs about the clothing. Ben, who was clearly coming out of his shell on all fronts and excelling in school back home, blurted out, "When in Rome, do as the Romans do!" It was a proverb attributed to Saint Augustine, meaning it was advisable to follow the conventions of any area that you were moving to, living in, or visiting.

Pumpkin commented, "Touché, my son!"

I had decided to lighten up the morning with some music and let Kamaria witness the Bad Love Gang at its finest. Once all nine of us were dressed in our Azurian outfits and had gathered around the kitchen/great room area in various stages of wakefulness, I put the Marantz boom box on a table and announced, "I thought a little music would get our blood moving for the day ahead of us."

Cleo reacted, "Of course you would, Bubble Butt! I hope you didn't pick out some crazy space song, just because we're billions of light years from Earth."

"Actually, I picked a light-hearted, feel-good, fun song that we all could sing and dance to, now that we are believers in Azur and deep space travel." I hit the play button and cranked up the volume. "I give you none other than **'I'm a Believer,'** by the Monkees!" The song was composed by Neil Diamond and recorded by The Monkees in late 1966, with the lead vocals by Micky Dolenz. It became the last number one hit of 1966, and the biggest-selling record for all of 1967. Over a million advance orders were taken, and it went gold within two days of its release. It reached rarified air as one of the few singles to sell more than 10 million physical copies worldwide. It hit number one on the charts in the US, Canada, Norway, South Africa, Australia, New Zealand, Ireland, Germany, Belgium, the Netherlands, and Austria. The song was number one on the UK Singles Chart for four weeks, in January and February of 1967.

There is something to be said for picking the perfect song at the perfect time. Despite still trying to wake up on a new planet, the entire Bad Love Gang took to the floor singing the words and dancing wildly to **"I'm a Believer."** I danced a modified jitterbug with Crisco; Ben quickly grabbed Kamaria and began to teach her how to jitterbug. Cleo made the rounds with Bucky, Goondoggy, Pumpkin, the Pud, and her brother Bowmar. In the middle of the song, Zaniah walked into the guest quarters and was looking at all of us, a bit stunned and unsure what to think. The Pud grabbed her hand and got her to join us for the last half of the song. A remarkable thing happened while we were all dancing; I started to feel a bit warm from the exercise of dancing and no sooner than I perceived it, the Azurian outfit I was wearing went into some type of cooling mode and kept me comfortable.

As the music faded, Kamaria was smiling and Zaniah, who still wasn't sure what had just happened, somewhat reflexively announced, "That was interesting. I brought the Flashback to take you to Blue Nova One's home. It is only a short drive from here. I noticed that all of you have Earth watches. Please finish getting ready and meet me outside in thirty minutes."

Day two, late-morning on planet Azur at Blue Nova One's home

Zaniah took us in the Flashback to Blue Nova One's home, a short distance away but higher up the mountain side. Her home was the Earth-equivalent of a palace, as she was second in line to Queen Azur. The surrounding grounds were a beautiful combination of manicured lawns, flower gardens, trees, fountains, small park-like sitting areas and walkways connecting everything. The oversized arched entry doors were heavy and led into a great two-story high hallway lined with statues of Azurian women and men: I did notice that the women outnumbered the men. Hanging from the ceiling above were stars, planets, and moons arranged like a galaxy that I assumed was the Danica Galaxy. Azur was easy to spot, as the glowing blue planet with three moons. Zaniah led us to a banquet room where a buffet-style brunch awaited us. A large circular table was perfectly set, with ten comfortable-looking chairs around it. There were two Azurian servers, one male and one female, working the buffet.

Zaniah announced, "Blue Nova One will be here soon. Please help yourselves to the food and take a seat at the table. You are on no particular schedule today. Blue Nova One is meeting with you by herself, and she will call me when you are finished here to come and get you. Please let your servers, Blue Ida Thirteen and Blue Elio Twenty know if you need anything. There are restrooms at both ends of this room. Please enjoy your day, and I'll see you again soon." She then departed.

We all took that as our cue to dig in and loaded up our plates. It was a beautiful and sumptuous buffet of fresh fruits, juices, milk, multiple casseroles, eggs, cheeses, pastries, and an interesting selection of nuts and different types of honey. There was no meat to be seen at all. Blue Nova One walked in after most of us were seated at the circular table, and we all stood and warmly greeted her. She filled her own plate and we all settled in together.

"I hope that you all were comfortable in the guest quarters last night and managed to sleep through that storm."

Bucky responded, "That was quite the storm. I got out of bed to watch it for a while. I can sure understand why you wouldn't want to try flying through one of those weather patterns."

"On a scale of one to ten, that storm last night was a six. Our weather patterns can be extremely fierce; most of our historic buildings were built into hillsides, like the queen's compound, because it was the best way to ensure structural integrity. We now know how to build anywhere, but it requires special materials and engineering methods. Last night does serve to warn you not to underestimate bad weather while you are here on Azur. When you see bad weather, play it smart and find shelter, or find a way to avoid it.

"As we eat, I thought it would be best to let you all ask me questions so we can get to know each other better before we get down to the subject of how we might be able to help each other. By the way, Ben, you made quite the impression upon Queen Azur's two children, Bella and Badar, yesterday. They have been asking the Queen nonstop this morning when you can come and play. I will definitely make those arrangements for you after we finish here today."

"I can't wait to see them again!" Ben answered excitedly. "They told me about riding their flying motorbikes. The Bad Love Gang has motorbikes on Earth, but they don't fly—unless, of course, you ride like the Pud!" We couldn't help but bust out laughing, because on one of our adventures late in the summer we had all practiced jumps off an inclined hill in the middle of a farmer's field with our bikes. The Pud decided to "be a hero" and really go for air on his 1969, ruby red, Honda SL 90. We were taking turns jumping one by one, so the entire gang was watching as the Pud gunned his bike across the field, hit the hill, and went airborne. For a moment, it looked like he might set the distance record for the day—but then misfortune intervened. Somehow the Pud lost his grip and slid off the back of the bike, pulling it vertical as he did so. He managed to roll and slide on the field after letting loose of the bike, avoiding getting hurt. His Honda SL-90 did not fare as well. The bike came down vertically, landing on the rear tire with the engine still running strong. It then bounced straight back into the air and arched into a head-first swan dive, oddly graceful, and plowed directly into Mother Earth. We couldn't believe our eyes! It was amazing to watch, but only if it was someone else's bike. The head-first collision wreaked havoc with the front wheel, front fender, fork assembly, headlight, and handlebars. But knowing that the Pud was not hurt, we all rolled in the field laughing for at least ten minutes. It automatically went into Bad Love Gang lore as an event none of us would ever forget.

After explaining the Pud's flying motorcycle story for Blue Nova One's benefit while the Pud cringed but tried to let go with the flow and laugh along with us, Ben unpredictably asked a serious question with the innocence of a child. "Blue Nova One, do you and the Azurians believe in God?" That got everyone's attention. The room went silent.

Nova enquired, "Why would you ask that question, Ben?"

"My real parents were very religious, believed in God and their heritage to God completely, and it got them killed. I'm curious if people on other planets get punished for their religious beliefs or believing in God." Pumpkin put his arm around Ben's shoulders. I was proud of how Ben was growing up so fast and thinking for himself. The Bad Love Gang was rubbing off on him in ways that would serve him well.

Nova answered, "We Azurians have some differences from and similarities to you on Earth in this regard. On Earth, you actually have many different religions your people choose from. You have sacred books supporting those religions, such as the Bible, Torah, Quran, Vedas, and many others. We look at God as a binary choice; we believe that there is only one God, and either you believe in God or you don't. Our views about this are perhaps less complex than yours, and at times, there is something to be said for simplicity of choice. We have had prophets like you've had on Earth, and their writings are collected in our Book of Ancients. They all point to the same God as the origin, creator, or source of the Universe. We would not think to punish our fellow Azurians based on their choice to believe in God or not. Everyone has that freedom to choose. I have observed that believing in God runs in families that believe in God, but the Spirit of God also moves among people who you would least expect to be believers. There is a mystery to it all, and that is OK."

"Do *you* believe in God?" Ben asked Blue Nova One.

"I do believe in God, Ben, and so does Queen Azur," she replied.

"That's awesome, Nova, outstanding!" Ben exclaimed with a big, boyish smile, making us all giggle. We relaxed a bit from the profound nature of what was being unexpectedly discussed.

Cleopatra joined the conversation. "Since we are talking about it, is God a male or female? And is he or she black, white, blue, or some other color?"

Nova responded, "The biology of our DNA and chromosomes make us what we are in flesh and blood. For example, you have two X chromosomes, and so you are female. Your brother, Bowmar, has an X and a Y chromosome and is male. Your DNA, influenced by other factors, determines the color of your skin. God is not female or male, God is God. God is not made of DNA or chromosomes like us. God is spirit, and God's color is God's choice. Of course, I am giving you answers as I understand things, but the God of the Universe must be magnificent beyond any capacity to measure. We mortals are the ones who seem to struggle to find ways to conceptualize, to understand or even to limit what God is like. To believe in God, you have to actually let go of all those intellectual struggles and believe. In some ways, I personally think it takes a bigger leap of faith to believe there is no God than to actually believe in God."

Pumpkin then asked, "Do you have evil, crime, or war on Azur? Like Ben, my parents were both casualties of World War II on Earth."

"Evil, crime, and war have all existed on Azur, but we have found ways to minimize their frequency and impact through the ages. We Azurians have the technology to explore other galaxies. We have visited many planets and studied other civilizations—especially your Earth, our sister planet. Evil and crime come in many different forms and seem to unavoidably affect all societies, some more, some less. Wars can be seen as evil and crime on large, concentrated, and sometimes protracted scales. Long ago, we made the decision to choose peace and to avoid wars at all costs. However, we are not naïve. We have developed ways to defend ourselves, but we are not a warring civilization and we consciously seek to maintain peace. One of the reasons you all are sitting here with me at this moment is to find a way to help us while keeping peace here on Azur."

Bucky interjected, "I agree that war is large scale evil—or as my fellow soldiers would say, 'war is hell.' Do you believe in hell? Or why else does evil permeate the Universe?"

"That is a question for the ages, Bucky." Nova replied. "I believe that God is good. Otherwise, if God was evil, the Universe would be a totally wicked place. But God has chosen to allow evil to exist for some higher reason. Perhaps it is related to the testing ground of choices in this life in the flesh. We are not robots of God; we get to make choices—some for better, some for worse. I know this: Working through conflicts is normal, and shapes our beliefs as we age. Perhaps in the spirit life after this life, God will decide to eliminate evil from the picture."

"So, you believe in Heaven?" Crisco enquired.

"That is what you call it. Because I believe in God, I believe that there is a spirit life waiting for me in the presence of God after death in this blue body. It is a source of comfort and confidence for me."

Bowmar then entered the discussion. "How long do Azurians live? What is your average life span?"

Nova smiled and tested Bowmar just a bit. "Before I answer, what do you know about telomeres?"

Cleopatra interrupted, "Before you start, my little too-smart-for-his-undershorts bro, answer the question in a way we can understand it!"

Bowmar tilted his head, smirked and pointed at his sister "Cleo, whatever you don't understand, you and I can have a little after-school study hall later to help you pass the testy-westy." We all broke up laughing at their typical sibling banter, and it seemed that Nova was studying our group interaction while answering our questions.

Bowmar continued, "DNA is the reproductive molecule of all of the cells in our bodies. It is the genetic blueprint for all our tissues and organs—heart, lung, brain, hands, feet, et cetera—but it also makes us who we are. Telomeres are protective caps at the end of our DNA strands. Those protective caps get shorter every time our cells divide during our lives. Eventually, as we age and get older, the telomeres get too short to do their jobs and our cells begin to age and malfunction. As the clock of life ticks, the candlestick telomeres burn themselves down to the ends of the DNA."

"Excellent answer, Bowmar," Nova confirmed. "Azurians live an average of one hundred twenty Earth years, and tend not to age until the end of that spectrum. We have found ways to protect our telomeres, such as an advanced childhood vaccine formula, mostly vegetarian diet, regular exercise, strict weight control, effective stress management, and proper sleep patterns. We don't smoke like you do on Earth, and we take steps to intervene early for alcohol or addictive behaviors."

I had been holding back and needed to dive into the proverbial pool at this point. "That all sounds great, Nova, but I have detected a shortage of at least two things that would help stabilize your telomeres a bit more."

"What's that, Bubble Butt?" Nova enquired.

"A sense of humor and a show of affection! I have not seen you or the other Azurians we have met so far have a belly laugh, or laugh out loud at all, really. No touching or hugging each other, either—there is no shaking of hands. You are all super-polite and accommodating, but I would have to say a bit over-intellectual and under-emotional. What's up with that?" I asked.

Nova answered, "Yes, I have been watching the nine of you and see your laughter and warmth exerted toward each other. Although we have not experienced an extinction event like Earth, long ago our planet did suffer and endure mass infections that threatened our survival. Our ancestors were forced to take strong measures to minimize interpersonal contact, and take steps to protect ourselves from one another. More recently, our modern medicine has developed techniques to deal with such infections, but some of our mannerisms or behaviors probably carried over from those dark times. I think we can learn from you, especially when I address our problem with you in a short while."

"It is obvious that exotic matter pervades your way of life here."

Nova, looking intrigued and impressed, enquired, "Why would you say that, Bowmar?"

"You use exotic matter to create wormholes to travel to distant galaxies, the anti-gravity properties are used in your Flashback vehicles, the flying motorcycles Ben wants to try out, and probably other modes of transportation we haven't seen yet. You use it for time-travel; even the Flashbacks are capable of instantly resetting the timeline by thirty seconds as a last-ditch safety measure. The exotic matter we have been using for the White Hole Project is the same blue exotic matter extracted from your stranded spaceship on Earth. You Azurians are blue people from the planet with blue exotic matter. Does the blue exotic matter influence your DNA in some fashion? I sense a close connection in all of this."

I was somewhat surprised by Bowmar's comments and questions, but it was totally him to move the discussion more directly into the realm of science and physics. I could see a small sense of wonder in Blue Nova One's face as she watched Bowmar talk, and then I recalled how she had mentioned Bowmar when she and I were working together to repair her spaceship in the south China forest. She had said to me, "And your best-friend, Bowmar... I miss him a lot!" I looked at Bowmar and his eyes were totally transfixed on Blue Nova One. *Maybe Bowmar has met his IQ match—or could she be his IQ superior?* I thought joyfully. At that moment, my music brain hilariously went out of control, connecting the funny dots of Bowmar's admiration of Blue Nova One, her knowledge base, and us being on the distant blue planet of Azur. It started playing **"Venus"** from the Dutch rock band Shocking Blue, released in 1969. The song topped the charts in nine countries, including certified gold for sales in excess of one million copies in the United States; the single sold over 7.5 million copies worldwide. Bucky saw that I was in a music trance and kicked me under the table to bring me out of it.

Blue Nova One, initially looking directly into Bowmar's eyes and then at the rest of us answered, "You are correct, Bowmar. Azur's nearly-unique blue exotic matter does thoroughly permeate our lives and culture here. For centuries, we have used an infinitesimal amount in our newborn vaccination formula, and it has been credited for having a stabilizing effect on our DNA telomeres to increase our longevity. It has interacted with our DNA through the years to contribute to our blue skin color. It has given us the technology to travel through time and to distant galaxies. We are still working to make discoveries to better understand exotic matter. Unfortunately, we see a shortage of blue exotic matter in our future, and that has us profoundly concerned."

Bowmar asked, "What did you mean when you said 'nearly unique?'"

"We have searched many galaxies looking for our specific type of blue exotic matter. As best we know, it exists here on planet Azur—and we have discovered that it also exists on your planet Earth. We call Earth our sister planet for that reason, and for another reason that we need to discuss next."

CHAPTER SEVENTEEN:
AN EARTHLY SOLUTION

"It isn't enough to talk about peace. One must believe in it.
And it isn't enough to believe in it. One must work at it."
—Eleanor Roosevelt

Day two, early afternoon on planet Azur at Blue Nova One's home

We all took a brief break to go to the bathroom, stretch our legs, and refill our plates. The two servers, Blue Ida Thirteen and Blue Elio Twenty, had restocked the brunch buffet. Much to our delight, there was an added assortment of sushi, sashimi, and prepared fish: the only meats that were ever served in the blue Azurian diet. Goondoggy, who had been quietly listening all morning, got us started again, "Before we talk about your looming deficiency of blue exotic matter, I'd like to know why you have us all wearing these fancy, shiny jumpsuits, or whatever you call them."

Nova replied, "It was what we developed as a way to stay interconnected but safe during the mass infections that threatened our survival. Initially, with the hood on and the hands covered on the earlier models, they provided a sterile, temperature-controlled barrier of personal isolation. They also had communication modules imbedded in the hood so that you could speak with your network of family, workers, or friends. Flash forward to now, and our clothing has evolved into a technological marvel. You are all wearing what amounts to a mainframe computer. Using nanotechnology to create computer microchips the size of molecules, the circuitry embedded in your outfits could power a small intergalactic spaceship.

"We call the outfit's built-in computer Luna. With your hood on, you can ask her questions or even carry on a conversation with her. As you continually use her, she actually gets to know you. In your future, it is called artificial intelligence; Luna will even make decisions for you, if you ask her. However, some decisions are best made by you. Luna keeps track of your biometrics and lets you know if you are pushing your cardio limits, or even if you are dehydrated and need fluids. She can give you a heads-up display of your environment day or night, and give you directions to get where you are going. With the hood up, you have a universal communication device at your command. You can ask Luna for language translation and she will automatically detect what language is being spoken around you and change your spoken words to that language, including some of the higher-intellect animal languages. If you are personally threatened in any way, which is highly unlikely, tell Luna 'protective shield' and she will create an electronic shield. The outfit material is impervious to the environment, especially important with our sudden weather patterns, and is virtually puncture proof—unless you play around with something as powerful as T. rex. We will get your outfits programed and activated before you leave my home," she concluded with a smile.

"Speaking of dinosaurs, Blue Max Ten explained the network of towers, poles and electronic fencing to keep the dinosaurs in their natural habitat. How do people get in and out of that habitat without getting zapped like the dinosaurs?" Goondoggy asked.

"The natural habitat of our dinosaurs is extremely dangerous and to be avoided, but if you accidently traverse the fencing, Luna and your outfit automatically disengage that segment of fencing so you do not get zapped to dust."

I looked at Goondoggy and said, "Don't you even think about it, if you're thinking what I think you are thinking!"

Goondoggy grinned. "Aw, don't be a party pooper, *Brontosaurus* Butt! Don't worry; I may be daring, but I'm not crazy."

"You *are too* crazy! When have you ever *not* been crazy?!" the Pud exclaimed.

"You're not very convincing either, my fearless friend," I responded as Goondoggy grinned and made peace signs, fingers held up in Vs at us with both hands.

Blue Nova One interrupted our exchange as everyone was giggling at me, Goondoggy, and the Pud. "Let's talk about how we might be able to help each other while you all are here on Azur. I mentioned that we have a looming shortage of what we call blue prime exotic matter. Although we failed in our recent mission to Earth, we actually have ample blue prime exotic matter here on Azur."

"What's the problem?" I immediately asked.

"The problem is where it is located," Nova responded. "It is located on the Republic of Azur, which is a distant island nation on our planet that did have its own ancient volcanic extinction event, destroying its dinosaurs millions of years ago. Subsequently, the island evolved to be very similar to Earth. The people there never discovered blue exotic matter, and in many ways, they are mirror images of you Earthlings. Now you know the second reason we call Earth our sister planet.

"They call themselves the Gazurians, and their diverse culture is a mixture of modern and old. Expert engineers and farmers, they are industrious and live in cities and rural areas. They raise farm animals and eat meat in their diets. They drink, smoke, play music, and they honor artistic abilities. Some of their artwork and music are amazing. Long ago they discovered gunpowder and fossil fuels, but they have yet to discover nuclear power. They know about helium and have elaborate airships, but must be very careful in the air given our planet's severe weather patterns. They are quite sea savvy and have surface and underwater ships.

"The Gazurians have various races and tribes sharing their island nation. They have had many civil wars through the ages, but now they somehow generally keep the peace. They elect new leaders every ten years; no one stays in elected office any longer."

Cleopatra quipped, "Sounds better than our government, where some politicians hold their seats for a lifetime of illicit profit and corruption!"

"How do you *really* feel about it, Cleo?" I wisecracked. Then I looked at Nova and commented, "It sounds like the Bad Love Gang would fit right in with the Gazurians, especially the music part. If we go there, I'm taking my boom box for sure! Why can't you just negotiate a deal with them and go set up shop to mine for your blue exotic matter?"

Nova, looking quite sober, responded, "We tried that many years ago, long before I became the prime princess to Queen Azur. Our drilling techniques were more invasive and primitive then, not nearly as well targeted and safe as they are now. We inadvertently caused an Azurquake—you would call it an Earthquake—that destroyed much property, including some of their most treasured ancient landmarks. Even their volcano showed some temporary activity as a result. The relationship between our peoples was tenuous before the quake. War broke out between us after, but we did not want war and there was never a winner or loser. Sadly, many people died on both sides. We have what you might call a détente with the Gazurians, and we live autonomously apart from each other."

"How is that working out for you?" I enquired.

"It is working in that we leave each other alone, and we blue Azurians have diligently searched the Universe for other sources of blue-prime exotic matter. However, something very important is happening now that could change the dynamics of our relationship with the Gazurians. Our scientists have detected significant impending activity of the main volcano on the Republic of Azur, called Mount Pelorius. Our planet's various islands are all formed by volcanos, and we have studied them extensively throughout our history. It is a force of nature that we Azurians understand, and can now predict with some degree of certainty. But altering the natural history of volcanic eruptions is a totally different proposition and extremely difficult, if not next to impossible, to undertake. We have painstakingly measured the active magma chamber of Mount Pelorius, and it is huge; it is either an island maker, or an island destroyer. In light of what we know, I opened a secret channel of communication with the current Prime Minister of the Republic of Azur, Danvinio One. Interestingly, he was willing to covertly speak to me and was aware of the radical change in the activity status of Mount Pelorius. His scientists are warning him that time is critical and their options are limited.

"I offered to send help, but politically, having any Blue Azurians suddenly around the Republic may create too many questions, causing panic or rebellion. This morning, before you all arrived here, I had another detailed call with Danvinio One and presumptively offered another potential solution to send help. I told him that we have friends from planet Earth, 11.5 billion light years away, who evolved to be nearly identical to the Gazurians—and would fit right in with their society, virtually unnoticed. I let him know that there may be a way to alter the eruption of Mount Pelorius that could be of benefit to the Republic of Azur, rather than an unmitigated disaster of historic proportions. He said that he was 'all ears,' and I laid out a concept for rescue. I made it clear that there were no promises, only hope based on science and execution of our plan."

Goondoggy, being himself and not even knowing the plan yet, blurted out, "Wow, that sounds utterly and completely rad! When do we go?!" In unison, we all yelled out, "GOONDOGGY!" That elicited a big smile from Blue Nova One, and we all laughed from the comic relief.

Still chuckling a bit at Goondoggy, I looked at Nova and asked, "Did you tell Danvinio One that you were sending the Bad Love Gang?"

"Not yet, but knowing the Gazurian culture, you all will probably leave some kind of mark there, if you succeed. Bowmar, I can sense your brain whirring. Tell us what you are thinking about how this might work."

Cleopatra, now sitting next to her brother, slapped his shoulder and said, "Yeah, and explain it in a way that makes sense to us Earth-lings, my cosmic-brained brother from the same mother."

Bowmar smirked and winked at Cleo in his brotherly way. "Deep within the Earth—or Azur, in this case—it gets so incredibly hot that rocks, minerals, and metals completely melt and become liquid. That superheated thick liquid is called magma. Because it is gener-ally lighter than the solid rock around it, magma rises and collects in magma chambers. The magma chambers are connected to the mouth of a volcano through what is called the central or main vent. Gener-ally, when volcanos erupt, the magma pushes up through the main vent and flows out of the mouth of the volcano. However, there can be so-called secondary vents, which are offshoots of the main vent. Some magma can escape through the sides of the volcano through them, particularly if the main vent becomes blocked.

"In fact, if the magma chamber cannot get through the central or main vent to the peak of the volcano, it can move sideways through a large secondary vent. That will make the volcano bulge out from the side; that bulge is known as a cryptodome, a somewhat hidden version of the lava dome you would expect to see at the center of a volcano's peak crater."

The Pud cynically interrupted, "I like that word, *cryptodome*. Maybe we can get some Kryptonite from that sucker, in case we need it for our future intergalactic space travels."

We all laughed, except Nova; she looked puzzled. Bowmar continued, "Some volcanic eruptions are explosive and some are not. The explosive potential of an erupting volcano depends on the composition of the magma. If the magma is thin and runny, gases can escape easily from it and it flows out of the volcano. Magma that has erupted is called lava. At temperatures north of a thousand degrees Celsius, or eighteen hundred degrees Fahrenheit, lava destroys whatever it touches—and its path is extremely hard to predict. Lava flows can be slow or fast. When they are large, fast, and very hot, they are called pyroclastic flows; these can be extremely destructive and deadly. With rock fragments ranging in size from ash to boulders that travel across the ground at speeds up to fifty miles per hour, pyroclastic flows can knock down, shatter, bury, incinerate, or carry away everything in their path. For example, during the 1902 eruption of Mount Pelée on Earth on the island of Martinique in the West Indies, a pyroclastic lava flow demolished the coastal city of St. Pierre, killing about twenty-eight thousand inhabitants.

"If the erupting magma is thick and sticky, gases cannot escape easily. Pressure builds up until the gases escape violently. In this type of volcanic eruption, the magma explodes into the air and breaks apart into pieces called tephra. Tephra can range in size from tiny particles of ash to house-sized, flaming boulders with the destructive power of bombs. Ash that erupts into the sky falls back to the planet surface like powdery snow. If it is thick enough, blankets of powdery ash can suffocate plants, animals, and humans. When hot volcanic materials mix with water from streams or melted snow and ice on the sides of volcanic mountains, mudflows form. Mudflows have buried entire communities located near erupting volcanoes."

The Pud spoke up. "That's not such a rosy picture there, Brainiac Boy. Why don't we just nuke Mount Pelorius and be done with it?"

Bucky replied, "The US Army Air Force did conduct trials with conventional bombs in Hawaii, trying to block or divert the course of individual lava flows on numerous occasions, starting in 1935. The results were a mixed bag, at best. Lava flows are very heavy, hot, and determined to take their own paths."

Bowmar added, "With regards to an active volcano, or one that is just about to blow, a nuclear bomb might alter the lava flow, or cause it to erupt a little sooner. The force of volcanic eruptions themselves is usually equivalent to nuclear explosions. It could just add radioactive fallout to the rest of the mayhem. Our best bet would be to find a substantial side vent pointed away from the Gazurian population, and try to make it the path of least resistance for the erupting magma and subsequent lava or pyroclastic flow."

Nova One had been staring at Bowmar during his explanation and was clearly captivated by his descriptions and thoughts. "Our scientific analysis of Mount Pelorius has shown a major secondary vent coming off the main vent. The good news is that it points north to the open sea, rather than any of the other directions that would have devastating effects to Gazurian population areas. The bad news is that the vent tapers as it approaches the outer north side of the volcano, and there is just the start of a cryptodome such as Bowmar described. We can give you precise coordinates to the location of the northern side vent, and we have very powerful non-nuclear explosives that will detonate using a built-in delayed timer. They will also explode when heated past two hundred degrees Celsius, or even if they are forcefully crushed against an object. You have to find a way to get those explosives to the coordinates of that northern, secondary side vent and blow it wide open so that the lava takes that pathway as the path of least resistance. If you succeed, there is enough lava to expand the geographic boundaries of the Republic of Azur to the north for potential future seaside settlements. That would be a benefit to the Republic, as opposed to an utter disaster with untold loss or extinction of life."

I gazed squarely into Blue Nova One's eyes and enquired, "If we are successful, what is the catch? What is the price for the Republic's salvation?"

Nova stared back into my eyes as if our brains were somehow connected. "You are perceptive, Bubble Butt, and my answer should be of no surprise to you. Prime Minister Danvinio One assured me that if we can safely help prevent the Republic's destruction, he will reopen a political pathway for us to negotiate a safe drilling treaty for blue prime exotic matter on the Republic of Azur."

The room instantly became quiet enough to hear a pin drop. "If we succeed, then we need something very valuable from you," I responded.

"I'm listening, BB."

"We have someone back on Earth named Hannah Lieb, whom we are determined to rescue from metastatic breast cancer. Our group as a whole believes that saving one life, Hannah's, would make rescuing the Republic of Azur an even trade." The Bad Love Gang around the table solemnly nodded in affirmation.

"BB, if you and the Bad Love Gang succeed, you will not only have the antidote for Hannah, you will have the admiration and the support of Queen Azur and the Blue Azurians for generations to come."

Looking at Blue Nova One and then the rest of the Bad Love Gang, I shook my right fist about head high and exclaimed, "*Yes!*"

CHAPTER EIGHTEEN:
GOONDOGGY IS MISSING

"I am a bit of a solitude person—a solitary personality.
I like being on my own."
—Anthony Hopkins

Day two, mid-afternoon on planet Azur at the palace garage

After finishing brunch together as a group, Blue Nova One directed her in-house engineer to individually program and activate our exotic Azurian outfits. It sounded like a crowded room, with everyone carrying on conversations with their personalized artificial intelligence Lunas. Nova contacted the queen's master of the household and confirmed that Bella and Badar were anxious to have some playtime with Ben. Bowmar, Bucky, Pumpkin, and I all stayed with Nova to begin planning the details of our trip to the Republic of Azur. We needed Pumpkin especially for his superb navigational skills and instincts to get us there and understand the precise coordinates of Mount Pelorius' northern side vent. With Pumpkin predisposed, Goondoggy offered to take Ben to the palace. Cleopatra, Crisco, and the Pud took a tour of the entire compound with Blue Zaniah Ten in the Flashback.

Using their heads-up displays and talking to the AI Lunas along the way, Goondoggy and Ben took the shortest walking distance to the palace. When they got close, they asked Luna to patch them through to Bella and Badar. Ben commented, "This is so much better and cooler than using our walkie talkies!" Bella and Badar were waiting for them on the expansive front lawn as they approached the palace, which was enormous but was also architecturally beautiful in regal details and eloquent in all respects.

Ben ran up to Badar and Bella. "Can we take those flying motorcycles out for a ride?" he asked. "I have been dreaming about those things ever since you mentioned them last night!"

Badar responded, "Absolutely! That would be a great way to show you around, and my bike is definitely faster than Bella's."

"Not on your life, little brother! You can eat my airspace while you dream of passing me!" Bella retorted.

Goondoggy enquired, "You got any adult bikes? Can I borrow one to take a ride, and catch up with the rest of our crew while you guys have fun?"

Bella teased Goondoggy a bit. Looking serious, she said, "Adults can't take chances like us kids, so only kids ride motorcycles on Azur." Goondoggy looked puzzled and disappointed for a brief moment, then Bella and Badar started giggling. "I'm just kidding," Bella reassured him. "This is the palace. I'm sure we have a motorcycle you can use for a while!"

Goondoggy looked at Ben, slapped him on the shoulder, and said, "These kids are all right! You're going to have fun today. Maybe you can recruit them to become part of the Bad Love Gang."

Bella and Badar led Ben and Goondoggy to the section of the impressive palace garage where the flying motorcycles were parked. There were four children's bikes and six adult bikes, neatly parked and ready to go. Ben exclaimed, "Wow"! Goondoggy said, "Set me free, I'm ready to ride like the wind!"

The bike frames and structures were made of the same polished chrome-like metallic material as the Flashbacks, but many of the accessories were fabricated from a glistening gold-tone metal, and the instruments were black and silver. The back of the bikes were wider than the front. Bella demonstrated how a retractable, transparent canopy would come out of the back and seal with the curved front windshield to cover and protect the rider in the event of bad weather. She hit the *Start* button and the bike automatically levitated six inches off the ground. A gold dial in front of the driver adjusted the baseline height of levitation to suit the height of the individual rider. Bella then systematically went over all the controls and pointed out an auto-avoidance program would keep the bike from striking trees when riding fast through the jungle or forest. The children's bikes were smaller replicas of the adult versions.

Ben enquired, "What do you call these awesome-looking flying motorcycles?"

Badar answered, "They are called Skylectras, and there is one thing that Bella forgot to tell you." He pointed to a switch on the dashboard. "So long as you are wearing one of our outfits, you want to throw this switch on; it synchronizes the Luna computer in your outfit to the bike's onboard computer so they are communicating with one another. Then you can tell the bike what you want and it will do it—like 'bank left as hard as possible without throwing me off,' or 'dive and stop a foot off the ground.'"

Goondoggy's mind was racing with possibilities. He looked at Bella and Badar and asked, "Could you excuse me and Ben for just a minute?" He took Ben's hand and walked about fifteen feet away. "I'm going to head out of here and let you, Badar, and Bella go for it and enjoy yourselves. But Ben, you have to promise me something, OK? You have to promise."

"OK, I promise, but what is it, Goondoggy?" Ben enquired.

"I'm going to take a Skylectra for an adventure and spend the night out in the Azurian boonies. I'll be back sometime tomorrow morning—maybe before everyone is up and about—but you can't tell anyone where I went. When they ask about me, just tell them the last time you saw me was when I dropped you off here with Badar and Bella."

"You're going to go check out the dinosaurs, aren't you, Goondoggy?" Ben questioned, with a slightly jealous look of boyish wonder on his face.

Goondoggy replied, "When we were little boys, Bubble Butt and my brother Willy dreamed of flying airplanes. Their dreams came true. I dreamed of seeing real dinosaurs, and now all the stars are aligned for me to experience that dream—so I'm going for it. It's now or never, buddy."

Ben smiled warmly at Goondoggy. "You go chase your dreams. Your secret is good with me, but you need to promise me that you'll be careful out there."

"I promise, Ben. If I get into trouble, I'll call you. Keep your outfit and hood on tonight while you sleep. If necessary, I'll contact you, but only if *absolutely* necessary."

"How about we talk at least once tonight anyway, so you can tell me what dinosaurs you see and what it's like?" Ben requested.

"That's a deal, Ben. I'll call you an hour or two after sunset to give you an update," Goondoggy agreed.

"Pinky swear?" Ben replied.

They hooked their pinky fingers together and Goondoggy said, "Pinky swear. I'll let you know if I see Fred and Barney out there, and if my Skylectra can outrun their car."

Ben giggled and exclaimed, "Yabba Dabba Doo, Goondoggy! Let's go have some fun!"

*Day two, late afternoon on planet Azur at the Queen's Island
Natural Dinosaur Preserve*

After departing the palace garage, Goondoggy practiced riding
his Skylectra using both manual controls and voice-activated controls through his Luna AI. He even took a trial run through some
woods using the auto-avoidance program, which was super-cool, but
he did make a mental note not to get too overconfident after flying
through some low-lying branches while avoiding tree trunks. While
riding and sightseeing, he talked to Luna about the dinosaurs on the
Queen's Island. Luna called it the Queen's Island Natural Dinosaur
Preserve and showed Goondoggy a heads-up display of the pole and
tower network creating the electronic fencing boundaries, as well as
the canopy covering the otherwise uninhabited portion of the Queen's
Island and creating the large, natural sanctuary for the dinosaurs.

Goondoggy asked Luna to take him to the best entry point to fly
with the pterosaurs that we had seen from the air the night before.
Goondoggy knew his Earth dino history. On Earth, the pterodac-
tyl was the earliest pterosaur, discovered in 1784 by Italian scientist
Cosimo Collini. The Pterosaurs first appeared on Earth in the late
Triassic Period and roamed the skies until the end of the Cretaceous,
living between 228 and 66 million years ago. Pterosaurs were not actually dinosaurs, but the flying reptiles that lived among the dinosaurs
and suffered the same fate of extinction. Modern birds didn't descend
from the pterosaurs, instead evolving from small, feathered, terrestrial
dinosaurs. Pterosaurs had powerful flight muscles, which they could
use to walk on all fours just like vampire bats and vault into the air.
Once airborne, the largest pterosaurs could reach speeds of over 65
mph, then glide at speeds of about 55 mph.

The Azurian outfit's AI Luna plotted a course to a heavily forested,
deep valley with towering waterfalls and a large river basin below. As

Luna guided the Skylectra to the calculated entry point, she warned Goondoggy, "We are about to cross the electronic canopy of the Dinosaur Preserve. Do you understand the danger and wish to continue, or would you like to abort?"

Goondoggy responded, "We didn't come here to abort, Luna. Dive down to where the pterosaurs are feeding, or resting; we'll start there." Luna put the Skylectra in an arcing dive past one of the grandest waterfalls, and Goondoggy was mesmerized by the awe-inspiring beauty of the surroundings as he approached the riverbed below. The showering mist of the waterfall created a late afternoon rainbow that made him smile. Luna put the Skylectra in a hovering position fifteen feet above the flowing waters of the river. Goondoggy took stock of the surroundings in every direction, then enthusiastically whispered to Luna, "Good work, Luna! You put us in the middle of the dino motherlode here!"

"I am uncertain of the meaning of this word, *motherlode*," Luna stated.

"It means you delivered on getting me into the middle of a lot of dino action, Luna."

"I am glad you are happy," she replied.

The river flowed from north to south, and along the west side of the riverbank downstream, a flock of *Pteranodons* were fishing from the rock outcroppings and cliffs. Their wingspans varied from ten to twenty feet, reminding Goondoggy of the large Albatross seabirds back on Earth. They had long beaks and prominent bony crests growing from the back of their heads, probably acting as a counterweight to the long beaks. Some of the *Pteranodons* dove from cliffs and snagged fish from the water, while others floated temporarily on the water and used their beaks or briefly plunge-dove into the water to catch their seafood meals prior to taking flight again.

Further upstream on the west side of the riverbank and in the nearby jungle was a herd of *Iguanodons*. There were two of them drinking water from the river, while the others were busy eating tropical vegetation. A few were standing on their hind legs to eat leaves from the trees' lower branches, while others were rummaging in the brush and grasses on all fours. Goondoggy was excited to see them because he recalled that on Earth, they were the first plant-eating dinosaur to be named, early in the history of dinosaur paleontology. He guesstimated that this particular herd of *Iguanodons* varied in length from 20 to 30 feet and stood about 10 feet tall on all fours, but 15 feet or more when standing on their hind legs. There were some younger small ones amongst the herd as well. He remembered that their "hands" were different from most other dinosaurs, in that they had five "fingers." There were three fingers in the middle, with hoof-like claws that were useful when walking. Another finger could be pulled in toward the "palm" to grasp with, and the fifth finger was a sharp, spiked thumb used for defense. The *Iguanodons* seemed totally preoccupied as they satisfied their late afternoon hunger cravings.

On the east side of the river, Goondoggy was thrilled to his childhood core when he spied on a pack of *Troodons* that were also out gathering food. The *Troodon* name was Greek for "wounding tooth," referring to the teeth bearing prominent cutting or wounding serrations that enabled them to enjoy an omnivorous diet. He had always been fond of *Troodons* because they had the highest brain-to-body-weight ratio of any known dinosaur, and were therefore thought to be among the smartest. Moreover, reconstructions of *Troodons*' brains showed signs of folding. The folds of a brain are called gyri, and the grooves between them are called sulci. These folds create more space for more neural cells to be packed into the same area for more efficient brain functioning and higher intelligence. Adding to the need for higher brain function, the *Troodons* had large, forward-looking eyes with advanced binocular vision, aiding in their hunting skills to target small, skittering prey, even at night. Goondoggy estimated that this pack of *Troodons* were 8 to 11 feet long and weighed approximately 75 to 110 pounds. He observed that they indeed had fast reflexes, moving to and fro on their two long, hind legs and using stiff tails for balance. They were handily catching ground rodents and reptiles, while a few appeared to be eating berries from some of the bushes.

It all seemed rather enchanting, like a dream come true to Goondoggy as he watched all the dino activity from the comfort of the hovering Skylectra and time slipped by. However, swimming upstream in the river and devouring fish of all sizes along the way was a lone *Spinosaurus*, the largest of all carnivorous dinosaurs (at least on earth). This one measured nearly fifty feet in length and weighed twenty tons. The *Spinosaurus* name meant "spine lizard," which described its very long spines growing out of its back to form what was referred to as a sail. These distinctive spines, emanating from the animal's back vertebrae, were up to seven feet long and connected to one another by skin. It had a long, narrow snout and a small crest above its eyes. Its mouth was much larger but similar in appearance to a crocodile's, with the species' characteristic uniquely straight teeth like knives that could spear slippery prey, such as fish. But it did not survive on fish alone.

The *Troodons* were the first to know danger was approaching. They all stood up straight and viewed the area downstream with alarm as the *Spinosaurus* came up out of the water on the west side of the river, its eyes on the smallest of the *Iguanodons*. The sheer mass of the *Spinosaurus* made for loud bass-sounding thuds on the ground as it made its move, rushing on all fours toward the *Iguanodons* with its sail spiking skyward. The *Troodons* decided to leave the scene on their side of the river and the *Pteranodons* took to the air. The *Iguanodons* began to move away as a herd, and it was quite the primal sight to see as the chase got underway. Then the *Spinosaurus* voiced a thunderous, guttural war cry as it closed in on the rear of the *Iguanodon* herd. Goondoggy commanded Luna to follow the *Pteranodons* and remember the location of the *Troodons*; he wanted to come back and spy some more on the *Troodons* before nightfall.

The *Pteranodons* headed south into the sky as a flock and followed the river basin below as they flew. Goondoggy was soaring with them at about 50–60 mph, imagining he was one of them and wondering where they were going. It was an incredible moment for him as the Azurian sun was beginning to set and the sky was a deeper hue of blue. The luscious green terrain below was rugged and carved by the river as it flowed all the way to the sea. As the river approached the sea, the *Pteranodons* went back into fishing mode and dove down into the water for some seafood treats. Goondoggy stayed for a while and enjoyed watching the animals' fishing expedition. Knowing that there was an hour or less of daylight remaining, he then instructed Luna to take him back to the where he had last seen the *Troodons* and land there.

Luna efficiently navigated the Skylectra back to the section of wilderness where Goondoggy had last seen the pack of *Troodons*. He found a flat rocky area, came in for a landing, and parked the Skylectra. He took a small backpack containing a blanket, flashlight, hunting knife, some packaged food, and an Azurian canteen from the Skylectra's small, rear storage compartment and then headed out on foot to explore the surroundings. He discovered a creek that obviously flowed into the river and hiked along the creek bed, knowing that the water might attract more wildlife to spy upon. This was Goondoggy at his finest: exploring the bush by himself, curious to find what he might and not fearing the unknown, but embracing it wholeheartedly. He did see some smaller lizards, a few rodent-like mammals, and several fish in the clear water of the creek. After hiking for about a mile, he came to a small opening in the dense forest just as the last remnants of daylight were fading into night.

He moved around the perimeter of the opening and crossed over a large fallen tree trunk. At the back edge of the opening, he made a fascinating discovery: a circular clutch of 22 dinosaur eggs. The *Troodon* females were known to lay two eggs per day over the course of a week or more. They laid their eggs almost vertically, with the bottoms of the eggs buried in mud and the tops of the eggs open to the air. It was thought that these eggs were brooded by the male of the species, but the Troodon pack must have still been out hunting for food. Darkness was falling, bringing a chill with it, and Goondoggy decided to pull the blanket from his backpack and lay it across the clutch of eggs. He then resolved to take a break, eat a snack, drink some water, and give Ben a call as promised. He moved a safe distance away from the clutch of eggs to take his rest and sat down.

"Luna, call Ben," Goondoggy commanded.

Ben immediately answered in a whisper, "Goondoggy, how's it going out there? Everyone here is worried about you, but BB said he half-expected you to pull a stunt like this. While we were all talking about you and wondering where you went, BB played a song in your honor."

"That sounds just like something BB would do. What song did he play?" Goondoggy enquired.

"He played **"Solitary Man"** by Neil Diamond, and said the song described you perfectly. He said it was his favorite Neil Diamond song." Diamond had been a successful songwriter for other artists, but released **"Solitary Man"** for his debut single as a recording artist on BANG Records in April 1966. It reached number 55 on the US Billboard Hot 100 in 1966. After Diamond became better known, having more commercial success with the Uni Record label at the end of the 1960s,

BANG Records rereleased "Solitary Man," again as a single, in 1970. It then reached number 21 on the US Billboard Hot 100, and number 6 on the US Easy Listening chart.

Goondoggy responded, "He picked a good one. I've had a few girls pull that crap on me, and I'm still standing—right out here, alone with all the dinosaurs! What did you tell them about where I went?"

"I only told them that I last saw you leaving the palace on your Skylectra. That's all I said."

"Good job, Ben," Goondoggy replied. Let me tell you about my day in the dino-boonies." He proceeded to tell Ben about all that he had seen in great detail. Ben was enthralled by Goondoggy's vivid descriptions, and feeling a bit jealous that he wasn't there to experience it all.

Ben then enquired, "What are you going to do about the eggs that you found?"

"I'm going to make a Flintstone cheese omelet when I wake up in the morning."

"Very funny, Goondoggy. That will make you a really popular guy with the *Troodons*," Ben cynically declared.

"They might have me for breakfast if I did that! No, I put a blanket over their eggs to protect them and keep them warm. I am hoping that they will sense or recognize that I am friendly. If I get a chance, I want to try Luna's universal communication function with them and see what happens. Anyway, Ben, I'll see you sometime in the morning, and give you the rest of the story then. Be a good boy and go nighty-night, now," he teased.

"I'll give you a swift kick in the crotch for saying that when I see you tomorrow. My karate lessons are making me into a lethal weapon," Ben shot back.

"I have balls of steel, Ben; it won't work. Have a good night anyway." They disconnected and Goondoggy sat with his back against a tree, comfortable in his temperature controlled Azurian outfit. Satisfied with his snack and water, he dozed off as the song **"Solitary Man"** played in his mind.

CHAPTER NINETEEN:
SINGLE-HANDED ACTION

"Boys like either dinosaurs or airplanes.
I was very much an airplane boy."
—Jim Lovell, Commander of Apollo 13

Day three, after midnight on planet Azur at the Queen's Island Natural Dinosaur Preserve

Sometime after midnight, Goondoggy was awakened by the sounds of running feet all around him. He opened his eyes and looked up to see that standing at his feet and also to his right, there were two *Troodons* staring down at him with their big, forward-looking binocular eyes. Many *Troodons* were running by on both sides. He immediately commanded Luna, "Give me language translation, *now*." Shockingly, Luna was able to translate between him and the *Troodons* in very simple, fundamental phrases.

The *Troodons* were communicating their worry to one another. The one at his feet looked at the one to his right and asked, "Friend or foe?"

Goondoggy responded, "I am friendly, I have covered your eggs to protect them. Why is everyone running?"

Luna's artificial intelligence made their simple responses easy to understand, "We are under attack, and we are here to protect our eggs."

Just as that was said, the *Troodon* to Goondoggy's right was literally grabbed away in the powerful jaws of an attacking *Carcharodontosaurus*. (*Carcharodontosaurus* means "shark-toothed lizard.") Its jaws were equipped with serrated, eight-inch, razor-sharp teeth that could slice through the flesh of prey like a hot knife through butter, reminding scientists of the teeth of the great white shark and the earth-extinct giant shark megalodon. Its head, with the jaws bearing those wicked teeth, was over five feet long. This particularly fearsome predator stalking the *Troodons* was about 42 feet long and 12 feet high, probably weighing close to seven tons.

The *Troodon* standing at Goondoggy's feet turned and ran as Goondoggy sprung to his feet and ordered Luna to give him a nighttime heads-up display. He grabbed the hunting knife from his backpack and asked Luna, "Can my protective shield be used as a weapon?"

"Yes, any menace or hazard that it comes in contact with will receive an electrical shock proportionate to the threat posed to you and me."

"Great! Turn it on now and give it the juice!" Goondoggy bellowed as he surveyed the battlefield with his night vision.

"I don't quite understand what you mean by 'give it the juice?'"

Goondoggy, a little impatient, yelled back at Luna, "For God's sake, Luna, get in the game here, lady! If you can provide an electric shock, then make it a big one. Don't pussyfoot around, OK?"

Luna replied, "OK Goondoggy, I got it. I am starting to like you more as we go."

"Good, Luna, maybe you'll make it into the Bad Love Gang one of these days." Goondoggy answered as his brain processed the scenario. The *Troodons* had positioned themselves strategically in the woods around their clutch of eggs, and their strongest members had formed an uneven line in front of the clutch. There was quite a bit of chatter going on amongst them. The *Carcharodontosaurus* was finishing devouring his first *Troodon* and taking stock of the others positioned in front of him. As soon as he swallowed his last gulp, he looked up at the moonlit night above and let out an earsplitting, chilling battle cry for the ages. Goondoggy knew he was about to attack the remaining *Troodons*.

Goondoggy, imagining himself as a medieval knight in the shining armor of his Azurian outfit, charged the beastly *Carcharodontosaurus* from behind and to the left of the animal, aiming for its massive hind legs. He yelled at Luna as he approached, "I'm stabbing this bastard in the foot with my knife while you give it the juice, OK?"

Luna, increasingly using her artificial intelligence programming to symbiotically adapt to her partner, responded, "OK; go for it, Goondoggy!"

He reached the left foot of the *Carcharodontosaurus* and drove his hunting knife down into the top of its foot as hard as he could. The electrical charge from his Azurian suit fired as he made contact, sending a painful, partially paralyzing shock up the predator's left hind leg. The *Carcharodontosaurus* screamed and looked down at its foot, enraged. The force of the strong electrical impulse threw Goondoggy through the air, back and to the left by about fifteen feet into a deep row of hedges that somewhat softened the landing. He asked Luna, "Why didn't you warn me that it was going to throw us back like that?"

She sweetly answered, "You didn't ask."

Goondoggy laughed at her and said, "OK, smartass; fair enough. Luna, we need to move!"

The *Carcharodontosaurus* saw Goondoggy clearly in the shiny, reflective Azurian suit, flying backwards into the hedges. The dinosaur couldn't seem to move its left leg and foot. However, it did manage to pivot counterclockwise toward Goondoggy on its left foot by using its good right leg to push and turn. As he swung around, he lowered his neck and long jaw to take a swipe at Goondoggy. Goondoggy was reaching up for a branch in the hedge above with his left hand to pull himself up. He saw the pointed jaw of the *Carcharodontosaurus* coming down at the last second, and tried to pull away as the monster's jaw clamped shut and severed his left hand from his forearm. It all happened so fast that Goondoggy was not really initially hit by pain so much as stunned by the visual shock that his left hand was gone. The end of his left forearm was bleeding profusely. He exclaimed, "Holy shit, Luna! That bastard just ate my left hand! Can you apply a tourniquet to my left forearm?!"

"Yes, applying tourniquet to your left forearm now," Luna replied. Goondoggy felt the forearm of the Azurian suit clamp down tightly on his left forearm and saw that the bleeding had stopped. Luna continued, "You lost a unit of blood, but your blood pressure and heart rate are sufficient to keep moving."

At the same time, the *Troodons* sensed an opportunity, given the temporary immobility of the *Carcharodontosaurus*. They attacked him from all angles, digging claws and teeth into the predator's body and neck. The *Carcharodontosaurus* roared and seemed to regain his footing. He had apparently had enough, as he turned and ran from the opening in the forest. The *Troodons* disengaged and let him go.

Goondoggy was pulling himself out of the hedges with his good right hand and couldn't believe his eyes as he saw a lone blue Azurian female riding a large Skylectra. She flew into the opening from above and settled into a hover right next to the hedge he was exiting. She was a welcome and beautiful sight, and he felt relief seeing her. Before he could speak, she introduced herself.

"I am Blue Delta Seven, the local grid precinct ranger for this section of the Dinosaur Preserve. I received a distress call from your Luna with the details of your location and predicament. That was a brave thing you did, trying to preserve the *Troodon's* eggs and confront the *Carcharodontosaurus*. I'd say he's a bit too big for you to take on by yourself, especially with just a knife. This story is going to go down in Azurian Dinosaur Preserve folklore!"

"I wish I could feel good about that, but I *am* missing my left hand," Goondoggy said.

"We have the medical technology to reconstruct your missing hand in about a day or so," Blue Delta Seven explained. "But there is a storm coming soon, and I need to get you to my home. I live here in the Preserve with the dinosaurs; we'll be safe there. As soon as the storm passes, I will take you to the infirmary so that they can get working on replacing your hand."

She dialed her Skylectra to hover an inch off the ground, making it lower than if it were parked on its retractable landing skids. She then proceeded to assist Goondoggy onto the rear seat. He was impressed by her strength, enough to nearly lift him up onto to the rear seat. The *Troodons* were resting around their clutch of eggs and Delta slowly hovered over next to them. She spoke to them using her Luna for language translation.

Goondoggy asked, "What did they say?"

"I told them you were hurt and I was helping you. They said that you were brave, and thanks," she replied, then ordered her Luna to take them home.

Day three, mid-morning on planet Azur in the palace infirmary

After the early morning storm cleared, Blue Delta Seven took Goondoggy directly to the palace infirmary and notified Blue Nova One and me (Bubble Butt) of what had happened. Blue Nova One contacted the chief medical officer at the infirmary, and arranged for

Goondoggy's left hand to be reconstructed using his own DNA for a bioengineering process coupled with advanced 3D bioprinting. The advanced medical procedure to rebuild Goondoggy's hand would take the Earth-equivalent of slightly less than 24 hours, and he would be confined to bed during that procedure. His left arm would be immobilized and placed in a bioengineering machine. The rebuilding process occurred in a fluid environment, but it was relatively painless—except for the perceived tingling and prickling of nerves being rebuilt and reconnected. When finished, his new hand would look like his original hand, as only his own DNA could recreate.

Bowmar, Bucky, Pumpkin, and I were all scheduled to spend most of the day with Blue Nova One, continuing to plan our trip to the Republic of Azur. Cleopatra, Crisco, the Pud, and Ben would join us late in the day to complete the planning process; Goondoggy would join us using closed-circuit video technology from his bed at the Infirmary. Before our day got started, we all decided to pay Goondoggy a visit to cheer him up a bit, since he would be stuck in one place all day.

When the eight of us walked into Goondoggy's room, he was lying in bed with his left arm already immobilized and enclosed in the bioengineering machine. Ben ran to the bedside and gave him a big hug. "I promise not to karate kick your balls of steel today!" Ben exclaimed. We all laughed and wondered what the heck that was all about.

I had brought the boom box with me, and told Goondoggy that we had rehearsed a song especially for him. He indicated that Ben had already told him about it the night before. I reassured him that this was something different as Cleopatra and Crisco positioned themselves on the right side of Goondoggy's bed, and the rest of us got ready to back them up. I hit the *Play* button, and the song **"I Want to Hold Your Hand"** by the Beatles loudly filled the room. Cleo and Crisco danced and sang to Goondoggy, teasing him and holding his right hand as they flawlessly performed. The 1963 song was the Beatles' first American number-one hit, and it started the British Invasion of the American music industry. It stayed at number one on the Billboard Hot 100 for seven weeks and became the Beatles' best-selling single worldwide, selling more than twelve million copies.

We were soon all laughing too hard to sing anymore. Goondoggy was smiling at us as the music faded. We asked him to tell us what happened, and he recounted his remarkable day and night at the Dinosaur Preserve, ending with his left hand getting chomped off by a giant shark-toothed lizard named *Carcharodontosaurus*. I started the banter by telling him, "It looks like you got dealt a bad *hand* out there, Dino Boy!"

The Pud remarked, "No more flippin' the bird for *you*, Goondoggy."

Bucky joined in the fun next. "I guess you won't be *handy* around the house anytime soon, huh, Goondoggy?"

Crisco chimed in, "I'd offer to help and give you a *hand*, but now you're asking for a little too much!"

Bowmar added, "Now you won't have to worry about people trying to force your *hand* to make you do something."

"When I ask you to help, I'm not taking that excuse that your *hands* are full anymore," Cleopatra said.

"Your right hand will never know what your left hand is doing!" Pumpkin wheezed between giggles.

We were nearly rolling on the floor with laughter as Goondoggy waved and stopped us. He said, "I gotta *hand* it to you, you guys are about as funny as a heart attack. At least I know first *hand* what it's like to play with real, live dinosaurs. And when we get back to school, I have a great excuse for not having to take any *hand*outs home. So why don't you guys stop overplaying your *hands*, and go do something productive while I get turned into the six-million-dollar *hand* man."

We all hugged Goondoggy and told him that we would visit with him about the mission to the Republic later on closed-circuit video, then check in with him again before going to bed. His left hand would be rebuilt and he would be ready to go with us to the Republic of Azur by the following day.

CHAPTER TWENTY:

JOURNEY TO THE REPUBLIC OF AZUR

"Security is mostly a superstition. It does not exist in nature,
nor do the children of men as a whole experience it.
Avoiding danger is no safer in the long run than outright exposure.
Life is either a daring adventure, or nothing."
—Helen Keller

*Day four, mid-morning on planet Azur at the Queen's Island
Space Center*

Blue Nova One personally took us to the Queen's Island Space Center, where the crews there had specially prepped a larger, modified Azurian Flashback and loaded it with all our needed supplies and the non-nuclear explosives that we would potentially use to blow open the northern secondary vent of the soon-to-erupt Mount Pelorius. We were all riding together in Nova's vehicle and examining Goondoggy's new, reconstructed hand. It looked great, and it was difficult to see the any scar lines from the advanced bioengineering procedure. The medical team did have him squeezing a custom-made, compressible ball with his new left hand to get all the newly reattached muscles, tendons, ligaments, joints, nerves, and blood vessels working in harmony. Goondoggy had warned us about not making any more off-handed jokes; we had decided to focus more on our mission at hand and give him a break, for the time being. However, it would be a continuing source of future teasing as the Bad Love Gang could never forget that story!

Nova gave us some last-minute details as we approached the Space Center. "I spoke to the Republic's Prime Minister Danvinio One late last night, and we agreed that it would not be wise for a Blue Azurian Flashback to arrive at the Republic in the light of day. Your arrival will be discreet and under the cover of darkness. In addition, we have pre-programed your flight plan to bring you in from the north to give you a good view of the north side of Mount Pelorius. You will be landing at the Republic's northeast seaport, just in case you get caught in a storm and have to come in through the sea as opposed to the air. Remember, the Republic's Gazurians are excellent sailors with both surface and underwater ship capabilities, and that superb seaport is close to the north side of Mount Pelorius. As you know, we have extensively reviewed all of the navigation parameters for your journey, mission, and north vent target with Pumpkin, and he is ready."

"We definitely won't let this mission become a damp squib, my lady," Pumpkin commented. (*Damp squib* is a British slang term for something that fails on all accounts, derived from the word *squib*, which is an explosive with the propensity to fail when wet.)

Nova continued, "You will be met there by Danvinio One and his Vice Prime Minister Stareveret Three. Between the two of them, you will have the complete cooperation of the Republic of Azur's central government. There is a piece of bad news that developed overnight, however."

"What's the bad news, Nova?" I enquired.

"Our scientists are reporting that the timetable for the major eruption of Mount Pelorius has accelerated; they believe it could erupt as soon as tomorrow afternoon, or any time after. Prime Minister Danvinio One confirmed that their scientists concur with that assessment, and that the situation there has reached a critical point. He said that he tried to send some of their airships to bomb the northern secondary vent location yesterday, as we have proposed doing, but the weather pattern and strong, variable winds prevented them from effectively reaching their target. All of you are heading into danger just by being in close proximity to that unstable volcano, and I do not want to minimize that reality with you in any way."

"This is pretty much routine behavior for Bubble Butt to put us all in danger, Nova," Crisco pointed out. "I am almost getting used to it... but I want to emphasize the word *almost*."

Cleopatra added, "Our motto is 'Live dangerously, have fun, don't die.' I keep trying to tell Bubble Butt that I want more of the 'have fun' part on these damn adventures. What the hell is wrong with you, BB?!"

Blue Nova One, now more accustomed to our group's dynamics, smiled broadly as I responded. "Winston Churchill said, 'The optimist sees opportunity in every danger while the pessimist sees danger in every opportunity.' I like to think that we are not *in* danger; instead, we *are* the danger."

"I like that mindset. It's better to be confident than full of doubt," Bucky said.

The Pud made us all laugh. "I like that bumper sticker that says, 'In case of emergency, run like hell!'"

We arrived at the Queen's Island Space Center, and the crew with our prepared Azurian Flashback was standing by at the ready. This special Flashback was equipped with a galley kitchen, restroom, and seats that could recline into beds. We knew that we had a long trip, nearly halfway around the planet. It would take most of the day, with us arriving at the Republic of Azur just after sunset. Bucky, Bowmar, and I would share the driving responsibilities while Pumpkin would monitor our course and navigation. The four of us were wearing our Azurian outfits with our Luna computers activated, programmed for the mission and interconnected with the Flashback. Most of, if not all of, the trip would be undertaken using autopilot, unless we faced an Azurian storm and needed to change course or travel underwater. The rest of the gang was dressed comfortably in their blue jeans and tennis shoes. We would all be dressed that way on arrival to meet with our sister planet "earthlings" at the Republic of Azur. For a brief moment, as everyone boarded and settled in, I found myself staring at the blue emergency *Reset* button on the dashboard that could take us back in time thirty seconds.

Blue Nova One boarded with us and watched as we all took our places and buckled into our seats. Then she said, "No matter what happens, I admire your courage and determination to undertake this mission in order to help us and your friend back on Earth. My team and I will be standing by here at the Space Center Communications Lab, if we can provide you with any additional help or updates. Godspeed to you all." And with that, she exited the Flashback.

Bucky took the honors of piloting first. He hit the *Start* button, the Flashback levitated in place, and the landing gear retracted. Then he commanded, "Luna, take us to the Republic of Azur." Luna responded, "As you wish," and we taxied out of the Space Center. The Flashback headed skyward with incredibly smooth acceleration and perfect pressurization of our passenger cabin. It was a beautiful blue-sky day as we quickly left Queen's Island behind and headed out over the open Azurian seas below. Bucky turned and looked at me. "The last time this group left on a mission flying into unknown danger together, you got us going with some music. You got anything in mind to play as we depart today?" The rest of the group nodded in affirmation.

"As a matter of fact, I do, but we are not headed to Nazi Germany this time," I answered. "This time we are trying to make peace, trying to change the outcome of a natural disaster, and trying to get a cure for Hannah's cancer to take back to Earth with us. The song I picked, well, maybe we could play it for the Gazurians, but for us, the lyrics typify this particular adventure." I hit the *Play* button on the boombox, cranked up the volume, and the sounds of **"It Don't Come Easy"** by Ringo Starr filled the cabin. Released in 1971 and written with the assistance of George Harrison, it was Ringo's first solo effort after the breakup of the Beatles. The song reached the number one position in Canada, peaking at number four on both the US and UK singles charts. I would play this song whenever things seemed hard to accomplish—just add a little love and get it done. We all sang together, and I could tell Bucky was glad he had asked. It got us psyched for the job ahead of us.

Halfway through the flight, we could see a massive storm front out ahead that stretched clear across the visible horizon. A wall of dark clouds stretched from the sea to the upper atmosphere, jagged bolts of lightning flashing in all directions. It was my turn in the driver's seat, but the autopilot was still engaged on our pre-plotted course to the Republic. I asked Luna, "Can we manually fly around that storm and stay on schedule?"

Luna replied, "That is not possible, BB. Get everyone buckled in now. I recommend that you give me new orders to replot our course going underwater until we are past the storm. You have seven minutes until we hit severe, unpredictable turbulence."

I told everyone that we were about to become submariners for the first time and to buckle in tight, then commanded Luna, "Take us on a new course underwater, Luna, and keep on our schedule to the Republic to the extent possible."

"Setting course now, BB. We will catch the fringe of the storm as we enter the sea," Luna warned. The cabin was mostly quiet as we descended toward the sea, the colossal wall of threatening storm clouds filling our front visual field. I tried to lighten the mood a tad by teasing everyone. "Any of you Bad Love Gang weenies get seasick?"

The Pud was the first to reply, looking a bit green. "I do, Captain Ahab, and I'm gonna see if that fancy Azurian suit you're wearing is puke proof in a minute."

Using a pirate's speech patterns I shot back, "Arrgh, keep your innards to yourself thar, Captain Pudwash!" It was a play on words from Captain Pugwash, a fictional pirate in a series of British children's comic strips and books created by John Ryan and popular in the late 1950s and 1960s. Pugwash was the pretentious but likeable captain of a ship called the Black Pig. Although he bragged of being the "bravest buccaneer," he was actually quite gutless and silly—but somehow, he managed to win anyway. His formidable arch-enemy was Cut-Throat Jake, captain of the Flying Dustman—a pun on the Flying Dutchman.

Cleopatra caught the pirate-themed drift and addressed me. "Listen here, you scurvy dog! Don't you be making us into shark bait; I'm not ready to visit Davy Jones' locker just yet."

Pumpkin exclaimed, "Well sink me and shiver me timbers! This seadog is ready to find some booty in the briny deep, and I'm not talking about you, Crisco!"

Everyone was laughing now and Crisco, seated next to Pumpkin, slapped the side of his head. "Listen, you scallywag son of a biscuit eater, me and my booty are keeping whatever loot we plunder—and leaving you with a salty wench to spend your life with."

We were nearing our entry point at the junction of the tempest wall and the Azurian Sea, which was indeed starting to rage with storm swells close to 20 feet high. I announced, "All right, you hearties, batten down the hatches. We're goin' in." We hit turbulence and high winds just as we angled into the sea; it was a jarring experience as we dove under the surface. The four rear sliding hatches of the Flashback automatically opened, and the extendable diving planes shot out of the sides. Rudders popped out of the top and bottom. We had seamlessly switched from flying mode to submarine mode in an instant. We could watch the underwater world around us as we dove to find smooth sailing, unaffected by the raging, stormy sea surface above. "How far down do we have to go?" I asked Bowmar.

My gifted friend answered, "I was just thinking about that, BB. The deal is that the deeper we go, the less you can feel the waves because they are basically a bunch of water molecules rolling over each other. Half of the wave is above the surface, and the other half is below. It's a matter of physics; the deeper we go, the more the base of the wave declines." Winking at his sister, Cleopatra, he continued, "In other words, the stronger and bigger the waves are up above, the deeper we must go to avoid them. For submarines on Earth, a rule of thumb is the waves are not going to bother anyone below one hundred sixty-five feet. And if they do, the boat can go even deeper."

"Bowmar is correct for planet Earth," Luna said, directly into our earpieces, "but our storms are more violent on planet Azur and the waves at sea are larger in their midst. We are leveling off at a nominal depth of two hundred fifty feet as our cruising depth. And before you even speculate, we are traveling at an Earth speed of forty-five miles per hour. Once we clear the storm above, we will get back in the air, make up time, and stay on schedule. I do recommend that everyone stay buckled in to the extent possible."

We passed the word along to those not in Azurian suits. At that depth, the world around us outside the canopy was dark, so I asked

Luna if she could turn on the lights outside. The modified Flashback had omnidirectional high-intensity lights that created a luminous envelope extending from our ship, allowing us to observe the sea life around us as we traveled. We moved smoothly underwater for a couple of hours. Along the way we witnessed some sharks, whales, various schools of fish of all sizes swimming in different directions, and perhaps most interesting, a large congregation of bright blue and yellow glowing bioluminescent jellyfish. We were fascinated by the beautiful colors in the depth of the Azurian ocean; it was almost like watching a fireworks display!

In the midst of seeing the radiant and shimmering school of yellow jellyfish, Crisco unbuckled and came over to whisper in my ear. I helped her find the cassette tape she wanted, then she announced, "Everybody sing with me!" She played the Beatles' song **"Yellow Submarine"** on the Marantz, belting out the lyrics. Released in August 1966, it was categorized as a children's song as well as psychedelic pop. The single went to number one in the UK, Austria, Belgium, Netherlands, Sweden, Norway, Australia, Canada, and New Zealand. In the US, it peaked at number two on the Billboard Hot 100 chart. The song inspired the 1968 animated film *Yellow Submarine*. We were all singing away together and as we neared the end of the melody, we came across a strange sight that prematurely stopped us from singing as the song faded in the background.

We came into a giant swarm of fish in front of us, swimming in the same direction. It was so thick that I instructed Luna to slow down in amazement. As she complied, Goondoggy pointed out that off to both sides of us we could see two *Mauisauruses*, also headed in the same direction. On Earth this prehistoric sea monster, restricted to the waters of New Zealand, was named after the Maori god Maui, who mythically pulled the islands of New Zealand up from the sea floor with a fish hook. The *Mauisaurus* was a plesiosaur, a swimming reptile rather than a marine dinosaur. We estimated that the necks of the *Mauisauruses*, with 68 cervical vertebrae, measured about 45 feet long. They had long, slender bodies and flippers like sea turtles. They looked like a snake strung through the body of a sea turtle with no shell. Their overall length was about 66 feet, and their long necks were flexible as they made it their business to easily consume fish that were swimming all around us.

Bowmar was the first to recognize that something was wrong, "Why are we and the sea life all of a sudden traveling in the same direction? Are they running from something?"

"Yeah... Briny Brain, I don't like it either; something smells fishy to me too," Goondoggy agreed.

Everyone was starting to look all around outside when off to our rear port side, disaster struck. Cleo was looking in that direction and let out a blood-curdling scream that got all of us looking to the same place. A giant megalodon, the largest shark to ever prowl Earth's oceans and still living on our sister planet of Azur, had come from behind and underneath us to attack the fins of our Flashback. We estimated that this particular megalodon exceeded 75 feet in length. Its massive jaws, containing 276 serrated teeth, were opened 12 feet wide as it approached us, the perfect carnivorous tool for ripping the flesh of its victims. Like the land-based *T. rex*, these sharks also had a ferocious bite force. While humans have been measured to have a bite force of around 1,317 newtons (a physics measure of applied force), great white sharks have a bite force of 18,216 newtons—and *T. rex* had a bite force of up to 57,000 newtons. The megalodon made *T. rex* look puny, with a bite force of up to 182,000 newtons! Megalodon would first attack the flippers and tails of its prey, severing its ability to swim away before going in for the kill and a meal.

This particular colossal megalodon had been tailing us, and all the fish around us were fleeing. We must have looked like a shiny, tasty, new meal as it locked on and violently clamped down on our left hydroplane and rear rudder. Then it viciously shook us from side to side, and started to dive with us in its mouth. It was like a wicked roller coaster ride in the sea, and nearly everyone was screaming and panicking. Luna spoke to those of us wearing the Azurian suits loudly and sternly. "Danger, danger! We are experiencing major structural damage with no recovery available!"

We were being pulled down to the left (port), and I yelled, "Hang on, we are time traveling!" With my adrenalin surging, for a moment that seemed like eternity, I had trouble reaching the blue emergency *Reset* button on the right side of the dashboard. With all my strength, I pulled myself up to the right and punched it.

Our modified Azurian Flashback instantaneously disappeared from the clutches of the megalodon's jaws and was reset thirty seconds back in time. "Yellow Submarine" was again fading in the background, and we were just noticing the giant swarm of fish in front of us that were swimming in the same direction as we were. I suppose it was momentarily disorienting to the group as a whole, but I was laser-focused in the driver's seat, acutely aware of each passing second. "Full-power, Luna! Give it everything we've got and get us the hell into the air NOW!" I commanded.

Luna calmly replied, "We are not quite out of the storm above."

I briefly lost my temper. "MOVE IT, woman! *Floor* it! Get us airborne, dammit! NOW!"

She did as commanded and we accelerated to full power in an upward trajectory toward the surface. Bucky, sitting in the rear bellowed, "The megalodon is chasing us!" The Bad Love Gang as a group turned and looked through the rear canopy. The megalodon was actually gaining on us. Goondoggy observed, "Wow, that thing is fast. Can you believe it's gaining?"

Crisco punched Goondoggy in the chest and screeched, "Who the hell are you rooting for, Goondoggy?"

I noticed the throttle was not all the way to full power on the dashboard, so I took over and slammed the throttle all the way to full. We lurched forward and upward even faster, and Luna warned me, "Too much power could cause us to lose stability." I responded, "Not enough power could cause us to lose stability if that enormous shark catches us and bites us in our ass again." I could see the light of day at the surface in front of us. We started to shake and shimmy just a bit from our increased speed, so I held the wheel firm. "When we break the surface, you launch us like a rocket. Got it?" I demanded. Luna answered, "Got it, BB."

When we reached the surface, the megalodon was too close for comfort. We launched into the stormy air like a ballistic missile launched out of a nuclear submarine. As we cleared the surface of the sea and accelerated into the sky, the shark came flying out of the water directly behind. The megalodon clamped its gaping jaws shut with snap, only to belly flop back into the ocean with a giant splash and an empty mouth. Everyone on board shouted for joy, a little manic with relief. I yelled, "Sorry to leave you behind, Meggy, but we have to get back to school!" The ride in the air was rough, but two minutes later we breached the other side of the storm's dark, heavy cloud wall and burst out into the clear blue sky, pulling tendrils of clouds behind us as we shot through.

Thanks to the Flashback's emergency reset button giving us a second chance at that thirty seconds of our lives, we were unscathed. Everyone breathed a sigh of relief as heart rates slowed to normal. Ben asked me, "What did you mean by telling Meggy the megalodon that we had to be back at school?"

I smiled at Ben and said, "Listen and learn, young Grasshopper." I grabbed a different cassette, plugged it in, and hit the *Play* button. **"Maggie May"** by Rod Stewart blared throughout the Flashback cabin, and everyone started singing together. The song, released in July 1971, was Stewart's first big hit as a solo performer. It successfully launched his solo career, becoming sort of an anthem for our generation of coming-of-age teenagers. In October 1971, the song began a five-week run at the number-one position in the UK and simultaneously topped the charts in Australia, Canada, and the United States. As the music ended, Cleopatra commented, "I wish I'd never seen Meggy's face! I'm gonna have nightmares about those big, beady, blank, black staring shark eyes."

The rest of the flight to the Republic of Azur was uneventful, and our flight plan reliably brought us in from the north after darkness had fallen. Bowmar, Pumpkin, and I changed out of our Azurian suits and into our blue jeans; Bucky was dressed in the same casual military outfit that he had arrived on Azur wearing. Using the nighttime heads-up display on the front of the canopy, we all could see Mount Pelorius, its cone smoldering blue-hued smoke, on our approach to the North-east Seaport on the island of the Republic. Staring at Mount Pelorius, Pumpkin observed, "We might be bloody well snookered; I sure hope this mission doesn't go pear shaped." It was one of his favorite slang phrases from the Royal Air Force, used to describe expeditions and flights gone awry.

Bucky pulled rank on Pumpkin. "Failure is not an option here, Sergeant Nelson. I don't plan to die on this island, so get your brain in the game, buddy."

It was a calm, crystal-clear night, with all three Azurian moons brightly shining and twinkling stars galore in the sky above. We touched down between rows of docks anchoring Gazurian seafaring ships. We parked close to an enormous hanger at the Northeast Gazurian Seaport. The huge hanger doors slid open and two people walked toward us as we descended the steps out of the Flashback. It was Prime Minister Danvinio One and his Vice Prime Minister, Stareveret Three. They looked like they could be from Earth...only we were 11.5 billion light years away from Earth. He was a six-foot-tall, handsome and athletic black man with salt-and-pepper hair, probably in his fifties, wearing a short-sleeved shirt and casual slacks. She was a five foot six, freckled, fair-skinned redhead. The attractive woman, probably in her thirties, was dressed in a green military jumpsuit. Her deep green eyes matched her uniform.

Danvinio One was the first to speak. "I am Prime Minister Danvinio One; you can simply call me Dan. Welcome to the Republic of Azur, Bad Love Gang. This is my Vice Prime Minister, Stareveret Three." We all shook hands, and suggested that they call us by our nicknames going forward. Stareveret Three told us to call her Star. We all briefly exchanged small talk.

Dan continued, "When Blue Nova One explained to me that she could send a delegation from our sister planet Earth to help with our crisis, I was all ears. She knows about Earth because the Blue Azurians have become more or less dependent on blue exotic matter, and you have it there. We Gazurians of the Republic of Azur know about Earth for a totally different reason that we have kept secret from the Blue Azurians. Soon you will learn this secret, and Star and I will be most curious about your thoughts." Looking at Bucky, Dan enquired, "Is that military clothing that you are wearing, Bucky?"

"Yes. On Earth I was an Army Air Force captain, special forces, and I was a pilot during World War II. I was also the first Earth person chosen to travel back in time using a machine called the White Hole Project. That is how I met the Bad Love Gang, who were also time travelers. Now we have managed to use the White Hole Project to time travel and then space travel using technology from one of the Blue Azurian spaceships."

"That is perfect, Bucky," Star responded. "We have someone we want you to meet. I am also a military pilot. Dan and I will be taking all of you in our Gazurian Titan One Airship to the staging area tonight for our assault on Mount Pelorius tomorrow." I could see Crisco rolling her eyes at the exchange between Bucky and the attractive Star. I looked at her and discreetly pursed my lips, mouthing *No*.

"We really don't have much time. Our scientists are telling us that the eruption of Mount Pelorius is imminent," Dan stated soberly. "The volcano's magma chamber is of gargantuan size, even larger than anything that we initially envisioned. The central lava dome is bulging. If it erupts through the central vent, the Republic is in certain peril. There is the start of a bulge— a cryptodome—from the large northern secondary side vent, but it may be too late for us if we do not intervene as quickly as possible. It seems that the two eruption pathways are in competition with each other, but we need to give the northern side vent some help...and we need to do it *fast*.

"Pull the Flashback into the hanger so that it is hidden, and our crew will help you to transfer your supplies and explosives to Titan One. We must go now so that you all can get some sleep tonight. You'll get a nice view of some of the Republic by air, and I'll point out some of the highlights to you as we travel. I am glad that you are here; we are still holding onto some hope for an Earthly solution to this crisis."

CHAPTER TWENTY-ONE:

THE BERMUDA TRIANGLE

"The greatest unsolved mysteries are the mysteries of our existence
as conscious beings in a small corner of a vast universe."
—Freeman Dyson

*Day four, late evening on planet Azur, aboard the Gazurian Titan
Airship over the Republic of Azur*

B lue Nova One had told us that the Gazurians knew about helium, which was plentiful on planet Azur, and had a fleet of elaborate airships. She was correct; the Titan One Airship parked inside the colossal hanger at the Northeast Gazurian Seaport was impressive, even extravagant, in size, appearance, and finish. It functioned as Prime Minister Danvinio's equivalent of Earth's Air Force One, and made Earth's Goodyear Blimp seem nearly miniature by comparison. It was much more akin to the historic and famous class of Zeppelin airships back on Earth.

The Zeppelin was a type of rigid airship named after the German inventor Count Ferdinand von Zeppelin, who pioneered rigid airship design and development at the beginning of the 20th century. Zeppelins were first flown commercially in 1910 by Deutsche Luftschiffahrts-AG (DELAG), which became Earth's first revenue-based airline service. By mid-1914, DELAG had carried over 10,000 paying passengers on over 1,500 flights. The most famous Zeppelin airships were the 776-foot-long Graf Zeppelin and the 804-foot Hindenburg. In the 1930s, they both operated regular transatlantic flights from Germany to North America and Brazil. The art deco spire of the Empire State Building was originally designed to serve as a mooring mast for the Zeppelins, but high winds made this unfeasible.

Inadvisably using highly-flammable hydrogen gas rather than helium led to the famous Hindenburg disaster in 1937. The Hindenburg caught fire and was spectacularly destroyed on May 6, 1937 during an attempt to dock with its mooring mast at Naval Air Station Lakehurst in New Jersey. There were 35 fatalities (22 crewmen and 13 passengers) among the 97 people on board (61 crewmen and 36 passengers), plus an additional fatality on the ground. The tragic event shattered public confidence and marked the sudden end of the Zeppelin airship era.

The Gazurian Titan One Helium Airship was a fully integrated, stacked triangular design of two 500-foot-long rigid cylinders with another 600-foot rigid cylinder engineered between and atop of them. There were stabilizer winglets and variable position engine pods along the length of the giant airship, and large horizontal and vertical stabilizers with control surfaces at the tail end. All three rigid cylinders had rear omnidirectional engine pods. The flight surfaces and variable position engine pods were computer controlled for flight stability. Attached underneath all this lift power was a magnificently designed and super-spacious flight deck with viewing areas, meeting rooms, dining facilities, and private living quarters. It was an impressive use of modern structural engineering combined with old-world technology. But the Gazurians did not need to travel fast to cover great distances separated by thousands of miles; they needed to get from one side of the Republic to the other, and this mode of transportation had its own style and mystique. There was a soft, steady drone of the engines, but it felt like we were Peter Pan: silently and softly gliding up and away from the Seaport, headed inland.

Bucky went to the cockpit with Star to "co-pilot" Titan One with her, also known as flirting, and the rest of us joined Dan in a circular viewing pod underneath the main flight deck. Although I knew our time with Danvinio One was somewhat limited, I remembered Blue Nova One telling us that the Gazurians honored artistic abilities and loved music. I grabbed the Marantz Boom Box and my cassette collection, recalling how music had served me well in my first meeting with Blue Nova One in the forests of southern China. As we all descended a spiral staircase into the rear of the pod, I could hear Cleopatra down below. She exclaimed, "*Oh, my god!* I think I just went down the stairway to heaven!" I wasn't sure what she was seeing, but I rifled through my music collection, grabbed a tape, and got it ready to play.

I was the last to descend the rear spiral staircase into the viewing area, and stopped at the bottom of the stairs for a moment, stunned. *Breathtakingly spectacular* would begin to describe the view—barely. It was a generously-sized circular room built entirely with a thin, unobstructive, frame and crystal clear, thick panes making up all the walls and floors. A cushy, comfortable looking seating area circled the edges. It was the perfect setting to observe the world below and facilitate discussion. I could see the lights of a large city below and ahead of us, and we were moving towards it at a leisurely pace. Everyone was oohing and aahing at the sights below; the clear views gave us the feeling that we were suspended in air, like we were the ones flying. I asked Dan if it would be OK if I played an Earth song on my boom box. He replied, "That sounds good, Bubble Butt. I've had a long, hard day, and I love all sorts of music, so let's hear something from your planet."

I hit the *Play* button and perhaps our most classic teenage anthem from the 1970s, **"Stairway to Heaven"** by the English rock band Led Zeppelin, started to play. I couldn't believe it; we were flying in a giant Zeppelin-like airship on a planet 11.5 billion light years from Earth on a rescue mission, and we were playing the Led Zeppelin song that rocked at every Oakridge High School Homecoming and dance that I had ever attended. Our group's queen, Cleopatra, took Dan's hand and started slow-dancing with him. I started slow dancing with Crisco, then she danced with everyone else and briefly teased Goon-doggy that it would be his new left hand's first dance.

Released in November 1971, "Stairway to Heaven" was composed by guitarist Jimmy Page and vocalist Robert Plant for their fourth studio album, *Led Zeppelin IV*. I personally loved how the song had three sections, with each one progressively increasing in tempo and volume until the grand finale. The final hard rock section was highlighted by Jimmy Page playing one of the greatest guitar solos ever; he would use a double-necked electric guitar to perform the song live. On Earth, it certainly ranked among the most popular rock songs of all time, and it managed to catch Danvinio One's imagination. When we got to the grand finale, Bowmar, Goondoggy, Crisco, the Pud, and I all stood together, wildly playing our air guitars and lip syncing the final stanza while Dan and Cleo stopped dancing and watched our crazy antics.

As the music faded, Dan observed, "Wow! If that is Earth music, then we need to open up a direct line of communication to share our best with each other. It sounds like the love of money is a universal problem, which doesn't surprise me a bit. I know this; all the riches of our Republic can't buy our way out of this impending volcanic eruption and its path of destruction. That song also talked about change coming. If we can work together to avert this catastrophe, then maybe for the first time in Azurian history, we Gazurians can live in harmony with the Blue Azurians."

I commented, "We plan to succeed tomorrow, but whatever happens, they ought to play this song at the end."

Bowmar uncharacteristically exclaimed, "Amen to that, brother!"

"Cut the crap!" the Pud barked. "I'm not ready for the final curtain to fall any time soon. Let's just bomb the shit out of that volcano tomorrow and head back home."

"If you'll look directly below us," Dan directed, "we are now passing over our biggest city and metropolitan area, New Gazur. This is also our nation's capital, and my home. Close to ten million Gazurians live down there in New Gazur. Our Republic is a nation of diversity, and it has been a long and sometimes painful road to get where we are today. I was elected prime minister by popular vote seven years ago, and I have another three years to serve. Our brightest scientists are warning me that if Mount Pelorius erupts through its central vent, New Gazur will likely be a zone of total destruction. There has not been time to prepare or try to move the population away without risking widespread panic and total mayhem. My heart is very heavy and split in two by this predicament. We have no time... We are out of time, and if ten million people try to evacuate in a hurry, it would be an utter disaster. There is no guarantee that they even could get far enough away, and fast enough, to get out of harm's way. It is a no-win situation, and quite frankly, for the first time in my life, I am truly scared. It is terrifying to be at the mercy of an unpredictable volcano. That is why I did not hesitate to reach out to Blue Nova One to see if she had any constructive ideas on how to help."

Ben went over to Dan and sat next to him, putting his arm around him while Cleo gave him a hug. The city below was beautiful. Glowing brightly in the night sky, we could see gleaming bridges, buildings, and skyscrapers—along with parks and green areas of all sizes and shapes—confirming that the Gazurians were expert engineers on a large scale. Although we had seen much of that at the Northeastern Seaport, and in the scale and finish of Titan One, the city was awe inspiring. Dan then started to tell us a secret story about where we were headed. Simultaneously, up in the cockpit, Star was telling Bucky the same story.

Bucky, already admiring the attractive Star's aeronautical prowess as a pilot, was marveling at the broad view of nighttime New Gazur below. "We are headed to a top-secret Gazurian aerodrome that we call Zone Black," she informed him. "We think of it as a kind of military black hole; the secrets that go in never come out."

"We have a secret military site like that on Earth called Area 51. We're hiding a crashed Blue Azurian spaceship there, among other things."

"Well, that is interesting. And it further shows that we really are sister planets, because we are hiding four airships that landed here on the Republic of Azur almost exactly thirty Earth years ago. The fact that you are a Special Forces pilot for the United States Army Air Force from World War II on planet Earth is almost too much of a coincidence to be a coincidence. Tomorrow morning you are going to meet United States Navy Lieutenant Charles C. Taylor. Does that name ring any bells for you?"

"No, not at all," Bucky answered with a mystified look of surprise on his face.

"Can you fly a Grumman TBM Avenger, Bucky?"

Looking up toward the stars, Bucky mused, "My god, I keep getting asked this question about can I fly this or that, even on a distant planet! What's up with this picture?" Looking directly at Star, he replied, "The Avenger was the heaviest single-engine aircraft of World War II, edging out the P-47 Thunderbolt by about 400 pounds. It had a strong Wright R-2600-20 Twin Cyclone fourteen-cylinder radial engine that produced 1,900 horsepower. The plane carried three crew members: pilot, turret gunner, and radioman/bombardier. It had a .30 caliber machine gun mounted in the nose, a .50 caliber machine gun in the rear-facing, electrically powered turret, and a .30 caliber machine gun under the tail. There was only one set of flight controls for the pilot, and no direct access to the pilot's position from the rest of the plane's interior. It had a generous bomb bay for a single, 2000-pound Mark 13 torpedo, a single 2,000-pound bomb, or up to four 500-pound bombs. It was rugged like a truck, and flew like one. It was better than any previous American torpedo bomber—and better than our enemy's torpedo bombers. Hell yes, I can fly one."

Star smiled at him, delighted with his answer. "On December 5th, 1945 on your planet Earth, Lieutenant Charles Taylor led a squadron of five US Navy Grumman TBM Avenger torpedo bombers called Flight 19 from Naval Air Station Fort Lauderdale, Florida on a combat and navigation training mission. Lieutenant Taylor had logged more than 2,500 flying hours, over 600 of them in the Avenger, and had seen action in the Pacific Theater of WWII. A total of 14 airmen set out that day with Taylor, and the other four pilots had around 300 hours of flight experience. The squadron was to perform a routine training navigation exercise and bombing run over the Hen and Chickens Reef in the Bahamas, and then return to the NAS Fort Lauderdale. They were flying in an area on Earth known as the Bermuda Triangle. About ninety minutes after takeoff, Taylor reported that there was a compass malfunction and that they were lost. That particular day, there was a wormhole aberration in the Bermuda Triangle connecting our two planets. Immediately after getting lost, Taylor's squadron flew right into it. Four of the five Grumman TBM Avengers flew out of the other side of the wormhole over the Azurian Sea, coming right for the Republic. They were confused and low on fuel, so they landed here. One of the five Avengers and its crew is thought to be lost in time and space in the wormhole."

Bucky interjected, "My World War II timeline got interrupted on March 14, 1945, when I was sent back in time to November 14, 1944. On November 21, 1944, I traveled to the future with the Bad Love Gang to November 21, 1975. I wasn't around in December 1945 when Taylor's squadron went missing, so that may be why it does not sound familiar to me. But I think I was stuck in time for a while, like that plane that is assumed to be lost in that wormhole."

Star continued, "Of the eleven airmen who landed here, ten of them went on to start new lives in various corners of the Republic after they understood what had happened and accepted that they weren't going back to Earth. We retrained them so that they could assimilate into our culture. However, Lieutenant Taylor decided to stay with the four Avengers and work for the Republic at Zone Black. He has cared for those Avengers for your Earth-equivalent of thirty years now; he recently turned 58 Earth years old. He picked up smoking on Earth and continued smoking here. A few months ago, he was diagnosed with a lung tumor that has spread to other organs. He has lost some weight, but otherwise, you wouldn't know his days were numbered. Our doctors say that he has six months or less to live. Yesterday, I informed him that he would have visitors from Earth, and he was ecstatic! He knows about the impending eruption of Mount Pelorius and wants to help in any way possible."

The light bulbs began to sequentially illuminate brightly in Bucky's brain. "Did those Avengers ever drop their bombs and/or torpedoes on their practice run in the Bahamas?"

Star answered, "Two of the planes were carrying 2,000-pound torpedoes, and the other three were carrying four 500-pound bombs each. One of the torpedo planes went missing in the wormhole, so we have three planes with bombs and one with a torpedo. The day they went missing on Earth, they radioed that they had dropped their bombs, but they had not; they knew they were in trouble early in their mission and wanted to come back. Once they got caught up in the wormhole, they were in a space and time warp. Totally confused, they continued to send radio messages. When they came out of the wormhole they were again over the sea and approaching the Republic of Azur, which probably looked like their own mainland. It is possible that some of their radio signals went back through the wormhole to Earth before the wormhole closed. At the time Charles and all his squadron were debriefed here, we were certain that this had gone down as a total mystery back on planet Earth. When Blue Nova One told Dan that she could send a delegation from Earth to help us, that sounded too good to be true. I have rarely seen Dan get that excited."

Bucky resumed his brainstorming, full of ideas. "Sometimes those planes were loaded with dummy bombs for their practice runs, but that doesn't matter. Those World War II bombs and torpedoes wouldn't have the explosive power that we needed for this mission anyway. But we do have the explosives from the Blue Azurians with us, and those are potent enough to open that northern side vent. Now we have a way to deliver them to their target!"

"We were hoping that you could use the Avengers in some way, Bucky, but what exactly are you proposing?" Star queried.

"Here's what I'm thinking," Bucky responded. "Bubble Butt, Pumpkin, and I are all pilots and can fly three of the Avengers. Hopefully, Charles is still strong enough to fly the fourth one. We can attach all the Blue Azurian explosives that we have to the bombs and torpedo carried by those four planes. Pumpkin is a superb navigator as well as a pilot; he can lead the Avenger bombing mission directly to the Mount Pelorius northern side vent coordinates. We will all follow him in one at a time and drop our supercharged bombs on the belly of that beast to blow that side vent wide open!"

With an innocent look of hope and curiosity from an otherwise tough woman, Star softly enquired, "Do you think it will work?"

"If it really is possible to redirect the eruption of a volcano, then yes, it will work," Bucky firmly answered.

CHAPTER TWENTY-TWO:
READY OR NOT

"Dream as if you'll live forever. Live as if you'll die today."
—James Dean

Day five, early morning in the Republic of Azur at the top-secret Gazurian aerodrome: Zone Black

We had arrived by night at the top-secret Zone Black aerodrome. The Gazurian ground crews helped shepherd the Titan One airship into its giant protective hanger, engineered to withstand the severest of Azurian storms. All of us were given private rooms on board, but before we went to bed, the Bad Love Gang gathered in one of the meeting rooms and traded notes. Bucky, Pumpkin, and I had all come to similar conclusions about using the Avengers to get the Blue Azurian explosives to their target. We were all quite exhausted from the very long day of travel and the frightening emotional moments of nearly becoming Meggy the megalodon's meal. The Titan One guest quarters had the comfiest beds ever, and we all slept well. It felt like Titan One was a cruise ship in the sky.

We had agreed to meet Dan and Star for a pre-dawn planning breakfast, and they had a special guest waiting to meet us when our group arrived. The nine of us walked into the prime minister's private dining room aboard Titan One, and Danvinio One immediately introduced us to United States Navy Lieutenant Charles C. Taylor. He was wearing the naval military flight suit, the same one that he wore on that fateful day of December 5th, 1945 when he and his squadron went missing. Bucky was also wearing his military attire from his fateful night of June 17, 1942, when the Blue Azurian spaceship crashed at Area 51. The two of them approached each other, saluted, and then embraced. It brought on a flood of emotions for Charles, and he started to softly weep as he hugged Bucky and looked around at the rest of us. We then introduced ourselves one by one, including our Bad Love Gang nicknames, and Charles told us to call him Charlie.

Born in October 1917 in the state of Texas, Charlie had aged according to his Earth years. It was December 1975 on Earth, and he was 58 years old. His face was weathered from years of sun exposure in his youth on Earth and subsequently on the Republic of Azur, as well as from smoking tobacco on both planets. He had a receding hairline and graying hair. He was six foot one and looked thin, but not yet emaciated due to his recent lung cancer diagnosis. Amazingly, he still had a Texas drawl; that was fun to hear, since we had left Tater back on Earth for this part of our mission and had missed that southern flair. Both Dan and Star had briefed Charlie regarding our plans to use the Grumman TBM Avengers in an assault on the northern side vent on Mount Pelorius, attempting to redirect the impending massive volcanic eruption.

As a fancy breakfast was served to us all on beautiful china by the prime minister's staff, I decided to get us started with a surprise announcement. "I haven't mentioned this to anyone until now, but as we traveled through the wormhole from the Blue Azurian spaceship at Area 51 on Earth to the Queen's Island Space Center here on Planet Azur, I saw a Grumman TBM Avenger rotating in the outer rim of the wormhole. I knew the plane because Goondoggy's brother Willy and I had built models of it when we were kids. I guess I didn't say anything until now because it almost seemed like a dream at the time. If that is or was the missing Avenger and its crew, then there is still hope for them because they are stuck in time in that wormhole. I plan to report that to Blue Nova One when we get back to Queen's Island. Hopefully, they have the technology to go rescue that plane and its crew."

Charlie, still collecting his emotions a bit, perked up and stated, "That was plane FT-3 carrying Joe, Herman, and Burt; they were missing when we landed here thirty years ago. I was the commanding officer of Flight Nineteen, and I have carried the guilt of losing them ever since. I'd be happy as all get-out if they were still alive and could be rescued!"

Bowmar interjected, "Anything's possible, Charlie. BB, I want to talk to Nova about this with you."

Cleo, trying to be sensitive towards Charlie but a little annoyed at her brother, said, "Baby brother, you keep your quantum brain focused on us blowing a perfect hole in that volcano today so you get *the chance* to go talk to Nova again. You hear me?"

That made us all smile and relax a tad. Bucky asked Charlie, "Where are the four Avengers? And is it true that they are ready to fly?"

"For some reason, and now I feel like I know why, I decided to stay here and work at Zone Black these past thirty years. I have lovingly cared for those four Avengers like they were my family. All of them are airworthy, ready to fire up and fly right now. Y'all came in after dark last night, but there is a runway outside for the Avengers. They are parked in a hanger that is walking distance from here. Bucky, I understand from Star that you have flown the Avenger, and that you want to enhance our bombing payload with some super-high-powered explosives that y'all brought with you. Then you want to go bomb a big, bad hole in the north side of that volcano that's fixin' to erupt."

"That's right, Charlie," Bucky replied and then enquired, "Are you still airworthy?"

"You bet your sweet ass I am!" declared Charlie. My plane, FT-28, carries a 2,000-pound torpedo. The other three planes—FT-36, FT-117, and FT-81—are each carrying four 500-pound bombs. We never dropped those bombs—and they're live bombs, not dummies. I've never messed with them since I got here. In the Pacific theater, we discovered that the Avenger could dive from 6,500 feet at an angle of 45 to 60 degrees, drop its bomb or bombs at 2,500 feet, and come within 40 feet of a moving target. I can drop that torpedo by myself from the cockpit of my plane like it's a single 2,000-pound bomb. You're gonna need bombardiers to release those 500-pound bombs in the other three planes. Since we're not aiming at a moving target today, I'd say we can drop those bombs right in the ol' pickle barrel."

"Excellent!" Bucky exclaimed. "Charlie, welcome aboard the Bad Love Gang, buddy. We're all time travelers from Earth and less than six months ago, we went back to China in 1942 and volunteered for a few days with General Claire Chennault of the famed Flying Tigers to accomplish a mission. We called ourselves the Panda Bear Squadron. We are missing our pilot we call Panda Yang Four, so we'll give you that call sign today. Pumpkin is a pilot too, and his call sign is Panda Paw Two. He is also our navigator and has the precise coordinates for our target, the side vent on the north side of Mount Pelorius. He will go first and drop his bombs on the target, then we will follow one by one after him and bomb the same spot until the side vent opens wide and the volcano erupts out of the north side and flows into the open sea beyond. Bubble Butt here is our other pilot and goes by the call sign Panda—"

I interrupted and dumped some water on Bucky's fire. "Sorry, Bucky, but with planes called Avengers, we're using call signs from the 1960s comic book series. Your call sign is Captain America One, Pumpkin is Hulk Two, I'm Thor Three, and Charlie is Iron Man Four. We are the Republic's Bad Love Avenger Squadron, plain and simple."

"I don't know about the 1960s on Earth, but I can go with the call sign Iron Man Four. I like it; it kinda has a Texas twang to it," Charlie commented.

"Sorry to get real here, but I have some concerns. Flying in your planes, you don't have to worry about pyroclastic lava flows coming out of the north side of Mount Pelorius and moving towards the open sea. But remember what we talked about: If the erupting magma is thick and sticky, and pressure builds up until the gases escape violently, the explosion blasts magma into the air and it breaks apart into pieces called tephra. That tephra can range from bullet-sized pieces to plane-killing, house-sized, flaming boulders. It may not be the WWII Japs or Germans shooting at you, but it could be just like a wall of antiaircraft fire from hell itself coming right at you, if you're in the wrong flight path at the wrong time. Alternatively, your planes could also be smothered in clouds of erupting ash. There are a lot of unpredictable variables depending on how well you do with your explosives in opening that volcanic side vent," Bowmar cautioned.

Cleo stood and faced her brother, hands on her hips. "You forgot to mention the gale-force winds carrying radioactive plutonium particles that melt the skin off your body in ten seconds, making your eyeballs bulge with pain and then explode while your eye sockets bleed!" she exclaimed, rolling her eyes.

We all busted out laughing at the two of them as Bowmar tried to recover. "I was just trying to make sure that they knew all the dangers."

Ben jumped into the conversation then. "Dad, I'm going as your bombardier today."

Pumpkin tried to dissuade him. "If this plan goes balls-up, then I'd be absolutely gutted if anything bad happened to you."

"Well, I'd be gutted if anything bad happened to you, Dad. I'm not losing another parent in this life. I'm part of this Bad Love Gang now, and I'm going today. Like it or not, I'm your bombardier," Ben said firmly.

"Hey, Ben, you might just get a Bad Love Gang nickname out of this adventure today," I said. "Since each of our three planes needs bombardiers, we need to assign two others."

Cleopatra and Crisco simultaneously blurted out, "I'm not sitting back today. I'm *going*!" They laughed at each other for their synchronous outburst and high-fived.

I said, "OK, Crisco, you fly with me, and Cleopatra, you fly with Bucky. We will all be wearing our Azurian suits today so that we can communicate with each other in flight, get real-time information from Blue Nova One and her scientists if necessary, and put Luna to work if needed. Since Charlie does not have an Azurian suit to wear, I want the Pud to fly with him to be his radioman and communicate everything that is happening. That leaves Bowmar and Goondoggy to fly with Dan, and Star to monitor the mission and advise us from Titan One off-shore."

The Pud looked at Charlie and cynically commented, "Don't you be pulling any Texas Lone Star hero crap with me today. The last two words of our gang motto are 'don't die,' and I intend to live up to that today."

We all chuckled at the Pud, and Charlie smiled. "I have well over six hundred hours flying the Avenger, so I think you are a little safer than the rest of your crew here."

Dan added, "Star will fly Titan One. I am going to assign Jadedominic Eleven to accompany us and fly our rescue airship, Libero Three, just in case we need her talents. I'll have her meet us over at the Avenger hanger."

Star remarked, "Jade is by far our best rescue pilot. She could spot a thin black line out of place in a herd of zebras while flying overhead."

Crisco excitedly observed, "Wow, you have zebras here? They're my favs! I want to see them later."

I concluded the conversation as the Azurian sun was starting to rise. "We need to get changed into our Azurian suits and go practice flying the Avengers. I'll contact Blue Nova One for an update on the volcano's eruption status. Dan, please have your ground crews attach the Blue Azurian explosives that we brought with us to the Avengers' bombs and torpedo."

Day five, sunrise at the top-secret Gazurian Zone Black, in the Avenger hanger

All nine of the Bad Love Gang changed into their Azurian suits and activated their AI Lunas. I called Blue Nova One and gave her a full update, and she then requested that I patch Bowmar, Bucky, and Pumpkin in to the call. With all of us listening, Nova told us that Mount Pelorius had reached critical status, with both the central vent dome and the northern side vent cryptodome bulging. She repeated that the active magma chamber was larger than anything they had ever studied on Planet Azur. She also warned us that there could be quakes associated with the eruption. Nova let us know that time was short; it was now or never. We gave her the short version of our plan, then got moving.

Star waited behind and escorted us on foot to the Avenger hanger. The ground crews slid the large hanger doors open, and what a beautiful, impressive sight it was to behold. There were four Grumman TBM Avengers in two rows, facing outward. Charlie's plane was a model TBM-3, and the other three were model TBM-1Cs. Charlie had kept them all in pristine condition; they looked like they had just rolled off the assembly line. The TBM-3 immediately in front of us had a wing span of 52 feet 2 inches, stood at a height of 16 feet 5 inches, and had a Wright Twin Cyclone R-2600-20 engine with 14 cylinders in two banks of 7, giving 1,900 horsepower. The plane had a maximum speed of 267 mph at an altitude of 16,000 feet and had a service ceiling of 23,400 feet. It held 325 gallons of fuel: 90 gallons in each wing, and 145 gallons in the fuselage tank. Fully fueled, it had a range of 1,130 miles.

Standing with Charlie next to his TBM-3 Avenger was a striking green lady with bright green eyes and black hair in a Republic flight suit. Star introduced her as Jadedominic Eleven. We made our introductions, and she told us to call her Jade. Her brilliant green eyes seemed back-lit, totally exquisite and captivating. My outrageous music brain irrepressibly started to play **"Green-Eyed Lady"** from the American rock band Sugarloaf. Released in August 1970, the song was featured on the band's debut album. It was their first single and peaked at number one in Canada, reaching number three on the US Billboard Hot 100. I had always loved this song's lyrics, the electric organ, and the guitar action; now I imagined that it had somehow been written to describe Jade. Then I briefly questioned my own sanity, given the dire circumstances we found ourselves in.

Not wanting to beat around the proverbial bush, I commented, "We have been working with the Azurian Blue people, but were told that the Gazurian Republic had evolved just like us Earth people. I'm curious, Jade; how or why are you green?" The group looked at me a bit cross-eyed, like I was being insensitive. I just shrugged, looking at them innocently.

"It's a totally fair question to ask, Bubble Butt," Jade replied. "I am from a small immigrant tribe here on the Republic. Long ago, our own planet faced extinction and we were forced to find other suitable planets to live on. A contingent of my ancestors landed here on the Republic of Azur and were able to assimilate into the culture. The Republic is our home now, and we must stop this volcano from destroying it. Star has briefed me on your mission, and my crew and I will be standing by in rescue mode if any of you suffer misfortune."

I gave her a quick hug and said, "Thanks, Jade. Star told us you were the Republic's best rescue pilot. I hope that your services are not needed...but we're glad you are here, just in case."

The four Avengers had been fueled and the Blue Azurian explosives had been attached to all the bombs and the torpedo. We spent the rest of the morning reviewing the Avenger engine controls and gauges, the various flight controls and the bomb dropping procedures. We then took the planes up and flew as a squadron, running several practice dives on the southern side of Mount Pelorius, which was the closest aspect of Pelorius to Zone Black. While we were practicing, Star and Dan took Titan One and Jade took Libero Three—which looked like a much smaller, sleeker, and more aerodynamic version of Titan One—to an observation position north of Mount Pelorius, hovering over the sea. The central vent of Mount Pelorius was smoking as our Avenger Squadron landed back at Zone Black in the early afternoon. It was time for us to refuel, stretch our legs, empty our bladders, and then make our assault on the cryptodome of Mount Pelorius' northern side vent.

CHAPTER TWENTY-THREE:
THE FLIGHT OF THE AVENGERS

"The origin of volcanic energy is one of the blankest mysteries
of science, and it is strange indeed, that a class of phenomena
so long familiar to the human race and so zealously studied
through all the ages should be so utterly without explanation."
—Clarence Edward Dutton

Day five, early afternoon at the Gazurian Zone Black Aerodrome

Four WWII Grumman TBM Avengers stood in line at one end of
the Zone Black runway with their Wright Twin Cyclone radial
engines loudly rumbling. Pumpkin, call sign Hulk Two, and Ben
were in the lead plane; Bucky, call sign Captain America One, and
Cleopatra were second; Crisco and I, call sign Thor Three, were
next; Charlie, call sign Iron Man Four, and the Pud were last. All
of us, excluding Charlie, communicated through our integrated
Azurian suits with our hoods up. The Pud would relay messages to
Charlie over their intercom. It was time to stand and deliver, and
the fireworks were starting soon. Bowmar's voice came through to
all of us simultaneously. "Bad Love Avenger Squadron, Bad Love
Avenger Squadron, over." We acknowledged and he continued,

"We have a problem. Blue Nova One just spoke with Dan, and there is increasing quake activity across the Republic. This has been confirmed by the Republic's scientists as well. We are starting to see some magma and tephra blown into the air from the volcanic cone. It's time for you all to haul ass and get this show on the road, over."

Pumpkin, in the lead plane, responded promptly. "All right, my brainy mate...and we're not gobsmacked by that revelation. The ground is shaking here, and we can see the cone of the volcano smoking. We are off and running." He throttled up and accelerated down the runway, shouting "Tallyho, Avengers! Tallyho!" Ben exclaimed, "Tallyho, Avenger Squadron!"

One by one, we followed Pumpkin and roared away from the hangar. Halfway down the runway, we could see a few trees falling down, swallowed by the quake splitting the ground apart. The runway beneath us felt like it was buckling and rolling. As we all left the ground, we could see a fault line below. We knew from our research and discussions that quakes in volcanic regions could be caused by the movement of magma in volcanoes. Such quakes served as an early warning sign of volcanic eruptions; it meant we were on the clock, and time was running short.

We flew in a staggered formation off Pumpkin and Ben's right wing, with everyone following off the right wing of the plane in front of them. Starting from the southern side of Mount Pelorius, we flew northeast directly over the Gazurian Northeast Seaport. We were in a hurry, so Pumpkin had us level off at an altitude of 10,000 feet and an airspeed of 240 mph. Mount Pelorius was 9,500 feet high, and was fairly steep and tapered for the upper 3,000 feet leading up to the cone. The upper aspect of the colossal magma chamber had expanded and was directly connected with the central and northern side vents. There was more resistance through the side vent, as it tapered toward the outside surface. The northern cryptodome marking our target vent was located between 4,500 feet and 5,000 feet on the north face of the volcano, and Pumpkin had the coordinates perfectly plotted in his navigation brain. As we rounded the eastern side, more smoke and ash bellowed through the central vent and from the volcanic dome. Over our private intercom, Crisco said, "BB, I'm scared! That volcano is gigantic, and it's getting ready to blow."

Not knowing how to quell her fears, I quickly decided to sing a few lines of the song that I was pondering at the moment. It was Carole King's **"I Feel the Earth Move,"** from her Tapestry album. It peaked at number one on the Billboard Hot 100 chart in June of 1971 and stayed there for five consecutive weeks. It also peaked at number six in the United Kingdom. Crisco commented, "BB, you are just incorrigible. Fun, but incorrigible." She started singing along with me, taking her mind temporarily away from the fear.

A few lines into our duet, as we were flying west to the turning point for our bombing run, Bowmar's voice again came loudly through our audio hoods. "There is incredible scientific chatter coming through all the channels. Everyone is saying it's going to blow any second. You're out of time."

Pumpkin's voice overrode Bowmar's. "This is Avenger Hulk Two to Avenger Squadron, come in."

"We read you loud and clear, Avenger Hulk Two," we all replied.

"I am starting my bombing run. Captain America One, I want you following on my tail, a half-mile out. If the two of us don't open the vent, then Thor Three and Iron Man Four, you two go next. This is it, guys; let's see what these Blue Azurian explosives can do."

Pumpkin's Avenger turned left into a 45-degree dive toward the cryptodome coordinates he had seared into his navigational brain. Bucky adjusted his speed, staying a half-mile behind Pumpkin; he started his dive at the prescribed time. We held at 10,000 feet, with Charlie and the Pud following behind on our right wing. Turbulence was building in the air as the volcanic cone spewed more lava, tephra, and ash.

Down in Pumpkin's cockpit, he was laser focused on the bombing coordinates. He planned to have Ben release the four enhanced 500-pound bombs at 5,500 feet. Then he would bank hard left while pulling up and away. Half a mile behind, Bucky was planning the same but would bank hard right before pulling up and away. Both planes were buffeted by strong variable direction winds, and all the smoke and ash were clouding visibility. Nearing the release point, Pumpkin commanded Luna, "Give me a clear heads-up display of the bombing coordinates. And Ben, get ready to drop on my command." Luna did as ordered, then Pumpkin could artificially see through the limited visibility. Hearing Pumpkin's interaction with Luna, Bucky did the same. Ben's heart was racing as he prepared to release the bombs. Both planes were pelted with tiny fragments of tephra, which sounded like explosive incoming gunfire as it randomly hit the wings. At 5,400 feet, Pumpkin saw the cryptodome coming into the crosshairs of his heads-up display and yelled to Ben, "Bombs away, Ben!"

Ben released the four bombs and yelled, "Bombs away, Dad!" Pumpkin banked hard left while pulling up and seconds later, as their first four bombs were making impact with the cryptodome, Bucky and Cleopatra released their four bombs. Bucky banked hard right and pulled up. The first four bombs exploded with such force that the emanating shock waves burst against the underside of Bucky's plane, nearly throwing him and Cleo out of control. Bucky, struggling to regain control, temporarily angled down again and increased his airspeed before pulling up a second time. Cleo was panicked and yelling. "Have you got it, Bucky? *Have you got it?!*" Bucky cockily replied, "Like a cowboy riding a prize bull. Relax, Cleo; we're getting out of here."

Watching from Titan One through high-power binoculars at an altitude of 5,000 feet from well offshore, Dan, Star, Bowmar, and Goondoggy were fixated on the Mount Pelorius north face crypto-dome as the first volley of bombs exploded. Goondoggy was the first to see some evidence of an effect. "I see smoke and lava start-ing to flow from the lower edge of the cryptodome!" Indeed, there was a hole visible in the north face as the smoke cleared. Bright, burning lava was soon pouring out and beginning to run down the hillside. They started to jump up and down and exchange high-fives, but were visually stunned and stopped in their tracks when a large explosion blew outsized lava blobs and tephra from the volcanic cone. Dan's communication device buzzed, and Blue Nova's voice filled Bowmar's ears.

Dan was the first to speak, "Our team of volcanologists is telling me that the pressure in the magma chamber is continuing to build; the first bombing run caused only a temporary dip in the pressure graph. It isn't enough to change the direction of the eruption."

Bowmar confirmed that Blue Nova One and her team had come to the same conclusion and immediately radioed Bubble Butt. "Thor Three come in, over."

"I gotcha, Bowmar, how'd we do with that first bomb run?"

"You got a lava flow started, but it's not enough of a hole to relieve the pressure from the gargantuan magma chamber. Pressure is continuing to rise, on both the central volcanic dome and the northern face cryptodome. You need to make your bombing run now, BB!"

"Ten-four on that, Bowmar. It's getting a little rough up here, and we've had to evade some of that flying tephra. Visibility sucks, so we're using our Luna heads-up displays to see better. Charlie doesn't have an Azurian suit or a Luna heads-up to see through this crap, so he is going to have to stay right on my tail to make his bombing run. His 2,000-pound torpedo has the most Blue Azurian explosives strapped to it; it is our 'biggest gun' to fire on this bastard mountain. I know you're not religious, but you better say a prayer for us; this picture is not looking too rosy at the moment."

"OK, BB, I'm pulling for you. Get your ass in gear, and let that cryptodome know who the boss is!"

"Roger that, Bowmar, we are starting our bombing run now."

I radioed the Pud and told him to have Charlie follow my lead through the smoke and ash, because I could see the target using my Luna heads-up display. As I banked left and pushed the Avenger into a forty-five-degree dive for the bombing run, I spoke to Crisco over the intercom. "This is it, Crisco. We're making our run now, so get ready to drop our bombs on my command."

Crisco, sounding both rattled and angry, shot back, "I don't want to die today, BB!"

"*We are not dying today, Crisco, I promise!*" I yelled as the Wright Cyclone engine howled. Tephra assailed our wings and fuselage in a thundering crescendo. "Get your finger ready to go on the bomb release, now!"

I again called the Pud and told Luna to keep the communication open between him, me, and Crisco, "Hey Iron Man Four, tell Charlie to release his torpedo when he sees our bombs drop and then bank left to pull away. We are going to bank right when we pull away. Bucky said to be prepared for shock waves to hit the plane when those Blue Azurian explosives hit the cryptodome and blow. Warn Charlie about that as well."

"I got it, Thor Three," the Pud excitedly replied. "We are taking heavy hits from that damn tephra! Part of our canopy is cracked, and our plane is starting to look a bit like swiss cheese back here! Remember the last two words of our motto: don't die!"

"Amen to that, Pud!" Crisco exclaimed.

We were in a forty-five-degree hard dive nearing our drop point. The soot, smoke, and ash this close to the volcano was almost overwhelming, along with the high, variable winds. Our plane was being thrashed and whipped by forces of nature more powerful than WWII antiaircraft fire. I asked Luna for help, saying, "Luna, stay focused on the best drop point for these bombs and keep it centered in my heads-up display."

"Increase your dive angle to 55 degrees and lower your landing gear to increase the drag and slow you down," she directed.

"Did you hear that, Pud?!" I yelled.

"I heard it BB. I told Charlie the same," the Pud responded.

I felt like we were on a wicked roller coaster ride as the plane was tossed about by primordial forces in the midst of our bombing dive. The center point for dropping the bombs was nearly gyrating on my heads-up display and I could hear tephra tearing away at our flight surfaces. I'd heard Bucky say that the TBM Avenger handled like a truck. At the moment, I was thinking that it felt more like I was flying a bulldozer towards a big rock pile. I was fighting the controls to stay on course and at 5,300 feet, Luna suddenly cried out to us, "Bombs away, now!" Crisco complied immediately, and there was an ever-so-slight delay for the Pud to relay the command to Charlie, who released the torpedo at 5,200 feet. We banked hard right and Charlie banked hard left as our four explosive-boosted bombs struck the cryptodome, followed by the 2,000-pound torpedo heavily laden with the high-powered Blue Azurian explosives.

It was a non-nuclear explosion for the ages! The combination of our four bombs and the 2,000-pound torpedo—which had provided increased surface area to attach plenty of Blue Azurian explosives—was enough multiplicative force on top of the first bombing run to blast a substantial crater at the level of the cryptodome, at the very moment that the colossal magma chamber had reached its peak pressure. As the new crater blew open, the magma chamber released its peak pressure through the side vent. A mammoth explosive volcanic eruption released its pyroclastic flow down the north side of Mount Pelorius and out to the sea as planned. The volcanologists and scientists of both nations saw the magma chamber pressure being released through the side vent of Mount Pelorius, and were all jumping up and down with joy and relief at their respective stations.

Meanwhile, Charlie, the Pud, Crisco and I were fighting for our lives. The bomb and torpedo explosions, followed by the explosive volcanic eruption, had created a massive shock wave accompanied by flying ash and deadly geologic projectiles. The only salvation available to us was that we had turned laterally to the right and left away from the explosive crater that we had just created. The pyroclastic explosion flew straight out of the opened cryptodome toward the sea, but the fringes of the immense eruption caught both our planes, with crippling consequences. The Pud, Crisco, and I were still connected by Luna through our hood communication devices. I heard the Pud squawk, "We're hit, we're hit! A piece of tephra the size of a school bus just took off the end of our port wing!"

At almost the same moment, the underside of our engine compartment, the belly of our plane, and our extended landing gear took a direct hit from larger flying tephra. The plane shook violently and Crisco shrieked, "I can see a big hole in the bottom of the plane!" Our engine started to cough and smoke; I saw that our oil pressure was dropping and the engine temperature was rising. The Avenger actually held 32 gallons of oil, but we were obviously hemorrhaging that oil reserve underneath.

Using Luna, I contacted Bowmar while the Pud could listen. "Bowmar, this is Thor Three and Iron Man Four declaring MAYDAY, MAYDAY! We are both turning toward the sea to ditch."

Bowmar looking through his binoculars, responded, "We have Jadedominic Eleven in Libero Three standing ready to help. I can't see either of your planes yet." Just as he finished speaking, he then saw both of our smoking, crippled Avengers break out of the right and left sides of the heavy wall of smoke, soot, and ash, heading towards the sea. Bowmar declared, "I see you! I see you! Who should Jade get first?"

"I'm worried about sinking fast, with the hole in our fuselage underneath," I admitted. "We are rapidly bleeding oil and about to overheat. What do you think, Pud?"

"Charlie says he can manage to ditch next to you while Jade gets you two first."

"That's a deal!" I exclaimed. "Crisco, get your life vest on, buckle in tight, and the minute we come to a stop, get the hell out of there."

"Will do, BB," Crisco agreed. "You just get us down safely, or I'm not speaking to you anymore."

With our flaps down and keeping the plane feathered out the best I could, we gradually approached the sea below. The engine overheated, lost power, and locked up. I could see Jade in Libero Three in the distance, coming our way. I knew that we were missing at least half our landing gear, but could not tell if we were missing both sides. Nothing happened when I tried to retract the landing gear, so I knew it would be a rough landing at sea and warned Crisco. At the last second, I pulled up to try and drag the tail, with the front of plane coming in high to settle into the water as we slowed. It helped a little, but when the one remaining landing gear dug into the sea, the entire plane whipped and spun around violently. Crisco's head was slammed to the side, knocking her unconscious.

The plane stopped and I yelled at Crisco to get out, but there was no answer. I slid open the front canopy and could see her unresponsive form in the back seat. Water was starting to pour in through the hole underneath the fuselage. I quickly got out and accessed Crisco through the rear sliding canopy. Water was already filling the cabin around her, and she was moaning but unresponsive to my commands. Using all my adrenalin-enhanced strength, I unbuckled her and yanked her clear out of her seat, then pulled her onto the wing with me. I didn't want us to get tangled in anything or sucked down as the plane was sinking, so I dragged her as far out on the starboard wing as I could and then eased us both into the water, holding her tightly from behind as I went. Seconds later, our Avenger disappeared into the sea.

We were floating in the water together with our life vests on as Jade arrived overhead in Libero Three, and Charlie and the Pud were making their approach to ditch their plane nearby. Perhaps the splashing cool water was enough to help bring Crisco back into consciousness. She groggily enquired, "Am I dead, or alive, or is this some kind of a dream?"

Still holding her, I answered, "I'm here with you, Crisco. And if you ask me, it's a little bit of all three of those things."

EPILOGUE

"The aim of medicine is to prevent disease and prolong life;
the ideal of medicine is to eliminate the need of a physician."
—William James Mayo

Day seven, early evening on planet Azur at the palace

It was a historic gathering of Queen Azur's Royal Court and governmental dignitaries who celebrated saving the Republic of Azur from volcanic disaster, as well as opening peaceful relations between the Blue Azurians and the Republic of Azur. Seated at the head table with the queen were her husband, Blue Max Ten; her sister-in-law, Blue Zaniah Ten; her children Bella and Badar, along with Ben; and Blue Nova One. Invited guests at the queen's table were Republic of Azur Prime Minister Danvinio One, Republic Vice Prime Minister Stareveret Three, and Republic ace rescue pilot Jadedominic Eleven, who had plucked Charlie, the Pud, Crisco, and me from the Azurian Sea. Seated at the first table at a right angle to the queen's table were the eight other members of the Bad Love Gang, along with Charlie Taylor.

It was a magnificent evening of joyous celebration and a few Bad Love Gang antics, capped by Blue Nova One giving me two separate vials of medicine for Hannah Lieb back on Earth that would save her from a fate of metastatic, terminal breast cancer. Nova made it clear that we would have to administer the first vial of medicinal antidote to Hannah sometime after her first trimester of pregnancy. That meant we were going back to World War II Europe in early 1945 to find Hannah. The second vial of medicine was "optional," and would require the consent of both Hannah and Meatball.

Blue Nova One, with the queen's blessings, had two more surprises for me—and I had two special requests for her. I told her about the TBM Avenger number FT-3 and its crew, stuck in time and space in the wormhole connecting Earth and Azur, and asked her if they had the technology to rescue them. She replied, "That would be tricky, but I will look into it." Then I told her about Charlie Taylor's diagnosis of metastatic lung cancer, and asked her to give him the best medical care the Blue Azurians could offer; it would give Charlie new hope, and send another positive signal to the Republic. Nova enthusiastically said, "Consider it done, Bubble Butt." She then revealed her two surprises: the first was a potential life-saver, the second was potentially earth-shattering...

Saturday, December 20, 1975 at 11:55 PM local time, the Krovo/ Krovopuskov family home in the Sequoyah Hills neighborhood of Knoxville, Tennessee

Bobbie and Natalie Krovo, along with their Aunt Nancy Royer, had all gone to bed for the night at the Krovo family home in Sequoya Hills. The various surveillance devices installed throughout the home were under active watch by Ding's FBI team. In the summer of 1962, when building a pool in the back yard for his growing family, Borya Krovopuskov (Russ Krovo) had clandestinely constructed an underground escape tunnel leading out of their basement, around the pool, and out to the bluff overlooking the Tennessee River. The tunnel entrance from the basement was well concealed behind a false wall, and the exit was covered with earth and sod. Through the years, Borya had planned many routes to leave his house in Sequoyah Hills in a hurry, but tonight he, his wife Catherine, and a small KGB team were covertly coming up the Tennessee River with a plan to use the tunnel to secretly enter the house to get Bobbie and Natalie. Ding's FBI team was in for a rough night and the mayhem would not stop there...

ABOUT THE AUTHOR

Kevin L. Schewe, MD, FACRO, is the proud father of two daughters Ashley and Christie, and two granddaughters, Gracie and Olivia. He is a native of St. Louis, Missouri and now makes his home in Denver, Colorado. He graduated from the University of Missouri—Columbia with a Bachelor's Degree in Biology and from the University Missouri Columbia School of Medicine as an M.D. He trained at the Medical College of Wisconsin to become a board-certified Radiation Oncologist. He is a Fellow of the American College of Radiation Oncology (FACRO). Having practiced radiation oncology for 33.5 years, he continues to serve as Medical Director of Radiation Oncology for Alliance Cancer Care Colorado at Red Rocks in Golden, Colorado (accredrocks.com). He is an entrepreneur, having founded a cosmetics company called Elite Therapeutics (elitetherapeutics.com) and Bad Love Cosmetics Company. He serves as Chairman of the Board of a micro-cap renewable, green energy and animal feed company called VIASPACE, Inc. (viaspace.com).

The first Sunday of June every year is National Cancer Survivor's Day. Dr. Schewe co-chairs a yearly celebration of National Cancer Survivor's Day at the Red Rocks Medical Center in Golden, Colorado. Every year he writes a skit that he and the local doctors perform for the Survivor's Day crowd. The skit always has a musical theme from the 1950s, 1960s, 1970s, 1980s, or one of various Hollywood venues. The doctors are dressed in costumes for their parts and ask questions or pose dilemmas to each other. The answers to those questions or dilemmas are clips from songs, which the doctors lip sync and dance to in front of the crowd. There is a dance contest in the middle of the skit and everyone comes together and dances at the end of the skit. It is great fun and an uplifting celebration of survival for the cancer patients, their families, and loved ones!

Bad Love Beyond is Dr. Schewe's third novel in the *Bad Love Series*. His highly-rated first two novels *Bad Love Strikes* and *Bad Love Tigers* were released in September 2019 and June 2020 respectively, and have both been Amazon bestsellers. Follow Dr. Schewe on Instagram @realkevinschewe and at his author's website at kevinschewe.com.

COMING SOON

BAD LOVE MEDICINE
The Bad Love Series Continues...

Bubble Butt and the Bad Love Gang have the medicine or cure for Hannah Lieb's breast cancer in their possession. Blue Nova One revealed that they would have to administer the medicinal antidote to Hannah sometime after her first trimester of pregnancy. The Bad Love Gang must return to World War II Europe in early 1945 to find Hannah and give her the medicine. The group meets with Winston Churchill in his underground London "War Room." Churchill asks for their help with a mission while his sources try to locate Hannah and her family. Time and space travel are inexorably intertwined as the intergalactic future, the mid-1970's, the WWII-1940's, and the best recorded music in the history of the universe continue to collide with each other in dramatic fashion!

www.ingramcontent.com/pod-product-compliance
Lightning Source LLC
Chambersburg PA
CBHW020544020726
47494CB00006B/1909